THE UPRIGHT SON

The Ashmead Heirs, Book Four

by

Caroline Warfield

ARE YOU SIGNED UP FOR DRAGONBLADE'S BLOG?

You'll get the latest news and information on exclusive giveaways, exclusive excerpts, coming releases, sales, free books, cover reveals and more.

Check out our complete list of authors, too!

No spam, no junk. That's a promise!

Sign Up Here

www.dragonbladepublishing.com

Dearest Reader;

Thank you for your support of a small press. At Dragonblade Publishing, we strive to bring you the highest quality Historical Romance from some of the best authors in the business. Without your support, there is no 'us', so we sincerely hope you adore these stories and find some new favorite authors along the way.

Happy Reading!

CEO, Dragonblade Publishing

**Additional Dragonblade books by
Author Caroline Warfield**

The Ashmead Heirs Series
The Wayward Son (Book 1)
The Defiant Daughter (Book 2)
The Forgotten Daughter (Book 3)
The Upright Son (Book 4)

Dedication

To my readers, especially those who love my characters as much as I do and those who have waited impatiently for this book.

We must be willing to let go of the life we've planned, so as to have the life that is waiting for us.
(Joseph Campbell)

Life is really simple, but we insist on making it complicated.
(Confucius)

CHAPTER ONE

ALIGHTING FROM HIS carriage with a fierce frown, David Caulfield, the Earl of Clarion, glanced around the yard of The Willow and the Rose in Ashmead, his back rigid. The entire trip had been impulsive, and David did not give in to impulse. At least, he rarely did. His uncharacteristic behavior had made him uncomfortable, and now an accident forced him to seek help. The man who came out to greet him, Old Robert Benson, the innkeeper, was a man he respected. His appearance soothed David's unease, but the flicker of comfort dissipated quickly.

"We weren't expecting you, my lord!" David felt the innkeeper's words as criticism. The earl, a careful man, always sent word ahead for the inn to expect him, if indeed he planned to stop at the Willow at all, with Clarion Hall less than an hour away. Warning Benson was one of many courtesies he tried to exercise without fail. Then again, he usually planned more carefully.

It couldn't be helped. We didn't plan to stop. He swallowed at his own nonsense. It wasn't as if Old Robert was offended.

"Forgive the imposition, Mr. Benson. One of the grooms has broken his leg. I thought it wise to stop here rather than subject him to any more travel than necessary." The road to Clarion Hall from the Willow passed over a bridge across the River Afon and up a steep, winding road to a ridge overlooking the valley. The road had been repaired the year before, but David knew from experience that it was subject to erosion in the spring. The uphill ride would cause misery to a man with a broken leg.

"Kindly send someone for Dr. Farley. We'll also need a room for a few days," David went on, his jaw tight.

Old Robert gestured to one of his workers and sent him at a run for the physician before he turned to the second carriage and the man being lifted from it. "Tommy Withers, is it?"

"Yes. Luggage came loose on the nursery set's carriage just before Nottingham, and he climbed up to secure it. He fell with his leg caught in a binding. I suspect it is both dislocated and broken." David feared for the man being carried, pale and faint, into the Willow. Should he have found help for the man in Nottingham instead of pushing on? He thought not. *At least here at the Willow, we can be sure of the care.*

The innkeeper studied David's face, but the earl felt no harsh judgment. When the old man spoke, his words never failed to encourage people, even an earl. "Accidents happen, my lord. You couldn't have prevented it. You were wise to bring him here. You take good care of your people. You always have."

Unlike your father. The words hung unsaid between them. Old Robert had more reason than most to dislike David's father, the former earl. Benson had once been a groom at the hall and his late, much-loved wife a maid.

A third carriage lumbered into the yard. "I see Viscount Ashmead is anxious about Tom. You best reassure him," Old Robert said before going to see to the groom's care.

David approached the carriage containing his children and his daughter's governess. His son and heir, Edgar, Viscount Ashmead, peered out the window with more worry than a ten-year-old ought to endure.

"Are we stopping here, sir?" the boy asked.

David looked past him at Lady Marjory, his daughter, younger than her brother by two years. She was always a poor traveler, and her pale face and the manner in which she leaned wearily on

Miss Walters, her governess, twisted his heart. She needed her own bed. "I think not," he said. "Go on to the hall. I will follow you as soon I've seen to Tom."

"Tommy was careless." Ashmead frowned.

"Perhaps, but he's paying a price for it. It is our responsibility to care for him." The earl stepped back and ordered the coachman on to the hall before doing the same to the carriage loaded with their baggage and other servants.

The Willow's able employees, as it turned out, had the man's care well in hand. David joined Old Robert in the taproom to wait for Dr. Farley and accepted a pint of the Willow's famous ale gladly.

"Congratulations on the christening of your niece, my lord." The innkeeper smiled warmly. "I trust all went well." Their tangled family connections would have kept him well informed, but the elderly gentleman had the good manners not to ask David why he'd left so soon after the celebration.

David nodded rather than speak. How could he explain it anyway? Two days of children, cozy conversation, and conviviality had left him drained. He'd had a surfeit of family. *That's why you're so morose. It must be.*

"I understand Lady Madelyn and the little one are both well. Gwen, is it?" Folks around Ashmead still referred to David's sister as Lady Madelyn as she had been as a child. Once a duchess, she now preferred "Mrs. Morgan."

"Yes. Gwen. She has her father's black hair." *Gwen.* Not even a proper English name, that. It made the adorable sprite sound like a Welsh princess. Perhaps she was one. No Caulfield, that one. He'd held her briefly in church, and she'd blinked up at him with her father's knowing eyes. And wormed her way into David's heart.

"Perhaps that is as well. We've had a surfeit of red hair, have we not?" the innkeeper said.

He referred, at least in part, to David's father's unfortunate philandering that had left his stamp on the looks of far too many people they knew. Those words from anyone else would have caused David to rear back, insulted. From this man, who had raised one red-haired Caulfield by-blow as his own, the words were merely a sad fact.

"Aye. My sister expressed similar sentiments." David puzzled over her preference to be plain Mrs. Morgan, but he couldn't fault her. She positively glowed with happiness. He had been surrounded by besotted couples, Bensons and Caulfields both. He shuddered at the thought. That alone probably had driven his hasty departure.

Soon after, the doctor arrived, and having heard the man pronounce Tom Withers likely to heal nicely, the earl left.

Within an hour, he stepped, alone, through the entrance of his country house. As he trudged through the massive door, his boots echoed across the polished parquet floor of Clarion Hall. He stopped and stared. The echoes bounced off the cavernous ceiling, up the curving walnut stairs, and against the stone hearth. Nothing buffered the sound or softened the effect. Designed to impress, to inspire awe, and perhaps to intimidate, the place neither warmed the heart nor welcomed a weary traveler.

His servants were scattered across the rear of the manor, unloading baggage and preparing to provide efficient, if largely invisible, service. Even the carriage that had brought him had been driven around. His children, he assumed, were ensconced on the nursery floor. Did they feel the same way, coming into this mausoleum of a house? He stood alone in the silence, pausing to wonder why he still felt like a visitor in his own home.

David Caulfield had been an earl for six years, and he had never questioned that impression before. He blamed his sister and all that cozy nonsense over the christening. The feeling would pass. What he needed now was a vigorous ride to drive out the cobwebs.

He burst into his quarters to find his valet unpacking. The man dropped everything to locate his boots and turn him out for riding.

Probably glad to see the back of me, David thought, striding toward the stables, startling the grooms seeing to the carriage horses and equipage. With a flurry of "yes, my lord," one scurried off to saddle David's favorite mount. David followed him deeper into the stables at a more sedate pace only to stop at an unexpected sight: his son patting the nose of his horse.

At ten, Edgar Harold Charles Caulfield, Viscount Ashmead, his heir, possessed a quiet dignity. David had done everything he knew how to be a good father to the boy, the father he himself had never had. He often felt like he fell short.

The boy turned and gave the earl a proper bow. "I didn't expect to see you, sir. I hope you don't mind that I came down. I had been trapped in the carriage all day and—"

"Of course," David said. "It appears we're both in need of a good ride. Shall we ride out together?"

The joy lighting the boy's face startled David almost as much as the lad's next words. "I would like that above all things. You're usually too busy, and I know you don't like to keep to my pace."

Is that true? If the boy says so, it must be. David frowned. *Of course, he is with his tutors much of the year, giving us little opportunity.*

It wasn't quite the gallop David had planned, but there was something satisfying about riding with his son, expounding on the land and its people. Their people. The boy showed himself to be an excellent rider and a good listener.

This was peace. David resolved to do it more often.

THANK GOODNESS THE weather has turned warm. Lady Delia Fitzwallace sighed when her youngest son fell into the creek. Again.

She had given in to her children and joined in the hunt for frogspawn after Alfred, her eldest, announced he wished to set up an experiment in an old horse trough in the kitchen yard so he might watch them hatch. Reading about a subject never satisfied that boy. He needed to get his hands around whatever it was. Last month it had been pullies and levers.

Now Alf stood knee-deep among the weeds where the stream pooled to one side, while Penny—at eight, two years younger than her brother—held her skirts and walked along the bank studying the water for signs of amphibian reproductive matter. She'd only slipped in twice and then only to her ankles.

Percival, the active four-year-old, presented the biggest challenge. He slipped on the rocks, trying to mimic his older brother—whom he adored—soaked his mother's gown when she hugged him close while chastising him, and then promptly wiggled down to do it again, much to Alf's disgust.

"Stop it, Percy! You're roiling up the water and chasing away the frogs," Alf said.

Delia reached for Percy. She managed to grab one arm when Penny piped up, "There are riders coming, Mama."

Delia glanced back over her shoulder to see a man and a boy approach. She and the children rented the Clarion dower house. In the four months since they'd taken up residence, she had never seen the earl, having been told he preferred London, particularly when Parliament was in session. The rider's haughty expression, distinguished bearing, and thick auburn hair left her in little doubt that she saw him now.

Since she was caught at her least dignified, embarrassment distracted her. She wasn't prepared when Percival yanked on her arm and overturned her balance. Flail her arms though she did, she could do nothing to prevent her tumble into the water.

"Hogswallop!" she grumbled and immediately prayed the earl hadn't heard her. She rose, striving for as much grace as she could muster, with weeds clinging to her sodden gown and a squirming toddler pulling on her arm.

Man and boy pulled to a stop. "Good afternoon," she chirped before they could speak.

Clarion—for it must be him—blinked. The boy looked up at

his father as if to ask how to behave.

"I don't believe I know you," the earl said, staring at her muddy hems.

"Do you know everyone?" she asked, intrigued. She stepped up onto the bank and pulled Percy with her.

"Everyone who would freely do whatever it is you're doing on the Clarion estate." He waved a hand as if to encompass the entire scene. "May I ask your identity and your purpose here?"

"Of course. We haven't been properly introduced. I am Lady Delia Fitzwallace. We have the privilege of renting the Clarion dower house. We have a five-year lease." She wasn't sure why she added that last, except perhaps a fear this stern man might turn them out.

He appeared startled by her title, and Delia suspected he may have taken her for a tavern trollop of some sort, though the children might have given him a clue if he'd cared to consider it. As it was, she had failed to use her proper form of address as Lady *Vincent* Fitzwallace, stubbornly refusing to go by her late husband's name.

He didn't dismount. "I am Clarion," he pronounced with a slight inclination of his head. "I am pleased to make your acquaintance."

He didn't look pleased. Delia gave a proper curtsy, somewhat hindered by the state of her gown.

Does one introduce children by name to an earl? She couldn't remember and rather thought not. "Children, make your obeisance to the earl, if you please." They did. Alf and Penny had fine manners under normal circumstances. They managed. Even Percy produced a damp and rather dramatic bow. He returned to staring gape-mouthed at the horses.

Clarion cleared his throat. "This is my son, Viscount Ashmead."

The unsmiling boy, his expression uncannily like his father's, inclined his head with all the hauteur of a prince of the realm. He looked to be Alf's age, and yet he had the mien of an old man.

The silence stretched until Delia broke it. "As to what we are about, we are hunting frogs' eggs. We thought to observe the transition from egg to tadpole to frog."

"It is a scientific endeavor," Alf added.

That broke through the little viscount's stern expression. He gazed at Alf with interest.

The earl's silence unleashed an imp in Delia. She made her eyes wide with faux innocence. "Oh dear. I hope the harvesting of frogs' eggs isn't some sort of poaching. I would hate to run afoul of the law so soon in our tenancy."

"Of course it isn't!" the earl snapped. "The Clarion estate can spare a few frogs. I—I'll leave you to it." He moved his reins as if to turn but thought better of it and looked back at her. "Do you generally allow your children to run free across the estate?" he asked.

"Do they appear to be unsupervised?" she retorted. Given her appearance, she wouldn't have blamed him if he said yes, but she was prepared to defend her mothering if she needed to.

His bewildered expression rewarded her. "Of course not," he said.

"They have been instructed to stay clear of the main house. Their greater temptations are your stables and vicinity, but they have accepted the need to respect that area as well. They know not to touch the property of others. They know better than to ramble through plowed fields or growing crops. They—"

"Enough! I take your point. Good day, madam." With an inclination of his head, he and his son turned, and Delia's children watched them ride away.

"He's not a happy man," Penny said.

Understatement, that. One of her father's dictates gave Delia a twinge of regret. He always said, "You never have a second chance to make a good first impression."

You'll never live this one down, Delia, and more's the pity. For all his stern reserve, the earl was an attractive man, and one who appeared to care for his son. She admired that in a man.

With a sigh, she locked this regret away with the others she'd endured. She refused to let life's disappointments weigh her down.

"Alf, there! I see an egg mass," Penny crowed behind her. And so she had. Delia turned to share her children's delight.

She put her stern landlord out of her thoughts.

CHAPTER TWO

D AVID SAT IN the sunny breakfast room two days later with London, York, and Nottinghamshire newspapers in a neat pile while he perused the first, making notes of items of interest, potential legislative concerns, or anything impacting the well-being of the realm. His steward, newly returned from London, where he had attended the christening as well, sought him out there.

"Good morning, my lord." Eli Benson's habitually cheerful greeting brightened David's dreary morning. Benson declined the offer of coffee, however, declaring that work had accumulated on his desk, though he had only been gone just over a week. "Perhaps we can meet this afternoon, after I've had time to go through it. I wanted to alert you to my return and ask if you have anything for me to address." He stood by the door with his hands behind his back, poised as if eager to get to work.

"Good to have you back. Things seem to be running smoothly here, though I did hear the tenants had questions about culling trees to preserve for winter fuel. The north portion along the ridge should suit. It didn't sound urgent." David frowned over a thought that intruded. "One question, though. What do we know about our tenants in the dower house? I encountered them the other day." David had been in London since January. The family had moved in while he was gone, under Benson's supervision, no doubt.

"Lady Vincent Fitzwallace? Widow. Charming lady with three pleasant children. Fanny has been teaching the daughter composition along with Amy." Benson's wife, Frances, was a writer, and her young sister, Amy Rundle, lived with them in the steward's cottage. Fanny Benson was also David's half-sister, one of his father's string of children born outside his marriage. David had grown fond of her and her mother's children with Rundle.

"Fitzwallace? Isn't that the Duke of Awbury's family name?"

"Lord Vincent was the fourth son, I believe."

"Was?"

"She is a widow," Benson explained.

David found the idea of a duke's daughter-in-law wading in his stream to be ludicrous. Except he'd seen it for himself. He'd taken her for a farm wife. He knew Awbury to be as high in the instep as they came and pretentious to boot. *What would he make of his son's relict wading in pursuit of frogs' eggs? Nothing good.*

Benson frowned. "Lord Vincent was a bit of a wastrel, one gathers, living on the woman's money, they say, but I found nothing to her detriment when she applied to rent. She has been perfectly punctual about the rents and rather an ideal tenant."

"Who are her people?" David asked.

"Merchants. Graham Shipping," Benson replied.

"Graham? Money indeed." David bit his lower lip. Awbury must have hated having his son tainted with trade even as he enjoyed the influx of money. *The old hypocrite.*

And now she was his neighbor. "Am I correct she has a five-year lease?"

"Yes, sir. You saw the contract, but—did I act in error?"

"Not at all. You are undoubtedly correct."

After Benson left him, David gathered his notes to take back to his desk. He and Benson often conducted estate business over breakfast, or in the steward's office. For his research and parliamentary work, David preferred his desk in the library, where sunlight flowed through a row of tall windows, rather than the depressing little room that had been his father's study. He planned to spend the morning in the library, martialing arguments regarding the need for formal policing in the City of London, issues that had swirled through Parliament last session and were bound to come up again. This time, David intended to be ready with arguments in favor.

With his head full of his unusual neighbor that particular morning, that plan held little appeal. When he opened the door to his library, the sight of his son halfway up a ladder, looking at books, pushed it right out of his thoughts.

The boy peered over his shoulder and climbed down carrying a book. "I'm sorry, sir. I expected you to still be taking notes in the breakfast parlor. You usually don't come to your desk for another half hour."

Am I really that predictable? "Don't apologize, Ashmead. You're welcome to use my books. Can I help you with something?"

"No, thank you. I think this may have what I want." He held up a volume of *Shaw's General Zoology*.

David studied his son's face. "Do you have the correct volume? There are fourteen of them." He glanced at the title. "Were you looking for birds?"

The boy's face colored. "Frogs, actually."

"Ah. I think I know which volume you need." David reached up and fingered through the set, pulling out the third volume. "Here you are. *Amphibia*. That should have what you want. Shall we take a look?"

It wasn't difficult to find chapters on frogs and plates to illustrate them. David found what he sought on page twenty-nine, a plate illustrating the common frog, its tadpole, and its eggs. "Is this what you were looking for?"

Absorbed in the drawings, the boy nodded.

"It is an unusual life cycle, isn't it?" the earl said.

His son's head bobbed again. "I just kept wondering after we saw those children. No wonder they were so…"

David's lips twitched. "Messy?"

"I was going to say dedicated," his son replied, glancing up.

It was not the word David would have chosen. "Curious, perhaps?"

"Yes, curious. Although I'm curious, and yet I don't think I would be curious enough to stain my trousers in the mud."

A smile slowly transformed David's face. *No, I certainly don't think so.* "It would be interesting to witness the process, though, wouldn't it?"

"Indeed, sir. For the sake of science." The boy closed the book. "May I borrow this book?"

"You certainly may. You're always welcome to my books." The little viscount rose to leave, but his father had an idea. "Do you suppose the Fitzwallace children would share their findings with you? We could pay them a call and inquire."

Hope bloomed on the boy's face. "Do you think they would show me what they found?"

"We can but express interest and hope for an invitation."

"I would like that very much, sir."

"Shall we say, two o'clock? We will ride over and present our calling card."

David's mood improved at the thought. He would see his neighbor again. He found her as interesting as his son found the frogs, and was just as curious to see her in her natural habitat, if indeed his dower house qualified as such a thing.

⇛⇚

Wednesday was music day in Delia's structured calendar of child-rearing. On Wednesdays, Amy Rundle, the steward's ward, came for her piano lessons and Penny got hers as well. Midafternoon, they began dancing lessons, for as Delia told them both, a lady must know how to dance. Besides, it was fun.

This particular Wednesday, even more fun ensued when she finished drilling the girls in the formal patterns of English country dances—a reluctant Alf joining in—and she showed them some of the less inhibited steps she remembered from her childhood in Jamaica. She had never joined in the celebrations then, being only a child, but the sound and color remained vivid in her imagination. The dances ranged from looser versions of the English ones to glorious movement accompanied by the African drums she kept in a cabinet in the corner.

Delia's memory was impossible to recreate, but the children soon had variations of their own and urged one another to silly gyrations, breathless with laughter, giving her hope they might burn off all their energy.

She didn't hear the knock at the door, and it took Parsons, her butler who also filled a footman's function, a minute to get her attention.

Parsons stood at the door, holding a calling card between two fingers. "The Earl of Clarion wishes to know if you are in, madam."

"Hogswallop," she muttered under her breath. *The man has a positive gift for catching me at my least dignified.*

The children danced on, oblivious. Delia clapped her hands. "Off with the lot of you. Upstairs."

Alf grinned at her. "Off we go." He marched through the door with a bouncing step, humming wordless music of his own invention. Amy and Pen grinned and followed his lead.

As the children danced from the dining room, toward the stairs, Parsons spoke up. "The young viscount accompanies the earl, madam. I took the liberty of showing them to the drawing room. You may wish Master Alfred to accompany you."

Too late. The dower house was a spacious foursquare building. The drawing room lay across the entranceway from the dining room they converted to a music room every Wednesday. Alf and the girls, arms waving about them, danced right by it. Viscount Ashmead, his eyes wide, gazed at her dancing children from the doorway.

Alf noticed the boy and stopped. "Welcome, my lord," he said. He ruined his perfect bow with a cocky grin. The girls didn't notice. They danced on up the stairs, giggling.

The frowning earl came up behind his son, tapped his shoulder, and gestured into the room with his head. Ashmead blinked and did as his father bid.

Delia took a deep breath, put one hand on Alf's shoulder, and ordered a tea tray. "Let's demonstrate that we are civilized, please," she hissed at her son.

Alf stiffened his back and pulled his hand down his face. The grin disappeared, and an expression of proper gravity took its place. He offered his mother his arm as if he was a fine gentleman and not a mischievous ten-year-old. It was all she could do to restrain her laughter. If she gave in to it, she would set him off.

The earl stood at the mantel, his son at his side. An eyebrow twitched, her only clue that he noticed her son's transformation. Delia stood, with her hand on a ten-year-old's arm and her hair no doubt askew, and tried to pretend earls called on her regularly. There was a time when they had. She really should have told Parsons she wasn't in, but she'd never had patience with that particular hypocrisy.

"Good afternoon, my lord. Will you sit and take tea?" She gestured to the comfortable chair next to the hearth.

Alf led her to the settee and took her hand like a gentleman to help her sit before moving behind to stand at her shoulder. Her visitors sat across the room.

"We weren't expecting you," she said, scrambling to locate her supply of polite conversation.

"We were not here to greet you properly when you took up residence. We thought to rectify that now," the man said smoothly. Too smoothly. The boy, she noticed, watched his father's every move, seeking clues for how to behave, no doubt.

"It is kind of you to call. I pray your travels from London were comfortable. The roads were muddy in winter, but I generally find them much improved this time of year."

Seriously, Delia? The roads?

The earl murmured some nonsense about travel. "Are you

finding the house comfortable?”

“Quite!” Delia brightened. “It is everything I might have hoped for the children. Spacious and comfortable. It is the countryside I sought, however. I wished something more salubrious for the children than Bristol.” *Also, something far from interfering in-laws and overbearing brothers.*

“Bristol is your home?” the earl asked.

“For much of my life. Kingston before that.”

“You lived in Jamaica?” His voice rose the slightest bit; the news had surprised him. Bristol hadn’t. Delia regretted bringing it up. Sometimes the less one said, the better.

JAMAICA. THAT EXPLAINED the dancing. *She sits there, the perfect English lady, but how unrefined is this woman?*

She spoke softly. “Yes. My mother’s father owned a plantation on the island. I was born there. My father brought me to England when I was eleven.”

“Your people are in shipping, I believe,” David said, remembering Benson’s report. The Duke of Awbury must look down his nose at her relationship to trade. Belatedly he realized she might fear he would do the same. “Quite successful,” he added lamely, feeling gauche.

Her chin twitched, and David would swear her entire form turned to steel. “Quite so,” she said through tight lips.

She definitely assumes I share Awbury’s narrow views. He needed to change the subject. “How did your scientific endeavors go the other day? Were you successful?” His son’s attention sharpened, fully alert. He nodded at the boy.

“I… I brought a book. It has illustrations of various frogs and their eggs. Did you find any?” the boy asked.

Young Master Fitzwallace—David recalled his name as Alfred—smiled. “We did. A lovely mass of slime. My sister is quite disgusted by it,” he said gleefully. “It’s called frogspawn, by the way. Would you like to see?" He looked to his mother for permission as Ashmead looked up at David.

"I would like that quite well." His son sighed.

"May I see the book first?" Alfred Fitzwallace asked.

Ashmead rose, and Lady Fitzwallace pulled down the writing desk on the secretaire that stood in the corner. "Lay it here," she suggested.

Soon the boys were in a discussion about what sort of frog might have left its eggs in a Clarion stream. "Probably the common frog. It will be impossible to tell until they hatch," Ashmead said somberly.

The other boy nodded. "Let's go out and see if there's any progress this afternoon," he suggested.

Ashmead handed David the book for safekeeping. "I won't be long, sir. I merely wish to see the progress," he said solemnly. "Science," he murmured.

David's hostess watched them leave, her affection for her son obvious. "I gather that is the reason for your unexpected visit."

He couldn't deny it. "Your project intrigued him."

"He's welcome here anytime. No need for calling cards and formality among children."

Of course there isn't. But do I want him running free in this household? Amy Rundle clearly does. He couldn't quite imagine his son dancing with abandon the way he'd witnessed when they arrived. He certainly couldn't see himself doing so.

He must have become lost in his thoughts, for the woman peered at him quizzically. "The frog project requires daily inspection for progress lest they miss the miracles." A flicker of a pain, quickly gone, tainted her expression. "Would you prefer that your son stays away from mine?"

Blunt talk, that. Would he? He still wasn't sure but refused to admit it. "Certainly not. A visit or two as things progress would no doubt interest him. Perhaps you could send word when there are changes."

The wretched woman saw his discomfort and found him

amusing. "Have you ever watched frogs hatch?" she asked.

"No, actually." Even in boyhood, even in the relative freedom of the months his parents decamped to London, leaving David and his sister at the hall, he hadn't had that particular experience.

The lady pursed her lips as if suppressing laughter. "Or chickens? Ducks?"

David raised his chin. He would not be mocked. "Neither."

She leaned forward confidentially and lowered her voice as if confiding a secret. "Me, either. City dweller."

His shoulders relaxed. "I have less excuse. We keep chickens for the Clarion kitchens. Perhaps I should investigate the possibility."

Lady Fitzwallace beamed across the room at him.

"In the interest of science, of course," he added.

Her joyful grin took his breath away. His whole being gravitated toward the spirit of the woman, elemental and full of life. *No, not spiritual. Earthy and basic.*

For a moment, he thought he saw an answering fascination.

"Will you?" she asked.

No, this will not do! He pulled his raging attraction under control and deployed his polite mask. He swallowed to ease a mouth that had gone dry. *Wait. She means the chickens. Why not? Benson will know about chickens.*

"I'll see what I can do," he said.

"The children would like that," the woman responded.

Of course. Yes. The children. "My son as well, I suspect. I will suggest it."

An hour later, he trudged up to the hall and let his son's enthusiasm wash over him.

"...and Alf—he said I should call him Alf—is sure it won't be long. They've already changed shape. He promised to send word, but if I don't take a look every day, I may miss something, don't you think, sir?"

David, lost in memories of the life surging in Lady Fitzwallace's dark eyes, hadn't been listening.

"Did you hear me?" his son asked. "I think I should check back every day."

David nodded without thinking, his mind on the woman who'd tickled his senses. "What do you know about chickens?" he asked.

CHAPTER THREE

EXPECTING A LETTER from her business agent in Bristol, Delia walked to The Willow and the Rose, a few miles away. She could have sent Parsons, who generally used the pony trap to travel into Ashmead, but the day was fine, a hearty lunch was to be had at the inn, and the children needed the exercise.

She kept their attention focused with a census of animals spotted on the way. The rabbits appeared to be particularly numerous this year, and Penny, for one, delighted in them. Alf and Percy, on the other hand, enjoyed chasing and sending the little creatures running. Delia might not be a countrywoman, but she suspected they were excessively abundant this year. She made a mental note to ask Benson, the Clarion steward, for permission to set some snares. Alf might enjoy the exercise, and rabbit stew would be welcome.

An unplanned foray into a woodlot in pursuit of a mother deer and fawn delayed them, but they came across the bridge to the inn around noon to be greeted by the Willow's jovial innkeeper, who stood at the door on the stable yard side, waving at the departing royal mail.

"Lady Fitzwallace! Well met," Old Mr. Benson said. He nodded in the direction of the recently departed mail coach. "I don't doubt that expectation of mail is the reason for your visit."

"It is indeed. We made a day of it, and I brought the littles for the Willow's delicious fare," she replied.

Mr. Benson beamed down at Penny. "You're in luck, little miss. Annie Morris's cooking cannot be topped. Today we have the finest rabbit stew in the county."

Penny's face crumpled, and she turned her face into her mother's skirts. "Poor bunnies," she wailed.

Delia knelt and turned Penny's face to hers. "Rabbits are one of God's gifts for our nurture, Pen. It is their fate."

Pen sniffed, only slightly mollified. She looked up at the beloved innkeeper. "Could I have potatoes instead?" she asked.

The old man chuckled. "Aye, little miss, if you prefer." He opened the door to see them in. "The taproom is uncrowded this noon, Lady Fitzwallace, but the private dining room is open if you prefer."

Delia acknowledged that she preferred a bit of privacy with the children and thanked him.

"I'll have Clara see to you," the old man said. He lifted the mail pouch he had been carrying. "I'll have a look and fetch anything directed to you," he said.

Delia herded the children to a table covered in linen next to a sunny window adorned with chintz curtains overlooking the stable yard. Clara, familiar from previous visits, brought a basin of warm water and a cloth for washing.

"Thank you, Clara. You are an angel," Delia said.

"I almost forgot, Lady Fitzwallace. Mr. Benson sent this," Clara said, pulling two letters from her pocket.

Delia's heart sank. In addition to her business correspondence, one had come from the Duke of Awbury, her former father-in-law. It promised neither cheer nor encouragement. She put them both in her reticule and pasted on a smile for the waitress.

Alf caught Delia's attention. "Mama, look. Is that Uncle Jeffrey's coach?"

Delia peered out the window at a particularly grand vehicle—extravagant-looking, just the sort of thing her brother might own. But Jeffrey would have written if he was coming, wouldn't he?

As she watched, a familiar form emerged. "Barnabas!" Alf

crowed, starting for the door.

It was indeed Barnabas McKinney. Tall, meticulously turned out, and possessing all the innate dignity of his African forebearers, her brother's business partner called to the ostler and spoke to him urgently, setting the boy running for the inn.

Delia grabbed Penny's hand before she could run after her brother. "Manners, please. We aren't hoydens," she said, admitting to herself she was as excited as her children. Barnabas was one of her favorite people.

By the time she exited the private dining room and made her way to the door, Mr. Benson was well ahead of her. Barnabas stood with one arm on Alf's shoulder, explaining an unfortunate situation to the innkeeper.

"His attempt to hold us up was so ineffective as to be incompetent," Barnabas said, his familiar deep voice rumbling to Delia's ears. "He needs a good meal more than anything."

He spied her then, and a broad smile greeted her. Barnabas opened his arms to Penny and picked her up as if she weighed nothing to hold her on his hip.

"Mama is eating bunny stew, Barnabas. We didn't know you were coming," Penny said.

"Dear ones," he said, "I apologize for not getting word to you. I'm on my way to London on business. The decision was made two days ago—no time to write or send a messenger. In fact, I bring you a letter from Jeffrey now. I had planned to drive up for an hour or so."

"You were attacked!" The very idea alarmed Delia. She peered into the carriage to see a huddled form on the floor. She hoped the man was bound.

"I wouldn't call it that. One shabby man attempted to extract money. As I was explaining to this gentleman, hunger makes a man desperate." Deep compassion in his eyes, heavily laced with sadness, reflected other times and places in Barnabas's own life.

"I'm pleased to feed the man, as any Christian would, but we can't turn a brigand loose on the road, Mr. McKinney," Mr.

Benson said, wisely in Delia's opinion. "We'll alert the Earl of Clarion, the local magistrate. He's a fair man. He'll know what to do."

Would he? She thought of the stern man she'd last seen sitting uncomfortably in her drawing room and considered he had the sober mien of a judge.

A fair man? Possibly.

DAVID POURED OVER the *Liverpool Mercury* at the breakfast table, his notes on theft and intimidation on the docks of various English ports at his elbow. There had been an upsurge along the west coast in recent months. He found meticulous notes about numbers helpful in preparing for the legislative season. He rubbed the tense spot between his eyes. Aside from London with its Thames River Police, there was no adequate policing for any of them.

He put the paper aside when his steward, Eli Benson, entered, poured himself some coffee, and joined David at the table.

The business of the day took moments. As always, Eli had matters well in hand, needing only David's approval of one or two items.

David picked up the *Mercury*. "I'm expecting another edition and the *Chester Chronicle* as well. When will the mail be here?"

"The coach would have gone through this morning. I'll be going after it," Eli said, rising.

David lifted his eyebrows. "Hardly a steward's job! Where is John?"

"Nursing the stomach complaint making the rounds of the servants," Benson replied. "We're short-staffed."

"Using my land steward as an errand boy will hardly alleviate that problem. I'll go."

Eli grinned. "Using the earl as an errand boy is better?"

David smiled back. "I need a ride."

A trip to the Willow promised a hearty meal, fine ale, and a conversation with Old Robert, which always lifted David from his dismals. The glorious June weather only added to his satisfaction with life.

He crossed the bridge, at peace with the world, passed Corbin's Stables, and rode into the Willow's stable yard. The scene that greeted him clouded his mood.

A splendid carriage, one certainly finer than David himself possessed, had been pulled up against the side of the inn. Delia Fitzwallace and her children stood some feet away with Old Robert Benson, watching while the coachman and a fashionably dressed gentleman of African extraction pulled a man from the carriage.

The man's hands were bound, but when his feet reached the pavement, his knees buckled. David wondered briefly if he had been manhandled, but quickly decided not. His clothing, David noticed, appeared to be a much worn—indeed, a ragged— uniform of some sort.

Obviously one of the pathetic army of former soldiers, driven to crime by unemployment and desperation. They were, in David's opinion, a national disgrace—the disgrace being the nation's, not that of the men who had served it so gallantly.

Two men held the prisoner up, gently escorting him toward the door as if he was an elderly retainer rather than the sort who required binding.

David dismounted to follow the procession into the inn, and an ostler ran to see to his horse. Alfred Fitzwallace saw David first. "My lord! It's a good thing you came. Mr. Benson planned to send for you."

Old Robert turned around. "Clarion! It is indeed good. This poor creature attempted to rob Mr. McKinney here. We're putting him in the private dining room until you can sort this out. The wretch needs to eat before you question him, however."

A table had been set for four near one window. Benson urged

the men half carrying him to bring the man to a far corner and seat him at a long table.

"I'm sorry," the man rasped. "I just need food. Water. Please, water."

Old Robert must have anticipated him. Clara, the inn's friendly servant, came in with a pitcher of water and two mugs, one empty, one filled with ale. "Stew and bread are on their way as you ordered, Mr. McKinney," she said, smiling at the dark-skinned stranger.

"My lord, may I present Mr. Barnabas McKinney," Old Robert said. "Mr. McKinney, the Earl of Clarion, our magistrate."

McKinney gave a proper obeisance and murmured a polite response. He studied David as if weighing him. The man's slightest glance at Delia peaked David's curiosity. "He did no real harm, my lord," McKinney said, pitching his voice low.

David nodded. "Doesn't look capable," he murmured.

McKinney nodded. "Delia, you might want to take the littles to the other room," he said.

Delia? First-name basis? Who is this person? Lady Fitzwallace gazed at her children as if conflicted about McKinney's suggestion.

"I'll see to the young ones, Lady Fitzwallace," Clara said. "You stay with your friend."

The Fitzwallace children obeyed, casting glances back at the stranger as they were led out. Only Alfred appeared ready to balk.

"Go on now, Alf," McKinney said. "We'll talk after. I promise."

Benson followed them out, and the coachman went to see to the horses. Lady Fitzwallace stayed. She approached the table and sat across from the prisoner. David and McKinney joined her.

The prisoner gulped water until Delia gently reminded him to go slowly. "You'll make yourself ill. What is your name?"

"Joseph Holden, my lady," the man said, holding his mug with a shaking hand. "Was Private Holden. Now just Joe." He glanced up at David. "You the magistrate?" he asked mournfully.

"I am," David said. "When was the last time you ate, Private?"

"Four days ago. Six if you don't count a bowl of porridge a farmer's wife gave me," the man said.

Benson returned with stew and bread. "Eat slowly," he said. "You might best start with the bread." He left them.

David and the stranger waited patiently while their prisoner struggled to eat slowly.

"What brings you to Ashmead?" David asked McKinney.

McKinney glanced at Delia. "I'm on my way to London on business for Graham Shipping. I thought to visit some…friends."

Graham Shipping explained the connection to Lady Fitzwallace. David assumed the man to be a senior employee. "You were confronted on the road?"

"Brush on the road stopped us. I heard 'stand and deliver' and stepped out. He didn't put up much of a fight. We thought it best to bring him on here," McKinney said.

David suspected the gist was true but that some details were left out. He was happy to leave it. "I see." He digested the story while he watched Lady Fitzwallace break up the bread into small pieces and murmur encouragement. Their not-so-fierce brigand did not seem to distress the woman.

Finally, David gazed at McKinney. "So you met this man along the road, saw his obvious need for assistance, and brought him to the Willow to seek the charity of the shire. Do I have the story right?"

McKinney's dark eyes glittered. "Exactly right, my lord."

"Tell me, private, are you good with horses?" David asked.

Hope, heavily salted with caution, flared in the prisoner's eyes. "I won't lie to you, my lord. I'm only fair with the beasts, but I've a strong back for digging, hauling, or any work you want to put me to. Carpentry's my real trade."

"Do you know how to repair stuck doors or rotten steps? My kitchen door is in need of attention," Delia said.

Joe Holden perked up. "As well as any man and better than

most."

David frowned. Sending a would-be robber to a single woman's house was not wise. McKinney met his eyes in agreement.

"How about gardening? I need someone to mulch, and plant, and…"

"Delia, are you trying to poach the earl's new employee?" McKinney asked.

At "employee," Joe Holden sat a bit straighter.

"I suggest this," David said. "I will hire Mr. Holden on a trial basis. He can sleep with the grooms above the stables. If my steward finds him trustworthy and reliable, we'll loan him to Lady Fitzwallace when she needs him while he lives at Clarion Hall."

McKinney nodded. "Wise," he murmured.

Lady Fitzwallace smiled at the prisoner, who was engaged in scraping the last of the stew from the bowl. "I accept. I have no doubt about our new employee. I'll look forward to introducing him to Parsons, my butler." She rose. "Now I best go make sure Penny isn't grieving over every rabbit in the shire."

David and McKinney watched her leave. "She's a brave one," David murmured.

McKinney chuckled. "That she is."

THE INN SUPPLIED a gig for the earl to drive his new employee back to the hall, and he accepted gladly to Delia's astonishment. Vincent would never have ridden in such a poor vehicle, and she doubted he'd have traveled with anyone like Joe Holden. He'd probably have had the man delivered by the ostlers, if he'd even thought to hire him. Delia and Old Robert waited by the inn door while Barnabas spoke with Clarion.

"He's a busy man," she said.

"Clarion? He is that. People think being an earl is all privilege.

True to a great extent, certainly, but with it come burdens, at least if the man who has the title is honorable and responsible. Clarion is both."

"I had the impression the welfare of Clarion Hall fell to your son Eli," Delia said.

Benson's grin widened. "It does, and my son does him proud, but don't be fooled. Clarion cares about the land and its people. The thing is, he also cares about England. Parliament is his life. He trusts Eli to free him to concentrate on that."

That jogged a memory. Benson hurried over and handed up a bundle of mail. Prominent in that bundle were several newspapers. Clarion smiled, thanked him, and drove off with the horse he'd ridden in on tied to the back of the gig.

Barnabas rejoined her, wrapping an arm around Penny. "Now let's have a bite and some of this famous ale. Then I must be on my way. I only intended to be here an hour or two."

He followed the direction of her gaze. "I quite like your earl. He handled that wisely and well."

"He certainly is not *my* earl!" she snapped. *He isn't quite the man I thought he was, either.*

Barnabas's eyes twinkled at her vehemence. They took a table in the Willow's private dining room, and before long, he had the children laughing out loud, Delia right along with them. True to his word, he left for London an hour later, with Penny and Alf begging him to return soon. She missed his teasing as soon as he departed.

CHAPTER FOUR

ELIA FOUND REREADING Awbury's pronouncements did little to improve their tone. Pompous. Pretentious. Presumptuous. A plaguey, pestiferous bother. That was her father-in-law. She tossed it aside. If there'd been a fire in the hearth, she would have tossed it there, but the afternoon was too warm for one.

Awbury had somehow discovered that the Earl of Clarion had returned to Ashmead, putting him in a frenzy of concern lest Delia's "tendency to outré starts and disastrous decisions" reflect poorly on the Fitzwallace name. Reading between the lines, Delia suspected the earl's political influence somehow mattered to the duke. She knew her father-in-law's real fear was that her origins would offend Clarion's sense of the privileges and power of the upper classes. Her family history certainly offended Awbury, who'd had to hold his nose to allow his son to take her money. Having met the earl, she feared he would agree. After the incident at the Willow, she wasn't so sure.

"A pox on both of them," she muttered. She wouldn't honor the duke's rant with a reply, nor would she entertain the slightest worry that the Earl of Clarion had ignored her since the Willow a week before. She'd heard not one word about her new man of all work. She reminded herself that her only concern about the earl was that he honor her lease and not take offense over something and jeopardize her position here.

The distraction she needed flounced into the drawing room

and threw herself into the comfortable chair by the hearth, the one so soft a person could sink into it and enjoy the impossibility of maintaining a straight-backed ladylike pose. "I hate them," Penny announced.

Delia closed the fold-down desk on her secretaire and smiled at her daughter. "What have Alf and Percy done this time?"

"Not Percy."

Delia's brows shot up. "Then who has so offended you? You said 'them.'"

"Viscount Ashmead." Penny spat the words out with a sour face.

Delia, on high alert for insult after Awbury's letter, stiffened. The father may be high in the instep, but she would not suffer rudeness to her children from the son.

"They have decided sisters are a plague. They are quite in agreement. Ashmead told Alf girls aren't steady enough to be scientists."

Delia stifled a laugh. *Not class snobbery. Gender. The age-old male ego.* "What did Alf say to that?"

"Alf agreed with him. He said science required steady concentration."

Steady? Since when is Alfred Peter Fitzwallace steady? "Are you telling me the viscount is here?"

"Of course. He comes to check the tadpoles every afternoon, at least every day that his tutor lets him out. He has to work in the morning because he expects to go to someplace called Ee-tun. He seems to think it is someplace important." Penny sneered her words.

Eton. Of course he does. She had hoped to spare Alf that, but her brother, Jeffrey, insisted he must be enrolled. Delia wondered if the earl knew his son had been visiting her kitchen garden every afternoon for two weeks. She herself hadn't noticed. He must not have been staying long.

"Shall we go out and speak with them?" Delia asked.

Penny gave a dramatic shrug, but she rose. "I suppose we

could see if they are in trouble."

"Have they been so far?"

"Ashmead is too worried about getting his clothing dirty to get into any interesting trouble, no matter what Alf says."

That gave Delia something to ponder. They were in the kitchen before Penny added, "I'm not interested in any Clarion chickens anyway."

Delia stopped so abruptly Penny had to turn back. "What about chickens?"

"They're going to hatch, but Alf and his lordship"—Penny's sarcastic use of the honorific almost made Delia laugh—"plan to count the eggs, and something about breeds. Alf says some probably make more eggs, and Ashmead says they should weigh the babies. Science, they call it. I said baby chickens would be cute, and that's when they told me girls can't be scientists."

The earl remembered! "I might like to see baby chickens. We could go together," Delia said. Her daughter's grin sent all the negative miasma generated by Awbury's message flying out the window.

She flung the door open only to react in horror at the sight of her son dragging a little girl—kicking and squirming—off her feet and away from the tin horse trough in which they had placed the frogspawn. Clarion's son watched, bouncing from foot to foot in dismay and wringing his hands.

"Alfred Fitzwallace, what in the name of all that is holy are you doing?" She charged at her son and extracted his prisoner. The little girl angrily shook off Delia's hands and took a few steps away only to turn, arms akimbo, to glare at the boys, obviously none the worse for Alf's treatment.

"She shoved the tub. She was going to dump it over!" Alf shouted. "I had to stop her."

"It doesn't matter. A gentleman does not handle a lady roughly, Alfred. Under any circumstances," Delia said.

Viscount Ashmead nodded solemnly. "She's right, Alf, even if Marj did provoke us. Bad form." He glared at the girl.

"Apologize, Alfred. Now."

The boy mumbled something that sounded like an apology.

Delia peered at the stranger. "I apologize for my son's behavior, but why would you do such a thing?" she asked the girl directly.

"He"—the stranger named Marj pointed at Alf—"said sisters are a plague, and my brother agreed. They said girls can't look at their precious frog babies, even though she"—this time she pointed at Penny—"helped collect the gooey mess. Then she ran inside, and they tried to chase me away."

Delia gazed at Penny, brows raised. "Kindly introduce me to the friend you didn't bother to mention to me."

"I forgot," Penny muttered under her breath. "Mama, this is Marj."

"Lady Marjory," Clarion's son corrected.

Alf just manhandled Clarion's daughter. Hogswallop. Delia inhaled deeply and let it out slowly. The girl, she noticed, rolled her eyes at that. Delia prayed she would not have to deal with an irate earl on her doorstep. "Gentlemen—and I use that term loosely in your case, Alfred—young ladies have as much interest in nature as you do. Penny did indeed help harvest the frogspawn, has taken an interest all week, and if I remember correctly, helped carry stream water to refresh their home. What changed?"

"M—Lady Marjory turned up, and—"

The other boy cut off Alfred's explanation. "She followed me. She was not invited. One does not visit without an invitation." He screwed up his face. "Unless it is calling hours, and then you present your card to the butler." He returned his sister's glare.

Alfred went on. "The girls started giggling and calling the egg mass disgusting."

"I can see where that might be disruptive," Delia murmured, biting her lip.

Marj glance at Penny, mischief lurking in her eyes.

This one is very different from her brother, Delia thought. "Lady Marjory, do you wish to examine the frogspawn or not? I believe

Penny has had plenty of opportunity."

Clarion's daughter darted a glance at Pen and nodded.

Delia pinned her son with a look only a mother could master, and he edged away from the trough, keeping a wary watch on the girl.

Penny in tow, Delia approached the trough. The other girl came up beside her. "My name is Marj, Lady Fitzwallace," she murmured. "And I wasn't really going to dump them out. I just wanted to scare Ed."

Ed? "Is that your brother?"

Marj nodded. "My father calls him Ashmead, but he has an actual name."

The girls spent a moment staring down at the creatures.

"Look, Penny!" Delia said, startled at how interesting it was. "You can see them inside the eggs now."

"I know, Mama. I've been watching them grow." She cast a scornful glance at Alf. "All week."

Delia looked over her shoulder at the boys. "How long until they hatch?"

"We don't know," Alf said.

"It depends on the species," the viscount—who, it turned out, had an actual Christian name—said.

"When do they get legs?" Marj asked.

"Good question," Delia said. "Ashmead, can you find that information in that book of yours?"

"Of Papa's," Marj corrected.

"Actually, Ashmead and I are keeping records so we will know for next time. We don't need books to tell us what our eyes can discover," Alfred insisted. The little viscount did not look convinced, but he glanced over at Alf, dropped his gaze to his boots, and said nothing.

"Well, ladies, while they wait patiently, would you like to come in? Penny is painting fruit this week. Would you like to try, Lady Marjory?"

The little girl glanced longingly at the frog barrel and at the door, obviously hesitant. Her whispered correction, "Marj," almost went unheard.

"Does Miss Walters know you left the hall, Marj?" Viscount Ashmead asked.

"Yes." Her guilty hunch of shoulders put the lie to that. She had obviously eluded her governess.

"Perhaps she didn't hear you inform her," Delia suggested. "It might be best for you to cut this visit short and come to visit us another day. I believe there was some question about an invitation. I'm giving you one now. You may visit us whenever you have permission to do so." Delia gazed back at Ashmead. "You may both do so. With permission. I suggest you use the front door from now on. And, Alfred, may I remind you that you are to inform me when friends come to visit?"

"Yes, Mama," he muttered.

Clarion's children left, bickering as they went. Penny gave her brother a pointed raise of her shoulder and flounced back into the house.

Delia returned past the kitchen, requested a fortifying cup of tea, and collapsed into her favorite chair. "That went well," she said at the four walls of the drawing room. At least, she hoped it had. She still wasn't certain she wouldn't have an irate earl on her doorstep. She wasn't sure how she felt about that either, except he might try to break the lease, and she wasn't having that.

"A SUMMER HOUSE party here? Hell no! What is Danbury thinking?" David frowned at the visitor imbibing his best brandy. The Marquess of Danbury might be David's good friend and political ally, but they didn't always agree, never less so than over the necessity to entertain.

Rob Benson—Sir Robert, to be precise—lounged comfortably in a leather chair by the window of David's library and smiled placidly back. "Don't glare at me. I'm merely the messenger. He's thinking what you lot always think. 'How can we ply the right people with convivial spirits and convince them to give up a vote?'"

Sir Robert Benson had grown up at The Willow and the Rose, ostensibly the son of Old Robert, for whom he was named, but he had the rather unusual distinction of being half-brother to both the Earl of Clarion and the earl's steward, Eli Benson. It was a complicated relationship, but in recent years, they had come to a sort of peace with it, and Rob came and went at Clarion Hall with perfect comfort. Since Rob had been raised to a baronetcy, society tended to look the other way on his irregular birth, easing comradery and cooperation in London as well as Ashmead.

Rob leaned forward, elbows on his knees. "Actually, in this case, the question is, 'How can we convince the party to advance the Earl of Clarion to the position of home secretary?' That is it, is it not?"

David didn't deny it. He and the marquess had discussed the position at length, and Danbury had urged him to seek the post, neither man satisfied with the current occupant of the position. David wavered, but he rather thought, on the whole, it would suit him and enable him to do much good. There was, however, no urgency about the matter.

"Yes. And Danbury might better host shooting parties in the fall at his estate in Devon or the one in Yorkshire," David said. "He can afford to do the thing right. I can't."

"Liverpool has no interest in shooting parties," Rob replied.

"The prime minister has no interest in summer garden parties either," David retorted. "We cozied up to him during the Season often enough. I believe Danbury has other targets in mind."

The Marquess of Danbury was David's closest political ally and friend, and they were often of one thought as far as policy. Though both were members of the Tory party, neither man leaned toward hidebound attachment to old ways. Demand for change seethed in the country. Unemployment and inflation fueled it. The anger that had led to the Luddite uprising five years before had not abated. If anything, conditions made it worse. The vital thing was to manage it, not to attempt to bottle it up. Both agreed economic stability, moderate election reform, and carefully managed improvements for the working class were vital.

Political strategy was an entirely different subject. David endured the round of social obligations during the Season as the price of title and position, often urged to it by Danbury. He didn't much care for it. Danbury reveled in the social round. The marquess either failed to grasp the pitfalls faced by a single man in possession of a title or deliberately chose to ignore them. Sometimes David suspected his friend—or the man's marchioness—of deliberate matchmaking. A house party at Clarion would bring the matchmaking mamas of the *ton* out in packs.

"I still don't see why he thinks hosting a house party here will tilt things my way," David said. "Liverpool will refuse an invitation. I could probably write his formal note declining it myself."

"Rockford thinks—" Rob began.

"You discussed my ambitions with Viscount Rockford?" It infuriated David. "You have no right!"

"My employer didn't need me to bring it up; he sought me out. Rockford has his fingers in every pie related to the Home Department—crime, instability, unrest. Hell, he ought to be home secretary himself. He thinks you're the man for the job and Sidmouth should be pushed aside." Rob peered at David pointedly. "Rockford's support will carry you far."

True enough. Rob's employer, ostensibly a Tory, gave neither party full support, yet he haunted the halls of Parliament, a shadow figure both respected and feared by all. "But would he attend this hypothetical house party? It would attract some of those we need to convince if he did."

"You sound as if you're wavering," Rob said.

David shook his head. "We aren't capable of doing it properly, not on the scale the society dragons expect." To do it halfway would humiliate him and doom his chances besides.

Rob opened his mouth to respond but bit back whatever retort he had for that. "I understand you have a new neighbor. Lady Vincent Fitzwallace, is it? You could invite her."

David's hand stalled on the way to his glass. *I could. If I was interested. If—*

"So you're wavering?" Rob's gaze sharpened.

"No, I am not." Not about Delia Fitzwallace and not about Danbury's pressure. "No one has house parties in the summer. At least, most people wait until autumn. Besides, no one will come, because Parliament is still in session." David glared back at his brother's speculative expression.

"It is indeed, which begs the question, What are you doing in the country? Is it the new neighbor?" Rob asked.

"Don't be ludicrous. I was bored witless by this session's endless debate about the postal service by March. They are still going at it. Worker unrest in the northern industrial cities is spiraling, and the old boys wanted to natter over the finances of the postmaster general all spring. I couldn't bear it." David glanced up from under lowered lashes. "Besides, I made an error."

A wicked grin spread over his brother's face. "The Duke of Bellwood's granddaughter!"

David groaned. "You too? The whole *ton* must be buzzing about it."

"Oh yes, indeed. You danced with her twice at the Portland ball. Ladies would have it that you are courting her or, at least, that the elusive Earl of Clarion is at long last on the hunt for a wife."

"I signed her dance card once, I swear. I remember that much, but Danbury had cornered Bessborough and needed me. My attention was on Catholic reform. When I encountered her after supper and she chirped, 'This is our dance, my lord,' I totally forgot I'd already led her out. She's a forgettable enough little chit." David shook his head. "I was ambushed. Now the hounds are on full hunt. I thought it wise to avoid town." He stared into his drink.

"Your abrupt departure fanned the flames." Sympathy colored Rob's words.

David squeezed his eyes shut. "Has the young lady's reputation suffered?"

"Not enough that you owe her marriage!" Rob shrugged. "Perhaps a bit. What do they say? Her value on the marriage mart is somewhat tarnished—by her behavior, no doubt, not yours. She may have to settle for a baron instead of an earl."

David snorted. "She and her manipulative mother will manage. I plan to stay here and avoid the entire pack of them."

"Hence no house party." Rob's lips quivered perilously close to outright laughter. If he gave in to it, David would feel obliged to knock him off his chair.

The earl nodded. "Danbury's notion that those traveling north at the end of July would welcome the invitation for a brief respite may sound logical to him. Except Clarion Hall hasn't hosted a party since my—our—unlamented sire went to his just reward. Except the expense to do the thing right would be punishing. Except I dislike society affairs. Except every society matron with a marriageable daughter will suddenly remember some minor estate, the road to which passes through Ashmead. I won't do it."

"Danbury also thinks you need a wife," Rob told him.

David snorted. "Even less likely."

Rob eyed him thoughtfully but kept his counsel. He put down the crystal goblet and rose to his feet. "As it happens, married life suits me fine. You might want to consider it."

David rose to walk him to the door. "How long will you be here?"

"Lucy generally takes a week for her quarterly inspection of the operation at Willowbrook. Da wants to cuddle his grandson. We'll be on our way back to London next week. Unlike you, I can't escape the social round." Rob earned a living providing discreet security for the diplomatic corps. He paused at the door. "Do you really think the cabinet will convene hearings on the prince regent's unfortunate wife?"

"His spies have been providing increasingly lurid reports on her behavior with her Italian paramour," David said, his lips pursed in distaste. "He's been exerting pressure on Liverpool to do it, and yes, I believe they will."

"Rockford says he didn't need spies. The Italian press is full of it." Rob shook his head. "Prinny can be cruel, but the princess is regrettably foolish."

David watched his brother ride away. From his vantage point on the steps of Clarion Hall, the ground sloped gently down toward the river. Trees blocked his view of Ashmead and the Willow, but the rolling fields of the Midlands stretched out beyond, lush and green. Peace seeped into his heart. Love for England—the land and its people—propelled him always.

Danbury can handle the social maneuvering, while I take strength from my children and the countryside. I'll back him with correspondence, but there will be no house party.

CHAPTER FIVE

T HE FITZWALLACE HOUSEHOLD was in an uproar the day the first of the frog larvae, or tadpoles, began to emerge. That Penny observed them first put Alf's nose out of joint.

"It wasn't Penny's place," Percy announced, parroting his older brother with as much pomposity as a four-year-old could muster.

"Penny simply happened upon it, angel. It could as well have been you or me," Delia said, raising one brow pointedly at Alf. "What if they decided to hatch while you were sleeping?"

Percy glanced up at Alf for confirmation.

"I better send a message over to Ed," Alf said, his woebegone expression fraying his mother's patience.

"We ought to be celebrating!" she said. "And when did the viscount become Ed?"

"His sister keeps tagging along—"

"She was invited!" Penny insisted.

"She keeps tagging along and calling him Ed, so Penny did too, and then he said I may as well also."

What would their father think? Delia chased the question away as soon as it rose in her mind. It didn't matter what the earl thought. His children had been to visit the frog nursery daily, although Delia believed the boys had also found trees to climb and the girls had embarked on a project involving the construction of tiny huts in the narrow woods between the dower house and the hall, "in case there really are fairies."

The Caulfield children came to admire the tadpoles and brought news—arrangements to observe the chicken hatchery had been made. Soon the four of them were off with a stern warning to behave respectfully and to keep themselves to the chicken yard. She hoped they heeded her. The earl may have permitted the learning exercise, but he would not tolerate nonsense.

She trudged back into the house, climbed up to her sitting room, dug Jeffrey's letter from her desk, and flattened it out. He had, he wrote, completed steps to enroll Alf at Eton for Michaelmas term—at Delia's expense, of course. She could afford it; Papa had managed to protect most of her marriage portion from Vincent's excesses and left her a fortune upon his death. She didn't mind the money, but she begrudged Jeffrey's interference.

She let out a burst of breath. *Interference? Too weak a word. He's Alf's guardian and can override whatever objection I make.* She resented his power, and that resentment seethed when he chose to exercise it. Most of the time, Jeffrey left her alone, knowing full well she could manage her own funds and her children. Not in the matter of Alf's education. He had seized on the notion that placing Alf at Eton would advance the family's interests—or rather, that the connection would advance Jeffrey's own interests. He wouldn't budge.

She needed to set out her objections to Jeffrey more firmly. Eton would expose Alf to the worst sorts of snobbery. The school's reputation for misery was well known. Alf hadn't sufficient Greek and Latin to achieve there. He would be behind his peers, although he did have some—of course he did. Delia wasn't a fool. Vincent had hired a tutor for their oldest before he'd died, and the man had tried. Alf loathed lessons but had plodded through. The tutor had despaired and happily parted ways when they'd moved to Ashmead.

She stared at the paper, wishing for eloquence to convince her domineering despot of a brother that she knew what was best for her son. Jeffrey rarely listened—never once he had his mind made up that something was to his benefit. *Drat the man.*

Relief flooded her when Parsons tapped on the sitting room door and entered holding a calling card. Delia's heart raced. *The earl?* Had something happened with the children? Had he come to berate her?

"Sir Robert and Lady Benson have called, my lady. Are we in today?" Parsons asked with a questioning lift of a brow.

"We are," she responded with cheer born of her relief. "Kindly order a tea tray. I'll join them in the drawing room shortly."

More neighbors. Will they be friendly? Their titles weren't the highest. In Delia's experience, however, the newly raised aristos were the most conceited. Still, the very fact that they deigned to call made her charitably disposed. She checked her hair in a mirror and found it fine. Her gown, a simple day dress, was fashionably constructed of one of Graham Shipping's better muslins. It would do. She pinched her cheeks.

She was at the door before a detail struck her.

Benson? How common is that name in Ashmead?

Delia blinked twice at the man who rose to meet her. She had half expected someone who looked like the keeper of The Willow and the Rose. The man who greeted her resembled the Earl of Clarion so closely her breath caught, leaving her speechless.

His chin dipped. Delia thought she heard a sigh.

"Another woman stunned by the Caulfield curse." The woman sitting on her sofa smiled at her own wit. She, at least, appeared friendly enough.

Caulfield. This man must be one of the old earl's by-blows. Gossip had it there were many.

Delia gathered her wits. "Sir Robert and Lady Benson, welcome to my house," she said. She dipped a curtsey, struggling to remember what obeisance the widow of a duke's younger son owed a baronet and failing.

"Thank you, Lady Fitzwallace," Sir Robert said, extending his hand to assist her to her chair.

The woman on the sofa smiled. "We're home only briefly but wished to make the acquaintance of our new neighbor."

Parsons's arrival with the tea cart prevented a reply to that, and no one explained Sir Robert's resemblance to the earl, leaving Delia to the obvious conclusion. Delia ascertained their preferences and began to pour, confident the Sevres tea set and her well-schooled manners made the right impression.

"How are you finding Ashmead?" Lady Benson asked, the tea ceremony complete.

"Ashmead is delightful. I lived my whole life in the city. Nature is a continual revelation and joy. My children—"

"Are they here?" Lady Benson, who appeared to be an utterly unaffected lady, bounced forward with enthusiasm. "Fanny wrote that you have children. She says Amy is enjoying your daughter's company."

Delia took a deep breath. "Of course, you know Fanny Benson. This is all new to me."

"And confusing, no doubt," Sir Robert drawled. "I'll let the ladies explain our family's scandals at a later time." Rob earned a nudge from his wife's shoulder with that.

"Will we meet your children?" the lady asked.

"Not today. They have gone up to the hall to visit the chickens."

Lady Benson beamed. "What fun they must be having. For so long, Ed and Marj had few friends. Have you met the Corbin children? They're Rob's other nieces and nephews." She peered at Delia. "Too fast? I can see I've confused you."

Delia was, in fact, mulling over "Ed and Marj." Lady Benson was obviously on close terms with the earl's family.

"We caught you unprepared. We won't keep you. We came to offer an invitation," Sir Robert said.

"Please join us for dinner on Saturday. It will be a simple family dinner—without children but no formality. I apologize for the rush; we're only here for a week this time. Our other home is in London." Lady Benson beamed expectantly.

"I would be delighted to come," Delia said without hesitation. She quite liked this pair.

"Excellent! I suspect you already know the rest of Rob's family." The Bensons rose to leave, and Delia walked them to the door.

"I am so glad you can come," Lady Benson said. "Eli and Fanny will be there, of course. And Clarion." Delia's reaction must have been obvious, because her guest leaned toward her conspiratorially and whispered, "Don't let his stiffness fool you. He has a good heart." With that astounding observation, they were gone.

Delia reeled under revelation after revelation. Now she'd agreed to dine with his toplofty lordship. She didn't know what to make of it.

One other thought came into focus as she climbed the stairs to her sitting room. *What would Awbury make of the Bensons?* A sly smile overtook her, driving out concerns about the earl. This could be fun.

CHAPTER SIX

AVID DISMOUNTED IN front of Willowbrook, Rob and Lucy Benson's beloved home, handed over the reins to a groom, and took a fortifying breath. Dinner with the Bensons, fond of them though he was, always left him feeling awkward. He managed relations with his irregular half-siblings quite well one-on-one, but nothing in his upbringing had prepared him for social situations involving them and their extended family. Warm and welcoming though the Benson clan was, David always felt as if he put his foot wrong. What his parents would have said didn't bear consideration.

Climbing the steps, Delia Fitzwallace's voice floated through the window. Yet another complication on the evening. A flood of discomfort squelched his flash of excitement at the sound of her gentle laughter. He had no time to ponder his contradictory feelings before the master of the house opened the door to welcome him in.

Rob clapped him on the back with a sympathetic smile and pressed whiskey into his hand. The company had sorted itself out by gender while they waited for dinner. The Benson men, including Old Robert, sipped drinks and fell, as they often did, into a discussion of hacks and horses, the bread and butter of the Willow and of Corbin's Stables nearby. Emma Corbin was Benson's daughter, and Ellis, her husband, the stable owner. David had wondered in the past how Rob could stand such narrow conversation, different as it was from his world in London. Rob raised a glass in sympathy, his expression long-suffering but affectionate.

David's eyes and attention easily strayed. Across the room, the ladies stood deep in amiable conversation, and David's gaze went unerringly to one of them. His fantasies of Delia Fitzwallace's form and face had failed to do her credit. A faintly exotic tint to her skin and tilt to her eyes only added to her allure. If she were a siren—and he wasn't entirely certain she was not—ships piloted by besotted seamen would perish on the rocks below.

The object of his obsession had transformed into a fashionable lady this evening. When one of Rob's cheeky footmen—ruffians the lot of them and former soldiers all—presented a tray with glasses of sherry to the ladies, she accepted one with perfect poise and a gracious nod of her head to her hostess, the picture of a proper society matron. His earth goddess of the woods lay well hidden inside the woman wrapped in that delicious confection of a gown.

Lucy gestured toward the windows, and the ladies crossed the room to peer out at the lawns and gardens. He watched Delia Fitzwallace move with feline grace. When she did, the sarcenet fabric of her gown, falling in graceful folds down her back and over her trim derriere, shimmered, changing color from bright to deeper yellow and back again. It sported flounces on the hem, as had become fashionable, but far from the excesses he had witnessed in London, adding to an impression of understated grace. When she turned to laugh at something Fanny said, his eyes moved without conscious thought to her bodice. Modest when compared to many, it gave nothing to offend, and yet his gaze fixed itself there unbidden.

"Be careful lest my wife catch your tongue hanging from your mouth." Rob startled him.

"Nothing of the sort," David snapped. Rob's victorious grin added to David's discomfort. He'd been caught ogling, and he knew it.

"It never hurts to admire beauty," Rob murmured.

Is that what I'm doing? It felt like something much earthier than that. Lust befuddled a man's brain. His father's excesses had taught him that much. He was not his father, the deity be thanked, and this woman deserved better. He couldn't be easy around her, however. She alternately baffled, intrigued, and inflamed him. If lust was all he could muster, he was best to ignore her.

He turned to face his brother, putting Delia Fitzwallace out of sight. "You're returning to London on Monday?"

Rob nodded. "Do you have a message to deliver?"

"I'll send my reply to Danbury over to you. It will be the polite version. When you see him, give him my undiplomatic one."

"Which is?" Rob raised a brow.

"When hell freezes over," David said, drawing a chuckle.

"Got it. Even if it makes a difference to your ambitions regarding the home secretary position?"

Eli Benson glanced over at them at that, eyes sharp.

"You may help by not bantering any such thing around," David said.

"London already speculates on your ambitions. Can Ashmead be far behind?" Rob asked.

"Ashmead is a world away." At least, David hoped so. "Politics doesn't live here."

"It will when you host that house party," Rob said slyly.

David rolled his eyes. "I said—"

"When hell freezes over. I know you believe that. Danbury can be persuasive."

"Welcome to Willowbrook, David. I apologize for neglecting you." Lucy beamed up at him. She was his late wife's sister, and he'd always been fond of her. Her next sentence proved she could still irritate him. "What's this about Danbury? The house party? Are you going to do it?"

"You look lovely this evening, Lady Benson. You've become

the consummate hostess," he said, ignoring her and earning a glare. "I see you invited our neighbor."

Lucy accepted the rebuff. "Isn't she charming? She quite livens up Ashmead society."

He followed her eyes, and the sight of Lady Fitzwallace chatting amiably with Old Robert sent a jolt of hunger through his veins. He tried, futilely, to pull his enchantment with the woman back. Such attraction wouldn't do. David never gave in to his baser nature, and even if he were in the market for a wife—which he was not—Delia Fitzwallace was not the sort of woman he would choose as his countess and mistress of Clarion Hall.

Wife? Dear God. What brought that to mind?

The call to dinner put an end to fruitless yearning. Sooner eaten, sooner done, and he could take his leave without offending and return to the safety of the Hall.

ACCEPTING FIRST PLACE as his due, Clarion offered their hostess his arm and led Lady Benson in to dinner. He referred to her by her Christian name, as Lucy. If Delia hadn't remembered Fanny Benson telling her she was Clarion's late wife's sister, she would have found it out of character for him.

"Lady Fitzwallace?" Sir Robert bowed over Delia's hand and offered his arm to lead her in, the proper gesture of respect by a host for the highest-ranking guest. She accepted gladly. She could manage proper behavior as well as his toplofty lordship.

Delia had attended many formal dinner parties, including some frightfully formal affairs in her father-in-law's house. This wasn't like that, though conventional courtesies were observed. Clarion sat at his hostess's right, perfectly well mannered, conversing politely with those on either side. Still, she sensed reserve, as though he sat outside the family circle, looking in. Then again, this party was less Caulfield, the earl's family of birth, than Benson, centered on their patriarch, Delia's innkeeper friend.

"Are you comfortable in the Clarion dower house?" Sir Robert asked.

"Quite. I rented it for the gardens alone, but I've come to love the house. My brother…" *Do you really want to bring up Jeffrey, Delia?*

"He objects to you burying yourself in the country?" her host asked with a teasing light in his eyes.

"Something like that." He had objected to the size of the house. Her brother believed his sister and her children ought to live in a stately manor along the lines of Clarion Hall. She glanced at the earl.

Sir Robert followed her eyes. "Three years ago, he wouldn't have come." He shrugged and gave a self-deprecating laugh. "Three years ago, I avoided Ashmead like the plague myself. It has gotten easier over time, but we're still working on it."

"Fanny Benson explained the complexity of your situation, wrought, I gather, by the previous earl?" She hadn't meant to make it sound like a question. Fanny had been blunt. The old earl's debauchery and the disgraceful will in which he'd cut his legitimate children short and listed his bastards for the world to see had resulted in this complicated gathering. "A blessing in the end," Fanny Benson had called it.

"Every bit of it. Fanny and I are only two of the old reprobate's irregular children. That's the public scandal. The private crimes are worse. Our sister Maddy believes he meant to rub his behavior in Clarion's face. As if a real man sowed his seed where he could and the perfectly upright son was the disgrace." Sir Robert grimaced. "Not proper conversation, I fear, especially at dinner, even at one as informal as ours. I apologize."

"Don't apologize. Every family has its uncomfortable truths. Good families keep them out in the open." Secrets had almost choked Delia's family. One, buried deep, still did.

"I think even Clarion would agree to that," he said. "But sometimes it is hard to tell."

She peered down the table again. Sir Robert and Clarion

shared identical hair and eyes, remarkably similar builds and features, but little else. Sir Robert had none of Clarion's aloof dignity, and none of the deep well of sadness she glimpsed occasionally. Her host smiled easily, the earl rarely. Sir Robert called the earl Clarion. Family but not quite.

He called the earl perfectly upright. Delia knew from hard experience they were few and far between among the upper classes. Many titled men ignored their marriage vows.

"I understand your children have been watching frogs hatch." She turned her attention to Ellis Corbin, husband of Sir Robert's sister Emma, proprietor of a prosperous stabling concern, who sat on her other side. "My children did that two years ago. My oldest kept them in a corner of the kitchen. A mistake, that. We were overrun with frogs for a while."

"How many children do you have?" Delia let herself be drawn into a conversation on the joys and challenges of raising children.

Clarion, she noticed, spoke solemnly to Emma Corbin on his left. The party had proven to be quite outside Delia's experience, with a stable owner at one end of the table and an earl at the other. Awbury would have apoplexy, and Jeffery would chastise her for wasting time on a nobody who could not advance her prestige. Luckily neither was here. She found she quite liked Ellis Corbin.

Conversation flowed easily back and forth from right to left.

At the other end of the table, Clarion appeared relieved when Lady Benson announced that the ladies would withdraw. Her initial fear that she had previously judged him too harshly disappeared when he made his excuses and forced Sir Robert to see him to the door. He couldn't bother to stay and socialize.

Delia set about charming the Benson clan that remained behind. She would ponder Clarion's behavior another time.

CHAPTER SEVEN

"I T IS BEYOND enough!" Randle Craddock, Viscount Ashmead's tutor, shook with outrage, while the boy stared down at David's desk rather than face him. The boy's trousers were torn and muddy. Mud streaked his face as well.

"Do you have an explanation, Ashmead?" David asked.

"No, sir." The boy's head bobbed up. "Except…"

"Except?" his father prodded.

"Alf said fishing is better early in the morning."

Alf, is it? David vaguely remembered the truth about early mornings. He rarely fished, and never in Clarion streams. Not since Rob Benson had left Ashmead when they were fourteen. No, not since he'd come home in a similar state two years before that. His father had had him thrashed. Not for the state of his clothing but for the company he kept.

"Is that it? Alfred Fitzwallace recommended the best time for fishing?" The boys' logic intrigued David.

"Yes, sir. And the girls wouldn't know where we went if we left early," Ashmead added earnestly.

It was all David could do to suppress his grin over that bit of masculine superiority. "Does Lady Fitzwallace permit Alfred to wander off at whim?" He had envied Rob Benson that freedom once.

"Alf said his mother would be angry, him going off without saying where, but she would have told the girls and spoiled it."

That the lady might not be raising her children to be utter savages came as a reassuring thought. He had wondered. There was another matter, however, a more serious one. "Mr. Craddock tells me you went without his permission, avoiding your lessons. You know my expectations."

The boy hung his head. "Yes, sir. Lessons first. I'm expected to begin school in the fall, and I'm expected to excel."

"There is also the matter of lying," Craddock spat. "And disrespect. When I saw him sneaking into his bedroom, he locked the door behind him, refused to open it, and claimed to be feverish. I had to ask the housekeeper to unlock the door."

What would a wise father do? David had no idea. His own father would have ordered him beaten, should he have been in residence, and wiped his hands of the matter. Servants and tutors would have done the same in the man's absence. Clearly Craddock expected it as well. He looked almost eager in anticipation.

What would Lady Fitzwallace do? He dismissed that errant thought. David was prepared to overlook the state of the boy's appearance. Lessons were vital, however, and lying a matter of character. Surely a father was obliged to mold his son's character. He had no idea how he was supposed to do that.

David stood and peered down at his son. "Dishonesty is never acceptable in a gentleman," he said. *Common but unacceptable.* "I will not tolerate it."

"This isn't the first day he has missed his lessons. I—" the tutor growled.

David raised a hand. "Lying is only the worst of your offenses, Ashmead. You are confined to the nursery for...for the foreseeable future until I see a change in your behavior."

"But the frogs!" The boy's horrified gaze almost weakened his father's resolve. Almost.

"You will forgo your trips to the Fitzwallace household until there is a change in your attitude. Furthermore—"

The boy opened his mouth as if to argue, thought better of it, and dropped his eyes to his shoes.

"Furthermore, you will complete all lessons you have missed. Working both morning and afternoon should help. You will write an essay for me explaining the damage caused by lying and the importance of honesty. You may bring it to me when it is finished, but remain above stairs otherwise. No pudding at supper. Nursery tea only. Am I clear?"

"Yes, sir," the boy mumbled.

David glanced at the tutor. "See to it he is cleaned up and dressed as a proper young gentleman immediately."

The tutor's sullen expression conveyed his opinion. David wondered if he had done enough, but he wouldn't give the man the satisfaction of knowing he hesitated. "One last thing, Ashmead. You will treat Mr. Craddock with respect at all times. Am I clear?"

A nod seemed the best the boy could manage. He left, head hanging, but turned at the door. "What about the chickens?" he asked.

"You are confined to the nursery. Period. Lady Marjory will have to report on the hatchery."

The little viscount looked as if he had been stabbed in the back, but he didn't argue. Utterly dejected, he left.

An oppressive sense of failure weighed David down when he tried to return to work. He should have handled it better; he wasn't certain how.

FEW JOYS MATCHED a glorious June morning in the country. At least, so it seemed to Delia as she snipped blossoms from the beds around her house to adorn her sitting room. A smock covered her day dress and a wide straw hat sheltered her from the sun. Neither chilly nor too warm, the breeze soothed her soul, and the song of birds in the hedges lifted her spirits. There had been no further harangues from Awbury, and Jeffrey had not responded to her objections to his plans to send Alf to Eton.

Even the children were at peace for the moment. The girls had gone up to the Hall—at least to the outbuildings near the stable block—to check on the chickens. Alf was rusticating in his room as a result of disappearing without notice. Absent his brother's nonsense, Percy played quietly in the grass.

The moment of peace proved fleeting.

"They missed it!" Penny crowed, skipping around the side of the building, Marj with her.

Delia laid her shears in the basket with her cuttings and shaded her eyes with one hand. "Who missed it? And what did they miss?"

"The chickens hatched, and Alf and Ed missed it." Penny grinned widely.

"It serves them right for sneaking off yesterday," Marj added. "Ed didn't do his studies, lied to Craddock, and called Penny and me names. He is in so much trouble. Maybe not for that last but for the rest of it. And he tore his trousers and came home covered in mud."

Good for Ed—for the mud, at least. Delia didn't actually begrudge the boys wanting to avoid the girls' interference. Alf had been disciplined for not telling her where he'd gone when he'd disappeared for most of the day. A day in his room reading Latin wouldn't hurt him, and producing an essay in that language would do him good. She might have to ask Eli Benson to translate it, however.

The girls held hands and danced in a circle, chanting, "The eggs hatched, and they missed it," over and over.

Percy tugged Delia's skirt and demanded to see the baby chickens. Clearly her peace had fled.

"Oh, very well, show me these famous chickens." Delia handed her basket to Joe—who was working nearby and who promised to put the blooms in water—hung up her smock, tied her hat more firmly, and let the girls tug her along the path.

They cooed over the little balls of fluff running about the hatchery and stood for long moments, admiring them.

"Did you weigh them? And mark down which breed they are?" Delia asked, meaning to tease. Two pairs of eyes went wide.

"Science," Marj muttered.

"Exactly," Delia replied. "Is there a notebook being kept?"

"They didn't let us see it," Penny said.

"Pity. It is your chance to show them you can think about the science. If only you had a notebook." Delia looked pointedly at Marj, watching her quick mind at work behind her shining eyes.

"I'll be right back." In a flash, Marj disappeared into the house, leaving Delia, Penny, and Percy to watch the cheeping creatures.

"What's this, then?" An older woman Delia took to be the cook or her assistant came to the henhouse to gather eggs.

"Lady Marjory announced that the chicks had hatched. I'm Lady Fitzwallace from down the hill. I hope I'm not disrupting."

The woman dipped a curtsey. "'Course not. Look all you like. Lady Marj is that excited about a bunch of chicks." The woman shook her head as if the children's excitement was a mystery to her.

The cook smiled benignly and went about her business. Of course. A working kitchen had no practical use for the children's "science."

Marj erupted into the area just then, waving a pencil and notebook. "Ed let me have it, but I have to bring it right back."

Penny eagerly rushed to take a look. "We need to count them! Ed and Alf counted the eggs."

Delia ignored them, her entire attention on the man who had followed Marj out at a sedate pace.

"I wasn't aware we had guests, Marjory," Clarion said, his eyes on Delia.

Delia dropped a curtsey. "Hardly a guest. Merely a curious neighbor investigating your hen house. I hope my intrusion isn't a problem."

Something flared in his eyes. "Of course not! You did express an interest in the life cycle of my chickens, after all."

That she had. She turned to stare at them now, heart hammering in her chest. *Hogswallop, but the man makes me feel gauche—* And other things she didn't care to examine.

Clarion stepped up next to her, hands behind his back. She could feel his heat along her side. "What are we doing?"

Upon closer study, the earl's stiff posture and tense expression left her wondering if he was as uncomfortable as Delia felt. That he might be less sure of himself than he pretended touched her deeply.

Oblivious to the tension between adults, Marj answered him without taking her eyes from the chicks. "They hatched. We have to count them, sir. To tell Ed and Alf." With a dramatic tsk, she began to count over again.

"Where is Mr. Alfred Fitzwallace today?" Clarion asked.

"Confined to his room for a day," Delia said, keeping her gaze on the girls. "He disappeared without telling me."

"Only one day?" Clarion sounded shocked.

Delia's gaze snapped to his face. *Was that criticism?* "And working on his Latin. It seemed sufficient."

The earl appeared to be struggling with a thought or perhaps words he wished to say.

She didn't wait for further disapproval. "Did you really punish Viscount Ashmead for muddying his clothing?"

She'd put her foot in it now. His expression turned thunderous.

THE SIGHT OF Delia Fitzwallace sharing the girls' joy in nature's renewal sent David's wits packing. He envied her comfortable familiarity with the children, something he had never quite been able to achieve. As he stood at her side, any conversational skills he had deserted him. Again. What about this woman made him feel like a nervous lad accounting for his deficiencies every time he saw her?

And then the blasted woman attacked his parenting skills, aiming her barbs at his greatest insecurity with unerring accuracy. His entire body went rigid, and outrage covered his fear that he had somehow failed.

"Ashmead ran off without permission. He failed to do his lessons. He lied to his tutor. And yes, he came home looking like a ragamuffin and nothing like the gentleman he is meant to be. He is confined to his room—completing the Latin and Greek he has missed, offering recompense to Mr. Craddock, and contemplating his character flaws."

Whatever reaction he expected, if any, it wasn't mockery, but the corner of her lips—her very attractive lips—quirked up.

"Goodness. A weighty consequence indeed for one so young." She bit her lip. *Likely to keep from laughing*, he thought, infuriated.

"Ashmead is my heir. He will one day be an earl. He can't afford weakness of character or allow frivolity to interfere with his duty. The younger he learns that, the better." David needed to leave before he throttled her or did something unforgiveable. Like kiss her laughing mouth. "I'll bid you good day, Lady Fitzwallace." He turned on his heels and strode to the hall.

He wasn't fast enough. Her words reached him anyway. "The poor lad. Pity."

CHAPTER EIGHT

A S ANTICIPATED, THE Marquess of Danbury responded forcefully to David's "hell no." David expected a letter. He didn't expect the marquess to appear on his doorstep. Or that he would bring his wife. Yet there they were, two days after his altercation with Lady Fitzwallace.

Now the marchioness had him on a forced march, touring his own home. "Don't be ridiculous, Clarion," she opined. "This house is a perfect venue for a party." The formidable matron swept through the empty cavern that was Clarion's neglected ballroom. Her shrewd eyes took in the years of dust that coated chandeliers and the faded wallpaper, as if cataloging tasks was required. "The wallpaper will do once scrubbed down. Some potted ferns. A few strategically placed paintings. No one will look too closely at how faded it is. The chandeliers will take work but be well worth it. How long since this room had a proper cleaning?"

His father had died eight years before, and his mother had decamped to London soon after. "Eight years. Ten, perhaps—and we have no plans to do so now." He frowned at his friend's wife. "There will be no house party. Danbury, speak to your wife, please," David demanded.

The marquess chuckled. "You best surrender now, you know. She won't give up."

"Harris tells me there are a dozen and potentially fourteen

bedrooms in the guest wing."

David glared at his butler, who trailed after them, probably at the lady's bidding. "The guest wing has been closed these eight years as has this barn of a room, Henrietta. I do not plan to open them." The earl spoke with as much force as he could muster.

The Marchioness of Danbury laughed. "I understand there are more unused rooms in the family wing—including the suite in which you've housed us—you living here alone as you do. They would do for bachelors." She turned to Harris for confirmation. "And plenty of room in the nursery should it become necessary."

David rolled his eyes. "The two of you know me better than most others. You know my financial situation. A house party is not feasible. If we attempt one and it isn't up to standards…"

Danbury snorted. "Standards? Nonsense."

The marchioness brushed aside his protest. "Seriously, Clarion. The room is perfect. As for the rest, isn't that steward of yours a magician? One gathers he has turned the tide on your finances."

He had, at least to a great extent. Eli Benson had been brilliant. David still dreaded the thought of a house party and refused to let his friends bully him. "Benson is a land steward, not a banking wizard."

Unfortunately, both the Danburys knew Benson was more than that—steward, solicitor, man of business. David frowned at the butler. "Harris, isn't it time for supper? Or something."

"If my lady and lords would care to retire to the drawing room, I will alert cook that you have completed your, er, tour," Harris intoned, scurrying out the door with speed that came close to unseemly.

"You look like you need a drink, Clarion," Danbury said, clapping him on the back.

Brandy helped, or it would have if Henrietta Danbury had let up her assault. "This place is a treasure, Clarion, if a bit dull around the edges. You've let it go to neglect. A house party is just the thing to give it life."

David leaned forward, cradling his drink. "What are you

doing here, Henrietta? Don't you have an end-of-Season ball to manage yet?"

"It was last week, you negligent man, and you weren't there." She stared down at him, brows together, her shrewd eyes boring into him. "Do you think this is about impressing the *ton* with your fashion sense? Your consequence, maybe. If you want those who matter—matter to England, not to the social whirl, you widgeon—to pay attention, you have to be seen. You have to impress. You will not wiggle into the home secretary seat by hiding in the country. You won't escape the husband hunting mothers, either, but that is neither here nor there. Danbury and I left London earlier than intended because you are important. What you do is important. We need people in power who will hold the middle course, neither clamping down on dissent until it explodes nor throwing off all restraint. We need you. If clean wallpaper and country air does the trick, then you must do it."

The damned woman's astute political sense hit home as none of her social nonsense had. Danbury smiled benignly and lifted his glass. "Hear, hear," he murmured.

David leaned back and let his head sag backward. "You know I loathe the balls and superficial drivel."

"That's just what it is: superficial. You have to focus on the undercurrents and what's beneath." Henrietta Danbury shook her head. "If it is Bellwood's granddaughter you're worried about, don't. Her mother has moved on to other prey."

David grunted. He'd assumed as much. "Others will take her place. At a ball, I have to watch my every step around the lot of them."

"Surround yourself with ladies who have your interests at heart. When does Lady Madelyn return to Ashmead? She'll know what to do. We could have a council of war. Invite Sir Robert and his brother, that steward of yours, too. Their wives will enlist in the cause gladly."

The earl groaned. Now she threatened to turn his family on him. "Next you'll recruit Lady Fitzwallace."

The expressive brows of the marchioness snapped together. "Who? Lady Elbridge Fitzwallace and her spouse are in Paris."

"Avoiding Awbury, one suspects," Danbury added.

David waved a distracted hand. "It is nothing. I just meant—the neighborhood. Lady Vincent Fitzwallace has taken up residence in my dower house."

"Delia? Here? But how perfect." Lady Danbury's explosion of delight horrified David. It didn't bode well for his peaceful solitude. Her next words confirmed it. "She'll know exactly what should be done."

DELIA'S WEEKLY PIANO lessons for Penny and Amy Rundle were upended by a cyclone. Parsons bustled into the dining room, converted as it was every week to a music room, in a state. "A caller, my lady, a, ah, personage." He held out a heavy calling card, but Delia had no opportunity to take it. The Marchioness of Danbury swept into the room and pulled Delia into a warm embrace.

"Delia, darling, whatever are you doing living in Ashmead, of all Godforsaken places?"

Engulfed in the woman's embrace and wrapped in her spicy scent, Delia couldn't reply. Released, she gaped at the woman. "I—But what are you doing here, Henrietta?"

The arrival of her old friend delighted her. Vincent had insisted they live in London during her marriage. Delia had enjoyed the cultural delights of the capital but not the snubs and slights of the *ton* who found "that sea captain's daughter" beneath them, never mind that her father's shipping empire put him in a position to buy and sell half of them. The Danburys—tolerant, intelligent, and full of life—had been the one bright light in her occasionally dismal days.

"We've come to talk some sense into Clarion!" The marchioness punctuated that astounding statement with a shake of her head that sent feathers bouncing. "But what about you? You disappeared after Vincent's funeral. I expected you back after your year of mourning, but you failed to appear. One tried quizzing Awbury, but he merely growls about 'women who don't know their place,' and I have no patience whatsoever with the man."

"We need a good chat. Parsons, tea in the drawing room, please," Delia said. "Excuse me, Henrietta, while I sort the girls. We were at our music today."

The marchioness frowned. "Never tell me Vincent left you so poorly provided for that you are reduced to giving lessons, Delia."

The thought tickled Delia. "Goodness, no. My father was much too clever to allow that to happen. I'm quite comfortably off, thank you. I adore teaching the girls. You may remember Penny. This is Amy Rundle. Clarion's steward is her guardian, and her sister—"

"Is Fanny Hancock—or Benson now. I met them last year in London. Delightful couple. Good to meet you, Amy. Give your sister my best. With luck, I'll see her while I'm here."

The girls happily abandoned piano for the freedom of the outside, and Delia saw her guest to the drawing room.

The marchioness spread her skirts, accepted tea, and pursed her lips. "Now explain to me why you disappeared."

"I didn't disappear—not exactly. Awbury insisted I stay in the town house in London. I think he wanted me where he could watch my every move for fear that I would bring disgrace on his escutcheon. I wasn't having it. I went home to Bristol. Jeffery has Papa's barn of a house now, and there was plenty of room for us. After leaving me alone for a year, Awbury again demanded I return to "Vincent's house," meaning under his thumb. Awbury owns the damned place. I refused."

"Good for you, but why Ashmead? London is full of houses," Lady Danbury said.

"London was never kind to Peter Graham's daughter, present company excluded. It had no attraction to me. Bristol, however, is crowded and dirty. Children need air and—and nature."

"Nature? How would you know that, Delia? You are city born and bred."

"I guessed. I turned out to be correct. This house and this valley suit me down to my toes, and the children thrive here," Delia answered.

"And Awbury gave up?" A raised aristocratic brow conveyed a world of skepticism.

"He frets. He fears I'll give Clarion a distaste."

"Political vote swapping is a complex dance," Henrietta muttered. "Has he control over your children?"

"No! Yet another blessing for me and source of resentment for my father-in-law. Vincent did me one kind deed. He appointed my brother guardian. It is diabolical that he had to choose a man and not their mother, but better Jeffrey than Awbury. He mostly leaves me be. And so I was free to search out a comfortable country cottage."

The marchioness glanced around her drawing room. "It is…cozy."

"It suits. Now tell me again what you're doing here. What is this business about talking sense into the Earl of Clarion?"

"Danbury wants him for home secretary. The current government dithers while unrest seethes, and the home secretary alternately frets and threatens, unable to formulate any constructive policy for dealing with it. Clarion is perfect, but he does nothing, as if the appointment will fall into his lap as a reward for excellence. We're here to nudge him to make the right friends and sow seeds, but he isn't cooperating."

"Perhaps he doesn't want it," Delia said, trying to put the man she knew into the picture the marchioness painted.

"Oh, he wants it. I can see it in his eyes. But he refuses to do what is necessary."

Delia blinked at that. "Lacking the necessary charm?" It

wasn't a word she would attribute to her aristocratic neighbor.

"That's the least of it. He can hold his own in political discourse, but he hates to socialize and positively refuses to find himself a wife. He needs a political hostess. But will he listen to Danbury and me? No."

"It is difficult to socialize in Ashmead," Delia pointed out.

"Exactly. It's a backwater. I admit, however, it has more than its share of interesting people. Have you met Sir Robert Benson and his wife?"

"The earl's double? I have. Delightful people."

The marchioness chuckled. "Exactly. Ashmead's remoteness isn't fatal, but he must marshal his resources. A house party is the thing. The stubborn man refuses."

"That's why you're here? To convince Clarion to entertain?"

The marchioness beamed at her as if she was a particularly bright pupil. "Lady Madelyn, his sister, will be recruited to manage the thing. Have you met her? She wasn't often in London during your tenure."

"I have not. She's much loved here," Delia murmured.

"And now that I know he has you for a neighbor, things will fall into place. You would make a spectacular hostess."

Delia choked on her tea. "Me? Henrietta, he can barely stand the sight of me! We rarely speak."

CHAPTER NINE

HENRIETTA DANBURY RETURNED from her visit full of praise for Delia Fitzwallace, her ever abundant enthusiasm overflowing, to David's irritation. He must, she insisted, invite the blasted woman for dinner during their visit, a visit that couldn't be short enough for David's peace of mind.

Lady Fitzwallace was presentable enough and pleasant in company. He had no reason to tell Henrietta no, at least not without an embarrassing description of their last encounter in the chicken yard. *Or your unfortunate attraction to the woman.* Delia Fitzwallace confused and disoriented him, and that was the truth.

He pulled out paper to pen an invitation, determined to get it over with before breakfast. He planned to ride out with Danbury this morning. The marquess, at least, was good company, and David wanted to discuss the issue of crime on the west coast docks with him. A soft scratch at the door interrupted him. He ignored it, but it became more insistent.

"Enter."

"My lord, we have a situation." From the look on Harris's face, the situation was serious indeed. "It is Viscount Ashmead," he went on.

"Explain." David was already out of his chair.

"He appears to have injured his arm."

Striding to the door, David puzzled over it. "In the nursery?"

"No, sir. Young Master Fitzwallace explained he was attempting to, er, escape," Harris said.

"Where are they?" David demanded, struggling to keep his anger in check.

"The Fitzwallace lad has taken Mr. Benson around the side of the house to the viscount. He is apparently on the ground beneath the family wing." Harris couldn't keep the distress from his normally bland expression.

David left his office at a dead run, through the entranceway, down the steps, and around the manor. He found Eli Benson and Alfred Fitzwallace kneeling by his son's prone body. A moment of panic almost destroyed him before Ed's eyes, full of anguish, flickered open.

"I'm sorry, sir. I oughtn't to have tried it." The brown eyes so like his mother's fluttered shut, and the boy clenched his jaw against the pain. One arm lay at an odd angle. The side of the boy's face was abraded as if he had scraped it on the bricks.

David swallowed back sick. "Doctor—"

"John Footman has already been dispatched to Dr. Farley, my lord," Benson, ever efficient, said. "His lordship's legs and back appear fine."

"He landed on his arm. Maybe his shoulder," the Fitzwallace hooligan put in.

"I will deal with you momentarily," David snarled.

David brushed the hair from his son's forehead. "Ed, what hurts?"

"Arm. Caught in the vines, and then they broke. Landed crooked."

David gently probed his ribs with little reaction. "Can you lift your leg?"

The boy did. First one and then the other. David ran fingers through the boy's hair but found no bumps or cuts. He glanced up at the nursery window three stories up. A rope of sheets hung from the window two thirds of the way down, and the vines that normally adorned the stone had been torn away. Ed had been lucky. Fear abated, and anger erupted in its place. David shook with it, struggling for control. "We need to get you inside," he said through tight lips.

"I sent for—Ah, here they are." Benson glanced back at two grooms rushing forward carrying a wooden door and a piece of canvas, no doubt intending to use it to carry the boy.

"I'll carry him." David slipped one hand under the viscount's shoulder, eliciting a moan. There seemed no way to carry him without causing pain. He sank back on his heels. "No," he murmured. "I'll try to stabilize the arm while you pull him onto the board."

The viscount's pallor increased, but the process took little time. "Through the kitchen," David ordered the grooms. "There are fewer steps. Bring him to the breakfast room and lay him on the table until Farley comes."

He stood and brushed his hands, pointed at Alfred Fitzwallace, and addressed his words to his steward. "Benson, confine this miscreant to your office and send for his mother. I'll speak with cook about willow bark tea for Ashmead and wait with him until Farley comes." He turned his glare on the neighbor boy, anger so fierce seething beneath the surface he feared what he might do. "I'll deal with you when I've seen to my son."

He turned his back on them and trotted after his son's injured body, encountering the Danburys at the breakfast room door, concern writ in every line of their faces.

"The Fitzwallace boy caused my son injury," he growled without preamble. "That should put period to any dinner invitations. I'll speak with you later." He slammed the door behind him.

DELIA TRIPPED OVER her skirts at the head of the path leading to Clarion Hall, righted herself, and kept running. Eli Benson's spare note had alarmed her. *There has been an accident. Please come at*

once. The footman who had delivered the note trotted at her side.

Penny and Percy had been playing quietly in the nursery, but there was no sign of Alf. She left the younger ones in the care of Joanie, her maid, and ran until she reached the hall's massive front façade, pausing halfway up the steps to gasp for breath, her hand on her heart. The door opened before she recovered.

Clarion's impassive butler stood aside to let her enter. "Master Fitzwallace is this way," he intoned without waiting for her to follow him. He led her to a long hallway to the left of a massive marble fireplace, the largest Delia had ever seen. It and the rest of the entranceway might have left her in awe if she weren't desperately worried about Alf.

"Is my son badly hurt?" she asked, skipping to keep up with the man.

"Not at all, my lady. Viscount Ashmead is the injured party," he answered.

Dear God! What did Alf do? It was almost worse.

They passed a series of ornate doors, and she glimpsed rooms that spoke of the glory of Clarion Hall, but they didn't pause. They passed one door behind which she could hear muffled voices—concerned-sounding voices—but they passed on by.

Just beyond there, the hallway took a sharp turn to the right, and Harris led her through a plain wooden door into what she thought was the business end of the manor, the servants' domain. They came at last to the steward's office, where she found Alf crouched on a straight-backed wooden chair in the far corner, a study in dejection.

Her son leapt to his feet and threw himself at his mother. "It isn't my fault! Ed wanted to come, but he slipped, and now he is dying!"

Delia glanced over his head at Eli Benson behind his desk. He shook his head to reassure her.

"Not dying but injured, perhaps?" she suggested.

"I don't know. The earl made me come here, and I can't go see how he is. Mama, he went white, and his arm—" Alf shuddered.

"Look at me, Alfred Peter Fitzwallace, and tell me exactly what happened. Don't leave anything out." She glanced up at the steward. "And perhaps Mr. Benson can help with some details."

The boy gulped several breaths and pulled himself together. "The tadpoles have grown—you know Marj has been coming to see, right? She's been bringing notes from Ed. When he heard the tadpoles were getting legs, he begged to see them, but Marj didn't see how she could carry them up to the place where they have him locked up. He's a prisoner!"

"Hardly that," Delia murmured, but she sympathized. Clarion's punishment had stretched into a week.

"So Marj said she was filching sheets from the linen closet to make a rope, and I got worried. I thought I'd better go see if I could help. She ran up while I waited below the window."

"Wait. Where is the nursery?" Delia asked, alarmed.

"The children are housed on the third floor," Benson told her. "On that side of the manor, their windows are three and a half stories up. Foolish risk, Master Fitzwallace. Very foolish."

Delia breathed in. "Then what?"

Alf nodded at Benson's comment and ruined it by shrugging. "The sheets held, but they weren't long enough. He yelled something about the ivy and swung over there to grab it, but the ivy came loose when he started to come down on it, and then he just fell."

Delia squeezed her eyes shut, praying the boy would recover.

"Their rope hung down about two thirds of the way. He made it a good distance before he fell," Benson explained sympathetically.

"It was his plan, and he fell. I caught him, but he knocked me down and hit the ground. It wasn't my fault!" Alf insisted.

Alf broke his fall. Delia breathed a short-lived sigh of relief.

"Perhaps you didn't push him, but Ashmead would never have attempted such a hen-witted thing without your influence, Alfred Fitzwallace. Nothing like this happened before he met you!"

Delia rose and turned to face a very irate earl standing in the door, breathing fire. She swallowed her first retort. A boy had been injured.

"How bad are Viscount Ashmead's injuries?" she asked, her jaw and throat tight.

"We won't know for certain until Doctor Farley arrives, but it appears to be limited to his arm."

"Alf broke his fall," Delia said.

The earl ignored that. He glowered at Alf. "What were you doing at Clarion Hall? Did you call up to the window to entice him down?"

Alf shook his head energetically. "Marj brought a note from Ed. They were planning it, and I was afraid. I thought I better make sure—"

"Are you claiming all this wasn't your idea? Absurd. They've never done something like this before." The earl folded his arms, as if holding himself together.

Delia feared an explosion. "You're upset, my lord. Perhaps Alf and I should go on home. Do send word about—"

"Upset? I'm not upset; I'm furious. Your son has corrupted mine—and my daughter, too, if he's telling the truth."

"My. Son. Does. Not. Lie." Delia spat each word emphatically. "And *corrupt*? You think a boy seeking adventure is *corrupt*. God help England when her boys cease to seek adventure."

"He defied authority!" Clarion roared back. "He was attempting to disobey and sneaking. Now he's—That *adventure* as you call it could have killed him."

"Perhaps he might not have attempted to escape if you hadn't imprisoned him over some muddy knees!" Delia's temper had slipped completely and the guard over her tongue with it.

The earl reared back as if struck. "He is confined to the nursery and schoolroom—hardly prison. And it wasn't over mud—he *lied*. He neglected his responsibilities."

"No parent can let lying slip by unpunished, but confining

him for a week? No wonder he wanted to escape. The entire plan was his idea." Delia, arms akimbo, held her ground. "Abetted by his sister."

The earl's mouth gaped open, and Delia turned to Alf, giving the man her back. "As for you, young man, the next time someone attempts something as *stupid*—as utterly foolish as the viscount did, you will fetch an adult to intervene. You're distressed now. Think how you would feel if it had ended even worse. Home with you! We'll discuss your consequences in private."

"Consequences, madam? You haven't managed your son in the past, and I have no trust you'll do so in the future." The earl glared at Alf. "You, young man, are not welcome here. Not at the hall, not at the stables, not even in the damned chicken yard. You've leased the dower cottage. Kindly confine yourself to it. My children will be instructed to stay away and to have nothing to do with you, your sister, or..." He frowned at Delia. "Your mother."

He shuddered a breath while Delia stared at him, unable to formulate a response to that final insult.

She recovered first. "You have an injured son. I will ignore your insult."

"Let me be perfectly clear. Your children are to stay away from mine," he said.

"Avoiding you and this place will be a pleasure, my lord. I would not want my son to see any further ungentlemanly behavior such as you just demonstrated."

"Ungentlemanly?" he choked.

She thought he would actually explode then, so red was his face. "I'll bid you good day," she said sweetly, dropping into a curtsey. "Come, Alf. We're going home."

CHAPTER TEN

Parsons alerted Delia that she had company before she finished her toast the following morning. She found the Marquess and Marchioness of Danbury in her foyer, dressed for travel. They declined coffee or food, claiming they had already broken their fasts and stopped merely to say goodbye.

"Henrietta! Leaving Ashmead so soon?"

"We've stayed as long as we planned to," the marquess said.

The marchioness pulled a face. "And Clarion is in a state."

"What is the word about Viscount Ashmead?" Delia asked.

"The physician said it is a clean break and danger of infection is minimal," Henrietta said, shaking her head. "Poor lad. Hurts like the devil, though. He won't try that bit of foolishness again."

"I should hope not," Delia murmured. "Alfred should have alerted an adult when he saw what they were up to."

"Perhaps, but boys their age always think they can manage the problems they get into without involving us. Our boys did," the marquess said. The pair of them had four children, all well married now.

"You would have had a fit if Andy or Howard did something like that!" Henrietta said.

"Are you certain they didn't? I know for a fact they snuck out at night by the time they were twelve. They certainly got in scrapes we only uncovered later," he murmured. "They were well aware of how emotional you would have been if you knew they were in any sort of danger, and were bound to keep it from you."

"Do you think Clarion overreacted?" Delia asked. "You probably know he blames Alfred for the entire disaster—unfairly, I might add. He has forbidden his children from having anything to do with mine."

The marchioness pursed her lips. "Perhaps a bit." Her husband raised his eyebrows, and she continued, "Oh, very well, yes, quite a bit. Raising children alone isn't easy. He's had to rely on tutors and governesses. Worse, his own upbringing left much to be desired. He has no idea how to go on as a father."

"The only reason the accident happened is that he confined the boy to the nursery to work on his classics because he ran off without permission and came home a mess." Delia bit her lip. "And lied to the tutor," she added, trying to be fair. "A week may have been excessive, however."

"Perhaps. It certainly didn't leave him much room to maneuver regarding yesterday's debacle," the marchioness murmured.

"I confined Alf to two days upstairs and an essay," Delia said.

"A quick thrashing would have been easier," Danbury said. At the ladies' simultaneous gasp of horror, he went on, "Swift justice, quickly over, and move on. Dragging it on for a week is harder on the boy and the father both."

Delia couldn't like it, but she had to admit the "swift" part made sense. "So you're leaving. Have you given up the house party idea?"

"Certainly not! It's why we've stopped. Delia, darling, you simply must mend your fences with Clarion. His career impacts the well-being of many, and you could be so much help with our plans."

"I don't see what I have to do with it. Even if he agrees to the party—which I doubt will happen—his sister is a much more appropriate hostess than I am. Those high sticklers in the Tory party are unlikely to warm up to Peter Graham's daughter. They certainly didn't before."

"Things change, Lady Fitzwallace," Danbury said. "If I may be frank, the high sticklers may have their noses in the air, but they would rally around your brother's money."

Delia's eyes flew open. *Does Jeffery have political ambition?* She couldn't be certain. "Awbury would rather I didn't put myself forward, and his influence has to matter."

"We're not saying you don't have to tread carefully, my dear. We're just asking you to mend your fences with Clarion."

"As long as he is unjust to my son, that is unlikely," Delia insisted.

Lady Danbury patted her hand. "Just think about it."

Watching their carriage pull away, she did. The marchioness had said, "You could be so much help with our plans..." Delia had the uneasy feeling she didn't just mean the house party.

⋙⋘

DAVID SAT AT his son's bedside, shoulders wilting, head down, mind blessedly quiet for the first time in hours. Farley had pronounced Ed fit and assured David that the boy would heal with little danger of infection or complication. He'd suggested a bit—just a bit—of laudanum for the pain and promised to stop by in a few days.

David had slept late and awoke dreading the day and aching from a night in a bedside chair. News that the Danburys had decamped for London improved his mood. Ed's fretful discomfort did not. The boy slept on, having been dosed again in the deep of the night.

As the morning advanced, David felt ready to nod off again as well. When Ed awoke, he took only sips of water. The boy said little, covered his eyes with his good arm, and moaned periodically.

David had had too much time in the night to agonize over the accident and its causes. He knew he would have to address both, but that would keep for a day or two. He dreaded it. Had he truly been too hard on Ed over the fishing incident? Did his son feel so badly used that he had to "escape"? David thought not. He hadn't thrashed the boy as his father would have in such circumstances. Maybe it would have been better if he had.

Fanny Benson called midmorning, escorted to the nursery by her husband.

"How is the lad?" she whispered. "I came to ask if I might help."

"As you see. Uncomfortable. Unhappy with his father." He sighed.

Ed pulled his arm away and attempted a weak smile. "I broke my arm, Mrs. Benson."

"I brought ginger biscuits," she said. "They go well with willow bark tea and soothe the stomach."

Fanny offered to sit with the boy so David might rest. Helpless to ease his son, he left him in the tender care of Fanny Benson and left to seek his valet.

For two days, David haunted the nursery, ignoring Ed's irritable outbursts and coaxing broth and willow bark tea into the boy, spelled periodically by Fanny and once by Benson. When Craddock entered the sickroom, the boy turned his face to the wall. The tutor swept out in high dudgeon. Farley directed that they discontinue laudanum after forty-eight hours, deeming overuse a bigger danger than the arm.

On the third day, David stood in his library, cradling a much-needed brandy, morose and restless, when Harris announced that Lady Fitzwallace had called. The butler's disapproving expression conveyed what he thought of women who appeared at hours improper for calling, particularly to a house suffering illness.

"Shall I tell her you are not in?" Harris asked hopefully.

David nodded, thought better of it, and called the man back. "I'll deal with her myself," he said, putting down his glass and striding from the room.

He found her in the massive entranceway, where Harris had

left her. The butler had not, he noticed with satisfaction, taken her bonnet or shawl. She stood partially turned away from him, head down, hands grasped tightly in front of her. *Surely she didn't expect a welcome!*

"What is your business here, Lady Fitzwallace?" he demanded without greeting.

"I came to ask after E—Viscount Ashmead. We've heard nothing, and my children and I worry for him." She looked pale and subdued, not at all her usual vibrant self.

Good, he thought with satisfaction, *she may as well suffer. I am.*

"Your children ought to have had a thought before my son's accident. There's naught they can do now except additional harm."

A spark appeared in her eyes. *Anger? Defiance? Justification? Let her try.* He raised his chin and clung to his own outrage lest the niggling realization he preferred her with that spark rise to the surface.

She swallowed. Hard. He watched her neck move with it. "Please tell me his condition, and I will be on my way."

"He has a broken arm. He is in great discomfort." The woman paled at his pronouncement, but he continued his callous recitation. "Pain keeps him awake."

That should serve!

Worry and sadness radiated from her.

He weakened slightly. "There is no sign of infection as yet. There is no fever. Farley pronounced it a simple fracture and predicts full recovery with no loss of function. Are you satisfied?"

She nodded but had more to say anyway. "How is Lady Marjory taking it? She must need—"

"Your ideas about what my children do or don't need are unnecessary. Your interference in their lives caused enough trouble," he said.

Her head reared back as if she had been slapped. Her mouth opened and closed over whatever defense she might have made. She dipped a curtsey—a damned late one in David's opinion—

and left him there breathing hard.

He returned to his brandy, sank into a deep leather chair, and struggled to block out the sense of failure that overwhelmed him.

The blasted woman had him questioning the raising of his own son. She had no right and certainly was no example of a good parent. At least, he liked to think she was not.

Would it have been easier if Marjory had lived?

Memories of his short marriage overwhelmed him. He had defied his father to marry a squire's daughter rather than submit to a forced dynastic marriage. Marjory—sweet, compliant, and adoring—had been terrified of his parents. He didn't blame her. He had been too besotted—and noble after he let his lust carry him too far with her—to consider consequences. Ed had been born seven months after their wedding, and his father had never forgiven him, even after Marjory had died giving birth to their daughter. His marriage had been one of the causes of the infamous will.

I must be in dire straits indeed if I'm going over old pain in broad daylight. In the aftermath of Ed's fall, he had needed to tend to Marj, the coconspirator, more desperate to see her whole and well than to chastise her. Benson had found her sobbing in the nursery, thinking her brother dead. The steward had called David from Ed's side while Farley still worked on him, but Marj had hidden under the bed.

Afterward, he'd found her asleep in her bed as if all was well in her world. It had brought a smile, the only one he'd had that horrible day. She had been least in sight ever since, refusing to speak to him.

Am I an ogre to my children? He thought not. Marj had a flair for the dramatic.

CHAPTER ELEVEN

ONCE AGAIN, DAVID eyed the pile of newspapers, neatly stacked but precariously high, on the corner of his desk. Danbury's blasted interfering visit had kept him from his research, and things had piled up. Fretting over his children hadn't helped. Ed submitted meekly to David's orders. Too meekly. His pain had lessened, but he floated about the nursery with his splinted arm in a daze. He accepted willow bark tea for pain, worked at his studies diligently but without enthusiasm, and talked little. Marj refused to speak to David at all. After a disrespectful outburst earned her days with no pudding, she stopped even looking at him, giving him her back if he attempted to tuck her in.

He had done his best with his children. Fear that his best fell short haunted him. He shook his head as if to drive out his demons and picked up his pen. Not one story in the newssheet before him seemed important enough to note.

The fate of England is less important than the well-being of my children.

He chided himself for that bit of rubbish. The fate of England mattered to him *because* of his children. Didn't it? He set the pen back down.

Perhaps what he needed to shake off his dismals was a ride. He might ride down to the Willow and enjoy a pint of ale—and a chat with Old Robert Benson.

He was dressed, mounted, and halfway down the lane when people walking up the road caused him to pull up short. Delia Fitzwallace strode forward with a warlike expression, hand in hand with his daughter. Even glowering as fiercely as Boudicca, that unruly woman sent an uncomfortable shard of attraction right through him. Memory of her face in their last encounter added a large dollop of guilt.

He dismounted and waited for them to approach, trying to assemble his disordered thoughts. Temptation to lash out warred with a suspicion he owed the lady an apology. Desire to chastise his daughter for running off battled with the impulse to hug her. Confusion drove his good sense to the winds.

"What the devil is this about?" he snapped, immediately embarrassed by his rudeness yet determined not to give the woman the satisfaction of seeing it.

"This young lady arrived on my doorstep and threw herself on my mercy." Lady Fitzwallace, chin high and jaw tight, spoke as if every word was forced out.

"She made me come back," Marjory muttered, staring at her feet. Her head bobbed up. "But I needed to talk to her. I did." She cast a sour glance at the woman.

"I'm grateful to you for returning her," he said. It was true enough.

"I hope I don't regret it." The woman eyed him as if he was some species of monster who might eat his young.

His head jerked up. "I beg your pardon, madam?" Her outspoken disrespect gave his words a sharp edge.

The Fitzwallace woman shuddered and sighed, as if struggling for self-control. As well she might be.

"You forbade her from going to my house," she said. "I certainly didn't plan to shelter her like some sort of criminal. I brought her to face you. I merely hope you'll hear her out. She has some important things to say."

He studied his daughter, eight years old and worldly beyond her years. She met his gaze steadily, her expression comically similar to that of the woman who held her hand. More forceful than her mother had ever been.

She has backbone, my daughter. A niggle of pride overtook him. "Come inside, then, Marjory, and I will hear you out."

The girl clung to Delia Fitzwallace's hand and glanced up at the woman with pleading eyes. "Only if Lady Fitz comes, too."

Lady Fitz, is it?

Ignoring her gown, the lady knelt right there in his lane like the farm wife he'd first thought her, grasped both Marj's hands, and spoke softly. That he found it endearing was a complication for another day. "What did we talk about, Marj?" she said. "Remember the words."

"I'm to apologize and—and make my case," the girl replied. "But about Alf—"

Lady Fitzwallace tugged on the tiny hands. Marjory sighed, her gaze on the woman, and went on. "Defend but don't defy—and warn."

"I have confidence in you, Marj," the woman said.

David reached out to help the lady rise as a gentleman ought. She blinked, as if stunned by the gesture. He soaked in the troubled whirlpool of emotion in her expressive eyes, but his hand never wavered. She wore no gloves; David resisted the urge to tear his off, to feel the texture of her skin. When she placed her hand in his, their eyes holding, warmth flowed through him, setting off a flurry of improper thoughts followed by immediate irritation at his weakness.

The lady broke eye contact, whispering to his daughter. "Confidence."

Confidence. It must have been the magic word. Marjory walked directly to him and said, "I apologize for disobeying you by going to see Lady Fitzwallace, sir, but I would like to have a word, if you please."

Spoken like a diplomat. How could he resist? "Then we shall have a word." He glanced behind her. "Perhaps Lady Fitzwallace might be so kind as to join us." The sentence was out before he thought. He hoped he wouldn't be sorry. He didn't wait for an answer.

DELIA ENTERED CLARION Hall again, this time in the company of the earl. She rubbed the hand that had touched his along her skirt to keep from raising it to her face as she followed him to his library. Memories of Awbury standing behind his massive desk, glowering down at her after some mishap, haunted her. Vincent had warned her to avoid the duke's study, the place of all his childhood nightmares, at all costs. A visit there never went well.

Clarion surprised her. Rather than force his daughter to stand before his desk like a prisoner in the dock, he drew a small wooden chair up next to two larger leather ones by the windows and led the girl to it, gesturing Delia toward one of the leather chairs.

"Comfortable, Marjory?" he asked, setting his hands on his knees and leaning toward the girl. "Now tell me what this is about."

Delia's heart did a funny little bounce. Concern warmed the earl's emerald-colored eyes, his love for his daughter apparent in every line of his body. However inept and heavy-handed he had been with his children, he cared for them.

He was still entirely unfair to mine, she reminded herself, holding her resentment firmly in place.

"First, I'm supposed to ap-apologize," Marj said, wiggling a bit in the chair and heaving a breath. "I should have warned you or Lady Fitz what Ed planned." She peered at a spot over the earl's left shoulder. "Even if that would be telling, and I'm not a tattler, and Ed would be mad."

Close enough. Delia swallowed a laugh.

The little one gazed directly at her father. "I didn't know he would fall."

"But you could have anticipated the danger if you thought about it," her father said.

Marj stared at her lap and nodded. "I won't let him climb out the window again."

The earl opened his mouth to say something but closed it again. Delia could almost hear, "What about the next harebrained scheme?" He didn't say it.

"What else do you need to tell me?" the earl asked softly.

"Alf was trying to protect Ed. When I went and told Alf, he said it was a—a *stupid* idea and Ed could get hurt, so he went to manage the thing."

"Manage the thing?" The earl's outrage sounded palpable. Delia braced for an outburst.

Marj nodded vigorously. "That's what he said. He said if Ed insisted on doing it, he needed to be there to catch him. So he stayed down, and I went up." Again, she dipped her head. This time, her shoes, rubbing together at the toe, held her attention. "I was supposed to talk him out of it, but we'd gotten the sheets ready and—" Her head bobbed up. "I did tell him Alf said it was a bad idea." Her chin trembled. "I didn't know he would fall."

"Your defense of your friend is admirable," Clarion said, his voice strangled. "But I believe Lady Fitzwallace also said to warn me about something."

Marj bounced upright. "Yes. This is important, sir. Listen to me. Ed complains that you don't trust him. That you don't listen to him. First, it made him very sad but then angry. He is that upset to be doing Greek all day with Mr. Craddock. He told me the next time he escapes, you'll never find him. That's when I knew I needed to talk to Lady Fitz, because you don't listen. I'm supposed to go to an adult, but you don't listen."

The earl sank back, appalled.

"What else, Marj?" Delia prodded. "Tell him what you told me."

Marj bit her lip. "Craddock hits him, sir. With his hickory stick. On his knuckles when he gets the Greek wrong, and then the page is mussed, and he has to start over. I told Craddock to stop, and he told me I was a sassy-mouthed girl and tutors are supposed to hit. Is that true?" She gazed at him wide-eyed, waiting for the truth from her father.

Clarion swallowed, and Delia watched the play of emotion on his face. She had no doubt he'd suffered the same and more as a child and in public school. She suspected the need to protect conflicted with the need to teach them respect for authority.

"He said he'd hit me if I spoke up to him again," Marj whispered.

Clarion's expression hardened. What passed for toughening boys was one thing, threatening his little girl clearly another.

"No, it is not. Hitting fixes nothing. I've never raised my hand to either of you, and I didn't empower Craddock to do so."

Marj flew out of her chair and into her startled father's arms. "I knew it! You never hurt us. Please tell Craddock to stop. I don't want Ed to disappear where we can't find him." She burrowed her head into his shoulder.

"You can be sure of it, Marjory," he said, his voice thick.

Delia's heart gave an erratic bounce. Knowing she was de trop at that point, she rose, forcing the earl to also. Marj slid from his lap.

"I should go, my lord," Delia said.

"Thank you for bringing my daughter home," he said. "And—" He couldn't seem to formulate what he meant to say next.

Surely not an apology! Delia dipped her head. "Of course," she said.

Marj tugged her father's hand. "About Alf, sir. It isn't fair to blame him, and I know you're ever so fair. You told me your work in Par-leement was about justice," she said, wheedling.

"Marj, I don't think your father blamed Alf for the fall. He didn't. Not specifically," Delia said. *He just blamed Ed's newfound quest for freedom on him.* She understood upset about the injury, but she did not comprehend why he tried to make the boy behave as if he was an adult.

Clarion stiffened. His gaze intensified, but whether in censure or not, she couldn't tell. She feared the former. A profound disappointment settled over her at that thought. When he spoke, he startled her even more.

"Lady Fitzwallace, I need to deal with the war in my nursery just now. But we have much to discuss. May I call on you?"

She wondered later if she could have said no, but of course she didn't. Manners kept her from it. She wasn't sure she would like the conversation, but anticipation put a spring in her step anyway.

Chapter Twelve

T HE EARL DIDN'T disappoint. At the perfectly proper time for a
call, he arrived dressed in a perfectly proper manner for such
calls. Delia sighed. When Parsons announced him, she wondered,
not for the first time, why neighbors couldn't be a bit less formal
with one another. That she had taken care over her appearance as
well—armor for the coming diatribe—also irritated her.

He didn't ask where her children were, assuming most likely
they were confined to their nursery as proper children should be.
In a sense, they had been. The children had been told to remain
on the upper floors under threat of a week without pudding or
creek wading, and she wafted a prayer that they would stay there
until he left.

Parsons arrived soon after they were seated with the perfectly
proper tea service—including iced biscuits—and she used the
opportunity to demonstrate her perfectly proper hostess skills,
pouring and serving. She took a sip of her tea and choked on it
when he spoke.

"I came to apologize," he said.

The shock abated. In Delia's experience, men's apologies
ended in "but" or "that you" and were nothing of the sort. They
were veiled criticism. She waited for it in silence, but when he
didn't go on, she raised her brows in question.

"I was wrong to blame your son."

A bigger surprise. The breath she held seeped out. "Apology

accepted. May I offer you a biscuit?"

He took one, bit in, and gave a moan of pleasure. "Take care lest I steal your cook!"

"We buy them at the Willow," she replied with a grin. "What have you done about Craddock?"

"I sacked him." The relish with which he said the words tickled her even more than the words themselves relieved her.

"I started to simply order him to desist, but the bounder had the effrontery to tell me my children would run wild and that Marjory was already beyond hope. I told him his services were no longer needed. Then I spoke to Miss Walters, Marj's governess. When I suggested she could have come to me if there was a problem, it became clear the tutor had bullied her into silence. She also told me Ashmead's situation was, if anything, worse than Marj described."

Delia took pity on his obvious discomfort. "Raising children is challenging. Most parents of your class"—she didn't dare say *our*—"leave it to hired staff. I think you just suffered the biggest pitfall of that."

"My parents left my upbringing entirely to tutors, unless I caused a stir. Repercussions were swift and merciless when that happened," he said.

Delia felt a grin she couldn't stop. "I'm trying to imagine you causing a stir."

His returning smile was restrained and, she thought, rather sad. "You might be surprised."

She thought of Fanny's story about the previous earl, that he'd set out to humiliate the man in front of her. What sort of father did that?

Clarion's words lifted her from thought. "You don't. Leave the raising of your children to others, that is."

"No. We had a tutor, but I discovered he was Awbury's creature. Moving here gave me an excuse to part ways. Alas, that leaves Alf's education lacking. My brother, his guardian, has enrolled him in Michaelmas term at Eton." She almost burst out her fears about the sort of bullying he could expect over his grandfather and what society called the "taint of trade," but she kept it to herself. "I think their character too important to leave to others, my lord. A tutor can teach Alf Latin, but can he teach honesty, integrity, courage?"

"I heard similar words this morning from someone else," he said, peering at his tea.

Delia waited, having no response to that that wouldn't sound intrusive.

A moment later he glanced up and explained. "I decided to consult the best father I ever met, Robert Benson, proprietor of the Willow."

Delia's brows shot up.

"Does that surprise you?" he asked.

It did. She could only nod.

"He suggested, gently, that raising a future earl is no different than raising any boy. That freedom to make mistakes is the best school we can give our children. He didn't say I've been going about it all wrong. He's too kind for that, but I understood his message."

"Did he have any specific advice?" she asked.

"As it happens, he did. He suggested you and I become better acquainted before we unleash our children entirely. He explained we would be better off presenting a unified front to them. He didn't explain why he had been unable to do that when I was a boy. He didn't have to."

Delia didn't need an explanation, either. The dear man had raised the old earl's son. Rob Benson and Clarion were half-brothers. "What do you propose?"

"I'm going to tell my children that, when they wish to visit, I will come with them, at least for a time, and I ask you to do the same."

Delia blinked in the face of his steady gaze.

"Mr. Benson suggested we take them fishing." His lopsided grin made him look years younger. It almost wormed its way into her heart.

"I would like that," she whispered. She cleared her throat and spoke up. "The boys would love it. We have poles."

"That won't be necessary. I have equipment, first-rate tackle and some very fine flies."

"Flies, my lord? We've used bits of meat for bait." She tensed.

His superior smile set her teeth on edge. *Hogswallop. Have I been caught wrong again?*

"Bait fishing is tolerable for children, but the boys' peers will be expecting them to know how to cast and fly fish," he said. "Danbury maintains a trout stream, for example, where he manages to conduct business as well as relax. I would be happy to—"

There's a right and a wrong way to fish? Trust Clarion to take the joy out of it. She felt her comfort slip away. He must have caught her reaction. His words trailed off.

"Perhaps we ought to start with something simpler, my lord. Visits to the chickens and the nursery—visits here as they have been used to doing—and let the children decide what comes next." Delia didn't think she could bear having Clarion organize them into the correct way to fish.

The earl stiffened. "As you wish. Small steps toward accord?" He didn't look happy.

"Exactly," Delia murmured, fearful she had offended the man.

ASHMEAD LECTURED DAVID on the life cycle of amphibia as they walked to the dower house the next day. A note from Alfred Fitzwallace had caused an uproar over the need to visit, David's first opportunity to put the new policy in place. It seemed he had his son back, at least for the moment, and that alone made the walk a joy. He began to see the wisdom of Old Robert's advice.

Except when Marjory tugged his hand, competing for attention. He may be an earl, but there didn't appear to be enough of him to go around, and no one, not even his effective steward or other family, could do this one thing for him. Only he could be their father. The thought humbled.

She tugged again. "But, sir. Today is Wednesday."

Of course it was. "How is that significant, Marjory?"

"Wednesday is music day," she said as if that ought to be obvious to him. "Do you think they might let me join them?"

He had no idea, nor was he certain he wanted her to. Memories of Lady Fitzwallace dancing among her children with abandon battered his libido.

The path through the woods they called the shortcut let them out behind the dower house. Alfred Fitzwallace leaned out a window below the eaves, waving wildly. "I'll be right down! Wait until you see!" he shouted.

Ashmead urged David toward a sort of trough for horses, but he hesitated. "Shouldn't we inform Lady Fitzwallace that we are here?" Perhaps if it was "music day," they ought to politely leave.

Alfred burst out the kitchen door moments later. "The tails are disappearing. At least one is gone entirely!"

David peered into the mass of swimming froglets. They had piled stones at one end, and one enterprising fellow, a tailless one, had climbed up on it. Another followed him.

"Welcome, my lord. Have you come for the big day?" Lady Fitzwallace approached, poised and perfect.

Perfect? Yes, he thought that might be correct. At least, for this morning. She wore a periwinkle gown covered with tiny white flowers that flattered her form. Not that her form needed flattering.

"Big day?" he asked, dragging his eyes from the woman to Penny Fitzwallace and Amy Rundle, who followed her out. The smallest Fitzwallace clung to his sister's hand. "For your music class?"

Her laughter burbled up and echoed in his chest. "My, no. We have frogs! They took their time, but now we must set them free. I'm so delighted E—Viscount Ashmead is here to participate."

David looked at his son for explanation.

"The tadpoles eat plants, sir, and stay in the water. We've been bringing creek plants—at least, I was helping when I was permitted. If they are safe and comfortable—like they have been here—they take their time meta…meta*morpho*sing. Now they have, they must be returned. Frogs need to come out of the water to breathe, and they need insects to eat."

Alf reached in and picked up one of the frogs on the rock, cupping it in his hands gently. He grinned widely. "Wiggly! Want to hold him, Ed?"

Marj and Penny neared the trough, ignoring Alf. "There's another one on the rock," Marj said.

"Look, Marj, more!" Penny added, pointing to some swimmers.

The boys were absorbed in the creature Alf held. Ashmead brought up his splinted arm and cupped his hands, the fascination on his face.

"Be careful with it, Alf," Lady Fitzwallace cautioned.

Her warning came too late. The frog wiggled free and hit the ground. David feared they were about to deal with tears over a frog massacre, but the little animal was sturdier than he'd expected. It shook itself and hopped toward the weeds. The Fitzwallace toddler started after it, but his mother stayed him with a quick hand and, "No, Percy!"

In the blink of an eye, Marj scooped it up and returned it to the water. "It needs to be wet. It has to stay here until we take it to the stream."

A vociferous discussion ensued about the best way to transport. Lady Fitzwallace called for attention. "Gentlemen and lady scientists," she began, drawing smiles. "We have a large laundry tub and a dog cart to transport it. If we're careful, it should do. We have two large cedar buckets as well if it proves too small. All will have to be covered, for I fear we have jumpers among them."

"Can't we leave the ones that have tails, or are still without four legs, here?" Penny asked.

"It might prove difficult to sort them when you dip them out, Miss Fitzwallace," David murmured.

"The earl is quite right," Lady Fitzwallace said, agreeing with him for once. He struggled not to preen with satisfaction. "Besides that, they are changing so fast they will be happier in the stream."

The ones that survive the shock and aren't eaten. Lady Fitzwallace caught his eye, and he knew she had the same thought.

"Matt Ellis came up from Ashmead two days ago to see them. He warned us. He said they let them out too late and some didn't make it," Alf pronounced solemnly, giving his sister a superior glare.

Joe Holden had settled in as Lady Fitzwallace's man of all work, though he still slept above the Clarion stables. He pulled the cart up to the trough and produced a large tin ladle. The lady handed him the toddler—Percy, she called him—and asked that he be carried up to her maid.

When the children argued over turns, Lady Fitzwallace formed them in a line as effectively as any general. Alfred appeared a bit miffed, but when she endorsed his demand for care lest some fall to the ground, he was somewhat mollified.

The lad's warning had merit. Marj ended up with a wet gown, and several half-grown froglets hit the dirt. They were quickly scooped into the tub but were, he feared, the worse for wear. When Ashmead stepped up, pale yet grim-faced with determination, David leaned forward under the force of an impulse to help. A frown from Lady Fitzwallace made him think better. His son managed to transfer two scoops of water and wigglers one-handed without incident. Pride infused the boy's obvious relief. He didn't volunteer for another turn, however.

Joe returned and pronounced the job well done. He helped them cover the tub and buckets and went back to pruning roses.

They set off.

David hadn't expected to be dragooned into a quest down the lane and into the woods, overseeing a frog transport. His peers in London would be amused at his expense, if they weren't appalled.

Alf managed to pull the cart while the girls flanked the tub and buckets, steadying the boards they used to cover them. A few yards into the woods, when the bumpy path made it more precarious, David lifted the rear of the cart gently, and Lady Fitzwallace caught one bucket that threatened to slide off, preventing disaster. Ashmead trailed along, clearly frustrated that he couldn't be more help with his arm still in a sling.

When they reached the stream, David realized it was the spot at which he had first met Lady Fitzwallace. The memory of her rising from the water, her gown clinging to her seductively as she rose, battered him. What he remembered most, though, was the way she'd covered her consternation with dignity and a show of poise.

"Now what?" Marj asked. Even Alfred looked at a loss.

"Let's begin with the buckets," Lady Fitzwallace suggested.

"Good idea." Marj grabbed for one of the buckets before the boys could get a jump on her and flung off the lid. It teetered in her hand alarmingly, and David rushed forward to assist. Marj gave a yank away, and the bucket overflowed, all over his buff inexpressibles. Water soaked his front and half-developed tadpoles clung to him all the way down.

David vaguely heard Alfred give a shout and frantic words from both girls while they began picking up flopping bodies and tossing them into the creek. His attention was entirely absorbed by the wet to his trousers and Lady Fitzwallace's hands trying to undo the damage. Her very warm hands dabbing places they should not.

CHAPTER THIRTEEN

HOGSWALLOP! SLIMY AMPHIBIANS clung to Clarion's pristine breeches. Previously pristine. Now soaking wet. Delia had already been fretting over the mud on his perfectly polished boots. She acted without thinking, driven to sweep the froglets off, to dab at the wet, to dry his front with her shawl, to make amends for yet another disaster, to, to…

Oh, dear me. A jolt of awareness stayed her unruly actions. Her behavior was beyond inappropriate. His very masculine reaction to her ministrations, obvious and getting more so, set her face and neck in flames. Other more hidden parts as well.

She stood back, unable to meet his eyes, and babbled, "I'm sorry. I'm so sorry. I just—It—The bucket—"

"Yes, the bucket." His rich voice rumbled through her.

She glanced up, and his green eyes, pupils wide, gazed back at her and held. Her heart paused in its run, and her breath stopped entirely.

"Got the last of them, Mama!" Penny shouted.

"No thanks to Marj," Alfred pronounced.

The earl shook off the powerful force that held their eyes together. "Not at all, Mr. Fitzwallace. It was my fault completely," he said.

Delia wafted a swift prayer that the children were too busy to notice the byplay between them—and too young to observe the reaction in his breeches. "We need to get you home to dry quickly, my lord," she said.

"Not until we free this mass of amphibian life into Clarion's streams," he said. "Help me, Alfred. Ashmead, use your good hand to lift that corner. There's a good lad."

Delia drew the girls away and watched, thunderstruck, while the Earl of Clarion upended her battered laundry tub and dumped the rest of the frog mass into the stream. Splashing yet more water, laced with green bits, onto his boots and his son's trousers.

The children let up a cheer and scrambled toward the bank to watch their carefully tended charges swim, many darting to the shelter of weeds, the more developed ones crawling onto the bank and setting up a frog chorus. Delia groaned quietly.

Clarion, wet and muddy, beamed down at his son. Marj burrowed her way under one arm, and he tousled her hair. "Now, you two, I fear Lady Fitzwallace is correct. We need to go home so I can dry off. Harvey will be so unhappy he may threaten to leave me."

Marj wrinkled her nose. "Nothing makes your valet happy." She gazed down at her wet gown and dirty hems. "Miss Walters won't be happy, either." She shrugged.

Delia could think of nothing to say while they walked wordlessly up toward the road that stretched from Ashmead to Clarion Hall. She knew with certainty she would never be able to face the earl again.

THEY LEFT IN silence, pulling the cart. Whatever social skills David had deserted him, lost in a shower of dirty water and amphibian abundance. Lady Fitzwallace couldn't look him in the eye, no doubt mortified by his crude reaction to her well-meaning attentions, and the uncouth state of his appearance. He struggled to summon some polite phrase to put her at ease.

At least the children seemed happy. "That went well," he

said.

She jolted upright, brows high, and covered her mouth with both hands. He couldn't make out any words in the strangled sound she made. Moisture pooled in her eyes.

David stopped in his tracks. He hated a woman's tears, especially when he caused them. He opened his mouth to apologize, trying to find euphemistic words that would not shock the children.

She dropped her hands, and he realized with stunned disbelief that she was laughing. "What is so funny?" he demanded.

"'Well,' my lord? That went *well*?" She ran her eyes from boot tip to cravat, biting her lip.

He turned, continuing their trek through the woods. Irritation sharpened his reply. "The da—darling little creatures are free, aren't they? Safely back in the water that spawned them? Wasn't that the point?" His voice rose alarmingly on that last word. *Is this woman ever satisfied?*

David never lost his temper, but the Fitzwallace woman was driving him perilously close to—

"You're right, sir," Ashmead said. "Our mission was to free the frogs we raised. We accomplished our mission but not without injury—to our clothing, at least." David stopped his dogged march forward, grateful they had reached the road. His son's words stunned him to silence.

He looked around. Penny Fitzwallace had wet hems and dirty hands from grabbing up the froglets that had dropped onto the muddy bank. A streak of mud told him she'd rubbed her cheek to push back her hair that had come loose. Marj's state was as bad or worse, since she'd already dumped water on herself before they'd left the dower house. Ashmead's trousers were soaked to the skin, his boots muddy, and he'd managed to collect a smear of mud on his sling. Even Amy Rundle, who'd followed along, had wet hems and muddy boots.

Alfred Fitzwallace stood tall. "We couldn't have done it without you, sir. It was harder than we expected. Thank you for lending us your support." The boy had his share of damp. He also spoke with a surfeit of dignity and sense—more than the adults in this party, in any case.

"You are very welcome, Mr. Fitzwallace. Returning them to their natural place was the right thing to do," he replied. "Now I suggest we all find our homes and repair the injury Ashmead referred to."

Alfred nodded. "Yes, sir."

Lady Fitzwallace came up next to her son, her pride plain in her expression. "We'll bid you good day, then, my lord," she said. The lane to the dower house opened onto the other side of the road a short distance away. Her curtsey would have been at place in the drawing room of the highest sticklers of the *ton*. Or would have if her appearance weren't so at odds with it.

Her hands—the hands that had seen to the disaster on his breeches—were held safely in front of her to spare her delightful periwinkle gown. It had managed to stay unmarred, but a spot on her chin looked suspiciously like mud, as if she'd nudged it with the back of one hand. Her coiffure had come loose, and sagged over one ear. He admired the raven color, surprised it hadn't occurred to him until now that she'd joined in the entire outside experience without a bonnet. His mother would have had apoplexy over that. Such an odd creature Lady Fitzwallace was. Wonderous and full of life but—

But what, Clarion? He had no word for what he thought of her.

He inclined his head. "I'll see that Amy gets home," he said, his throat thick.

Lady Fitzwallace murmured her thanks and herded her little family on its way. As they left, Alfred lifted his sister onto the cart to ride the rest of the way. He wasn't such a bad lad.

David gestured his children forward, and they wandered on uphill.

"Wasn't that the best afternoon ever?" Marj enthused.

Best ever? Surely not. But David was oddly at peace. He didn't know what to make of it.

CHAPTER FOURTEEN

DELIA BELIEVED THE parting on the road was the last she would ever see of the Earl of Clarion, having blotted her copybook as thoroughly as she possibly could.

A few days later, however, a note arrived from the hall. Formal and neatly written by Ed, Delia's assumption being confirmed by the signature, "Viscount Ashmead." It read,

Mr. Alfred and Miss Penny Fitzwallace are invited to nursery tea at Clarion Hall this afternoon at two.

The postscript, however, was pure Marj. *Hurry. We have kittens.*

A frenzy of anticipation ensued. Delia finally sat the children down for some stern words. No running. No dirt. No rude words. And no water. "You may go if you can behave like the lady and gentleman that you are."

"You're coming too, Mama, so you can see how well we go on," Penny told her.

Fear froze Delia. She hadn't expected to face the earl again. "No, I—" But of course she was. She and the earl had agreed. When the children visited, they would follow. Her shoulders sagged. "Of course I am, dear. Give me a moment to get ready."

Delia rang for her maid and began searching through her wardrobe. "Joanie, I need to escort the older two to Clarion Hall. Please manage Percy this afternoon for me," she said when she heard the door open.

"A morning gown, my lady?" the girl suggested, pulling two likely candidates out.

"Not the periwinkle," Delia replied. *No sense in reminding him of the frog fiasco.*

With little fuss, Joanie dressed her in an attractive topaz muslin and arranged her hair in braids at the crown of her head. She added matching topaz earrings.

"Mama, quit fussing. We need to go." Penny pouted from the doorway. "You look fine enough for viewing kittens."

Fine enough for visiting an earl? Joanie handed her a fashionable high-crowned bonnet with a tasteful nosegay of burnt-orange daisies and chocolate-brown ribbons that complemented her dress and flattered her complexion. The bow she tied beneath her chin quite satisfied Delia. "Now I'm ready."

Penny rolled her eyes. "We're visiting the nursery, not the Prince of Wales."

Joanie handed Delia a soft shawl in complementary colors, the smirk on her face saying "we shall see" as clearly as if she'd spoken out loud.

Delia took a final look in her peering glass. *Girded for combat? Yes. I will do.*

DEEP IN AN analysis of two conflicting reports and two even more questionable newspaper articles about workers in the northwest industrial cities, David resorted to a multicolumn dissection of the details. All he ended up with were more questions, ones he needed to answer before drafting legislation, ones that likely would require the attention of Viscount Rockford's shadowy investigative organization.

Perhaps my brother-in-law might shed light. Brynn Morgan, Madelyn's husband, worked for Rockford in an entirely different capacity than Rob did. His expertise was assessment of engineering reports, but he might have insight. The press, of course, was free to print what they liked, but David's work would be easier if they kept to the facts, and government reports tended to base their "facts" on political assumptions.

"Excuse me, sir." Ashmead peered anxiously from the door. "I'm sorry to disturb you. You may remember we invited the Fitzwallace children to tea."

He did remember. Ashmead had spoken with him about it over breakfast. He'd begun having the boy join him, alternating days with his sister. Their company enlivened his mornings; he regretted not doing it sooner. Still holding his pen, David glanced at the clock on a shelf next to a bust of Shakespeare across the room. "It's early. When do you expect them?" It was just noon.

"That is the thing, sir." The boy looked apologetic.

"Surely they know tea is served in late afternoon," David said. *Even the Fitzwallaces aren't so backward as to not know that.*

"I said two o'clock. But Marj added a note to the bottom of my invitation. She told them to hurry," Ashmead said.

"Why on earth?"

"The kittens, sir. You may not know, but there are new kittens in the stables," the boy explained.

David sighed. "Incentive indeed. They may be here soon. I'll just finish up and—"

"They're here, actually. Harris put them in the drawing room and sent for me. I'm afraid Marj and Penny have already gone to the stable block. Alf is waiting for me. Lady Fitzwallace is going after them. She sent me to tell you she has it in hand. Those were her words: 'in hand.' You needn't accompany us if you are too busy."

Lady Fitzwallace was at Clarion. Of course she was. Remembering their last encounter, he felt a flush of heat.

They'd agreed they would accompany their children. David glanced down at his desk. The work called to him. The lady could certainly handle the children. She'd seemed to be able to command behavior the last time he'd seen her. He bit his lower lip in thought.

"May I go on, sir?" Ashmead asked. His face no longer looked as pale as his sling, for which David knew immense relief.

Lady Fitzwallace can manage the children, David thought, *but are her standards of behavior the same as mine?* Besides, he wanted to see her.

He put his pen down. "I will accompany you," he said, rising. He tugged his jacket into place and straightened his cravat. *Lady Fitzwallace…* He told himself his decision had far more to do with caution about his children than with a desire to see the lady.

With the boy's enthusiasm pulling him along, they overtook Lady Fitzwallace just as she reached the stables. She turned with a smile and dropped into a perfectly appropriate curtsey. The girls were nowhere to be seen, most likely inside. The boys didn't wait for their elders but hurried after their sisters.

The earl inclined his head, returning her smile. She had worn a delectable gown, one that complemented her coloring and caressed her form. When he pulled his eyes from that form, he noticed she wore a bonnet this time, one that would be the envy of Mayfair drawing rooms. "Shall I escort you to the famous kittens?" he asked, offering his arm, deeply warmed when she took it.

They paraded down the stable block as though strolling through Hyde Park. Their children clustered at the far end in a stall he knew to be empty—of horses, that was.

Lady Fitzwallace was uncharacteristically quiet, as if she could not conjure polite small talk. Perhaps she struggled to mention—or, God help him, apologize for—the incident involving his clothing. He preferred she not.

"What is it about animal babies that send children into parox-ysms?" he asked, drawing another smile, to his delight.

"Life, my lord! Life." She grinned. "Reproduction fascinates us all." The words out, she must have realized the less proper implication of them. She paled slightly and turned her head away, hiding her blush behind her bonnet.

"Indeed. We're surrounded with it here in the country. Frogs.

Chickens. Kittens. Bees. Birds."

Her head bobbed up, her smile back in place.

He couldn't resist adding a tease. "How did you ever manage to learn these things, living in the city as you did, my lady?"

She opened her mouth and closed it quickly, having no answer, and David wanted to kick himself. *What was he thinking?* He wasn't. At least, his brain wasn't doing the thinking.

Luckily, they had reached their children and the suggestive conversation was drowned in a chorus of cooing and exclaiming. There were five kittens, all in shades of gray and black. Their proud mother, a lovely gray shorthair, looked on, accepting the adulation as her due.

Penny sat in one corner, cradling a black one; Marj, next to her, set one in her lap, simply staring at it with rapt attention.

The boys' attentive expressions belied their attempt to appear less besotted with the felines. Alfred, once again the practical one, asked a good question. "Why are they kept in the stables?"

"They are working animals, not house pets," David explained. He hadn't been permitted pets as a child and didn't keep hunting dogs. He'd never questioned that Clarion Hall remained animal-free.

"Working? What work can cats do?" Alfred screwed up his brow in thought.

"The mother is one of the estate's effective crew of mousers, and her little ones will no doubt join her in the trade. Without them, the stables and the kitchens would be overrun," David explained.

"We could use a mouser," the boy said. "I watched Mrs. Parsons chasing one with a broom yesterday."

David gazed at Lady Fitzwallace, who had been watching the kittens toddling around with girlish joy. "Would one be welcome, Lady Fitzwallace? In your kitchen, of course," he said.

Penny gasped and rose to her feet, still cradling the kitten. "May we have one, my lord? Oh, Mama, do say yes."

Her mother gave David an impish glance. "We'll have to ask

Mrs. Parsons, of course, but a mouser would be a welcome addition."

A mouser that lived in Penny's room, no doubt. "The babies will need their mother for a while yet. Do consult your cook. If it appears to be welcome, you may take one when they are ready to wean," David said. "Look—the mother has become restless. You best put the babies back with her."

Penny kept her reluctance in check and put the little one right next to its mother. "Look! She's licking him!"

"Bath time in the nursery," Ashmead chortled. "Best get that other one back to its mama, Marj."

David noticed his own daughter was much slower to comply.

"We can check on them every day, Penny!" Marj announced.

Visions of daily disruption to his work for trips to the stall assailed David. "Perhaps not every day. You don't want to force Lady Fitzwallace to trudge up here daily," he said. "In addition, it isn't good for them to be handled so much when they are tiny. They are best left to their mother's attention. Perhaps you can check on them and send reports to the Fitzwallace family."

Marj stuck her defiant lip out, and Penny appeared close to tears.

"And they can visit later this week."

Lady Fitzwallace put an arm around her daughter's shoulder. "Thank you for your gracious invitation, Lord Clarion, and for the offer of a kitten for our house," she said, modeling perfect manners and giving her daughter a pointed look.

"Thank you, my lord," Penny mumbled.

Alfred and Ashmead had wandered to the stall that held Ashmead's own horse. Alfred stroked the beast's nose admiringly. David glanced at Lady Fitzwallace. Did she ride? He ought to ask. He ought to invite Alfred to hack out after Ashmead's arm healed. He tucked those ideas away for a later date.

"Did I hear nursery tea was on order?" he asked.

Soon Ashmead and Marj had them trundling along the path between the hall and the stables, happily discussing a game of spillikins they might enjoy upstairs.

They entered the house through the kitchen and paused at the narrow stairway tucked by the breakfast room that led to the nursery and family quarters. Marj had already started up them. David came to a decision. "Is my presence needed for nursery tea?"

"No, sir," Marj said. "We can manage fine, and the chairs are too small for you—remember?" She giggled.

"I can accompany them," Lady Fitzwallace said.

David had a better idea. "I suggest these young people—who have demonstrated today that they can act like proper gentlemen and ladies—have their tea, and you join me in the drawing room." Recalling, belatedly, the propriety of entertaining a single woman in his home, even a neighbor, he went on, "We could ask my steward to join us."

Lady Fitzwallace glanced up the stairs. "Are you certain?"

"I'll make sure Alf behaves, Mama," Penny said.

Ah, but who will make the adults behave? David thought.

CHAPTER FIFTEEN

DELIA WILLED HER hand not to quiver when she took the arm Clarion had offered. She breathed in and stiffened her spine, determined to show him—for once—the perfect manners instilled in her by her parents and a succession of governesses.

Clarion's unbending butler appeared before they reached the formal drawing room. He bowed and accepted her bonnet, to be placed, no doubt, on the table for that purpose in the hall's imposing entrance. Clarion had a quiet word, and the man departed with dignified tread, likely to order the tea tray.

Clarion led her into a room so large that the dower house parlor, dining room, and breakfast room would fit in it with space to spare. He escorted her to a settee and applied stops to hold the drawing room door open, performing the task rather pointedly in Delia's opinion. *Proprieties maintained, my lord. Duly noted.*

Moments later, a young maid appeared, curtseyed, and announced that tea had been ordered. The girl took a seat in the far corner and pulled out what looked like mending. *Proprieties indeed.*

"Benson, alas, is occupied with an inspection of fences," the earl explained.

And no doubt has better uses for his time than serving as my duenna. Her heart sank with the memory that she had made far less effort at propriety when he'd called on her.

That left them in silence. A glance at the earl confirmed her suspicion that he was as ill at ease as she was. She wondered what they might comfortably say about the children.

"Was your walk pleasant? It is a bit warm today," he said at last.

The weather? Really, Clarion, is that your best? "Yes, thank you. Quite pleasant. We generally take the short way under the trees. The woods always feed my soul." *Feed your soul? Striving for poetry, Delia?*

To her surprise, he smiled at that. She noticed, not for the first time, that his rare smiles always had a tinge of sadness. "I've always thought so. I'm most at peace in the country."

"I'm astonished by that. You spend so much time in London!" she said.

His smile faded. "Parliament is there. And the court. An earldom comes with responsibilities both here in Ashmead and in London."

And they weigh heavily on a man who takes them seriously. She had no doubt this man did. "Ed—Ashmead—seemed to think we were taking you away from work today. If you need to return to it, I will be quite content here," she said.

"Not at all. I'm capable of entertaining a guest, no matter what Henrietta Danbury may have told you." He stiffened. At least, so it seemed to Delia.

She felt her face heat. *Hogswallop. Have I given offense again?* She groped for something to say. "Old Mr. Benson told me you carry England on your shoulders. He said Mr. Eli Benson's job is to care for the Clarion estate to free you to do so…"

Now Clarion appeared embarrassed. "Benson exaggerates— but not about his son's skills. He is a treasure."

"Tell me, then—"

The tea tray arrived, cutting off what she meant to ask. Harris arranged the tea service on the table in front of Delia, cast a keen eye on the maid in the corner, and apparently satisfied, bowed out, leaving the doors propped open.

Harris obviously expected Delia to pour. She did so gladly,

grateful to show off her manners and grace. Glancing up, she found Clarion studying her intently, his expression filled with heat that made her want to squirm. She didn't.

Clarion accepted a cup and an iced biscuit without comment. *Perfect.*

"What were you going to say, Lady Fitzwallace?" he asked.

"I find myself curious about the workings of Parliament. Lady Danbury alluded to domestic security, I believe," Delia said, hoping she'd opened a door to his thoughts.

He considered her question carefully. "She is correct; it is a concern. Crime and disorder endanger us all."

"But one must understand what lies under disorder, not so?" Delia said.

She rather thought her response startled him, startled and pleased. His gaze intensified. "That is exactly correct. Violence and disorder will serve no one. We need well-managed policing for everyone's sake. Long-term, however, that is inadequate to prevent frustration from boiling over as it did with Joe Holden. He seems content working for you."

"Never say you're one of those radicals—universal suffrage, Catholic reform…?" she asked, brows lifted.

"No. Simply sensible about a man's need to feed his family, to find employment, to live with a modicum of dignity. If people are denied that, they will rebel… Especially when they have no voice, no choice in the things that matter to them."

No choice. No voice. As she had none in the matter of Alf's guardianship. As she hadn't in her marriage. Lack of control had almost driven her to—"You fear rebellion as they had in France?" she asked.

"Resentment and the ills of poverty, left unaddressed, will fester. Many of my peers, as you call them, fear any sign of reform will lead to revolution," he replied.

"Awbury is one of them," she muttered.

"Most likely, though he rarely commits until forced to take a position," he replied, studying her carefully. He shook his head as if to push the subject aside. "Tell me, Lady Fitzwallace, what is your objection to fishing?"

The abrupt change of subject flustered her. "I don't object to fishing. I rather enjoy putting a baited hook into a stream and waiting quietly for some poor fish to take a nibble," she answered. *There. Let him call that too plebeian.*

His lip twitched. This time, the smile met his eyes. "There is indeed more than one way to fish. We could do both, fly and bait fishing. Are you up for a competition?"

It was the last thing she'd expected from him. "I with my humble pole, you with your fantastic flies?"

"Let the children decide which side to take." His eyes narrowed in a dare.

"Are you proposing an outing?"

"I am. You bring Penny to see the kittens at the end of the week. I'll remain laboring over my reports. Then next week, I'll show you an excellent fishing spot. One down on the river," he said.

"I will agree on one condition." She raised her chin, one brow lifted high.

"What condition?"

"That you stay well away from the water."

He laughed then, a deep-throated laugh. "Agreed. I would rather not search for a new valet. Shall we say Wednesday?"

They finished their tea in pleasant accord, although the heated glances he cast her way gave her cause for unease.

Preparing for bed that night, she recalled the sensation of his eyes on her. The expression itself was familiar enough. Men had fluttered around her as soon as her year of mourning concluded. A personable young widow in possession of a fortune attracted them like bees to nectar. She had no trouble deflecting hints of marriage. She wasn't about to hand herself and her children into some man's control. Less respectable offers alternately offended and exasperated her. Not one tempted her.

But Clarion? She admitted to a slight attraction. *Oh, very well.*

The day of the frogs, it was much more than that.

He hadn't actually flirted with her then or today. The thought of the oh-so-proper earl flirting sent a ripple of amusement through her. She wasn't mistaken about those heated glances, however. She knew exactly what they meant. He was more likely to be direct if he wanted her. The thought of him offering a blunt and utterly improper proposition did not amuse one bit. It sent shivers up her spine. Of course, she thought, the upright earl would never do such a thing. He might seek out a discreet courtesan, but he would never approach a respectable neighbor.

Why is that so unlikely? He's a man of his class, and they all think a widow is fair game. What would you do if he did make such a proposition? Would you accept? She preferred to believe not but shocked herself by wavering. A mischievous thought intruded. Would her perfectly proper neighbor be perfectly proper in the bedroom? Would he insist on titles and remain buttoned up? The thought made her giggle.

She slipped between the covers and tried to sleep. She still had no answers to her questions.

ASHMEAD SIGHED WITH relief when Paul Farley removed the splint from his arm on Monday afternoon.

"Healing nicely," the doctor murmured. "It won't be much longer."

The boy's face fell when it became obvious the splint would be replaced. "At least another two weeks, I'm afraid," Farley pronounced.

"But we're meant to go fishing on Wednesday!" the boy complained.

Farley ignored the boy and set to work. After a few moments, he glanced up briefly. "A broken arm is an inconvenience but not as much as a broken neck. You might think on that the next time you're tempted to climb out a window."

"You will have to fish one-handed," David told him after he had seen the physician out.

"I may as well sit and bait fish," Ashmead complained, not that he had ever done anything else. He heaved a long-suffering sigh. "You may let Alf use my equipment."

"Generous thought but unnecessary. We have enough for both of you. How about if we see how you do?" David suggested.

"Yes, sir," Ashmead said, downcast.

His daughter was rather more displeased. David had proposed that they limit the expedition to the boys. Lady Fitzwallace had become quite irate on behalf of the female sex initially. She was even more attractive when riled, and David had been tempted to tease her just so he could watch, but that, he quickly realized, was beneath him.

When he'd explained that he would be happy to organize a fishing expedition entirely for the petticoat contingent in the future but that he thought time with just their sons might be good for them, she'd considered it and agreed. She'd made a generous offer. She would organize an activity especially for the girls at the dower house so they were kept busy. He found her even more attractive when he realized how clever she was.

In the end, he had agreed that Marj would visit the dower house under Miss Walter's supervision on Wednesday, two days hence, while he and Lady Fitzwallace took their sons fishing.

They had agreed to one more thing.

Consequently, when Clarion had spoken with Eli Benson about his requirements in a new tutor, he'd added some new specifications in addition to the usual education and background. Candidates must be able to show ability to maintain discipline without resorting to corporal punishment. That had brought a smile to Benson's face, but the steward had also suggested such a paragon might be hard to find. Clarion had waved his concerns away and added one more. The candidate must be ready for two students whose abilities might not coincide. Alf would join Ed mornings in the schoolroom.

Sitting in his office on Tuesday afternoon, at ease for the first time in days, he wondered if he'd lost his mind or found it. He'd gone from forbidding the Fitzwallace children to arranging even more interaction. Worse, he'd gone from avoiding Delia Fitzwallace to allowing her to charm her way right under the emotional armor he normally employed to get around such things. He reminded himself he was not his father, but he could see no respectable outlet should he act on his attraction.

"And tomorrow there will be fishing," he sighed to the empty room. A grin started in his belly and climbed right up to his face. He ignored his misgivings. Things were looking up.

CHAPTER SIXTEEN

A SMALL MUTINY threatening the fishing expedition kept Delia's mind off her roiling uneasiness about Clarion's obvious attraction. When she told Penny the girls were excluded from the fishing excursion, her daughter's outrage vibrated the windows. Notes were surreptitiously exchanged between households as Pen and Marj attempted a joint attack, demanding to be included. Delia almost wavered, but a missive from Clarion stiffened her resolve.

Our daughters threaten organized rebellion. This is our opportunity to present a united front. Do not weaken.

Delia's smile started on her face, blossomed in her chest, and warmed her being. He trusted her. *Organized rebellion indeed.* It appeared the man may have a sense of humor after all. She sighed, certain she stood in grave danger of melting when she saw him again.

Penny huffed and puffed but, when given the charge of entertaining her guest, began to soften. Ideas were suggested and rejected before she settled on cookery. The girls would spend the morning baking with Mrs. Parsons. There was some debate about whether to allow the boys any of the results. When Delia insisted that would be good manners, Penny announced they would also prepare luncheon to be served when the earl, Delia, and the boys returned. "And the boys must eat it," Penny insisted, chin high. Delia could only agree and hope the earl didn't flee from the results.

On the designated morning, she stared in the mirror, dressed in a simple gown, one she used for gardening, certain Clarion would turn up looking fine as sixpence, but unwilling to risk one of her better dresses on a riverbank. She reminded herself he'd already seen her in a faded work dress soaked to the skin after she'd fallen into the creek the day they'd met. She refused to think about the frog dumping expedition.

She raised a hand to her coiffure. Joanie, her maid, had done a splendid job, giving her a braided cluster at her neck. Attractive but simple. Perfect for a day outside. In their small staff, the girl served many functions, including helping with the children. Percy often fell to her care. That she turned out to be a gifted lady's maid had been good fortune. Still, Delia frowned at the simple gray dress, fashionably made though it was. She had no business dressing to entice. None. And yet—

"If I might suggest, my lady, your Turkish shawl would brighten the dress," her maid suggested, holding up the garment in question, a shimmering fall of color that appeared to change with the light.

"Brilliant, Joanie!" Delia said, taking it from her and trying a variety of arrangements. "How shall I ever manage it and a fishing pole?"

"Allow me, my lady." Joanie set to work on the silken shawl, arranging it in an attractive drape and fastening it with a brooch.

Sounds below alerted her that she had dawdled too long. She grabbed her bonnet, a flat crowned affair designed to keep the sun away, and hurried down the stairs only to stop midflight, breathless, at the sight of Clarion. If she thought him attractive before in his perfectly proper attire, he left her knees weak now, dressed as he was as a gentleman of leisure about to ramble in his woods. She had thought him a man chained to his desk; she'd been wrong. Buckskin trousers hugged muscular thighs. At the very least, he spent time on horseback! A black scarf tied in a simple knot topped his loose linen shirt, and a short jacket covered a simple brown waistcoat. As if his clothing hadn't impacted her enough, the appreciative gleam in his eyes made her mouth go dry. She made a mental note to give Joanie a raise.

Another pleasant surprise met her outside. A spacious landau awaited at her doorstep, an open conveyance with ample room for all of them, and equipment strapped to the rear.

She raised a brow in question. She had thought they might trudge down to the bridge across from the Willow.

"I thought to show you good spots along the Afon. Did I do the wrong thing?" he asked.

Touched by the concern she read in his expression and voice, Delia suspected she had been given a glimpse at the self-doubt he showed to few people. When her smile earned an answering one, she said, "Lead us on!"

She took his hand and allowed him to help her into the carriage.

LADY FITZWALLACE SAT on the camp stool David had brought, serenely bait fishing while he tried to teach the boys the fine art of fly-fishing. As if he was some sort of expert.

Casting surreptitious glances at her, he wondered if she found the tackle he'd brought pretentious. She didn't show it, but neither had she appeared impressed.

He had acquired the gear at an exclusive emporium in London for a trip to Danbury's fishing lodge near the borders. He'd used it perhaps twice. The wooden rod she'd brought, likely homemade in the time since she'd moved to Ashmead, bore no resemblance to it. Hers put him in mind of the few times he'd run off to fish with Rob Benson when they were boys before his father had put a stop to it. A wave of nostalgia tugged at his heart.

"Oh!" the lady called as she leapt up, pulling on her rod. The moderate-sized chub on her hook wiggled and fought.

Ashmead hurried over to net it with his good hand. "Well done, Lady Fitz," he crowed.

"That's one for me!" she declared.

Are we keeping score? If so, she's ahead by one. David had had no luck at all.

"Ugly fellow. What is it? Is it edible?" she asked.

The boys looked at David for answers. "Not particularly. Bony, I think. I've seen them used as bait for better fare."

"Shall we let him go?" she asked.

David removed the hook from the fish's mouth. He grinned and offered her the wiggling body. "Care to toss it in?"

She pulled her head high and declared, "No, thank you, my lord. You may," as grandly as any duchess. "But that is still one for me."

The relish she took in her catch belied her formal declaration. There must not have been much opportunity to fish in Bristol. Or London. Henrietta Danbury had told him the lady had lived in London throughout her marriage. He vaguely remembered seeing her once or twice, but of course, much of that time would have been during the last of his own marriage and Marjory's illness. And then mourning. The countryside, he suspected, was entirely new to her; she delighted in nature as much as the children. He let himself be pulled along by her infectious joy.

Two hours later, she was still ahead, three fish to two. If the graylings he'd caught and stored in his creel were better table fair than the bottom-feeders she pulled and tossed back, he was too much of a gentleman to point it out.

Ashmead, frustrated by his one-handed efforts, sat on an oilskin next to her, bait fishing for a while. He added one more to her count. Alfred continued trying to master fly-fishing a bit longer, but now both boys, bored, had taken to skipping rocks, which put a period to his casting.

David carefully wrapped his fishing gear and carried it up to the landau. One did not treat equipment carelessly. The waiting coachman took it from him to strap in place. The horses, the earl noticed, were happily cropping grass in the field behind the carriage.

"Are we leaving, my lord? Shall I hitch the beasties to the carriage?" his man asked.

David considered it for a moment. "It may be a while. The lady is still happily engaged. Perhaps another half hour."

Returning to the riverbank, he peered around. The boys continued to be contentedly and safely occupied. The place he had chosen was indeed idyllic. He'd done well, and Lady Fitzwallace showed no sign of losing interest. At a loss what to do or where to sit, there being only one camp stool, he stood by the bank with his hands behind his back.

The lady cast him an impish glance that said, "I'm winning," but she didn't verbalize it. She turned her beaming face toward the river.

In David's experience, ladies didn't fish and earls didn't sit on the ground, but the day felt perfect. He couldn't explain it. He pulled the oilskin he'd brought up next to the camp stool, sat next to her, and leaned back on his elbows. He let the sun, the breeze through the trees, and the ripples of the water soothe his soul as nothing had in a very long time.

The day and the company. That thought brought him to sit upright. He hadn't expected her to be quite so comfortable to be around. She'd managed, miraculously, to form a picture of perfect poise, her posture upright, her feet pulled together, her simple gray gown arrayed in folds over her knees, a glorious silk shawl draped gracefully around her shoulders...

A nagging impulse prompted him to roil the peace.

"Have you heard from the Marchioness of Danbury?" he asked.

"Goodness, no. I wouldn't expect to. Have you?" she replied, glancing down at him.

"No, but her handiwork is afoot. My sister Maddy informs me she will be in Ashmead in a week. She's bringing Lucy Benson with her."

"How is that the marchioness's work?" she asked, a blink reinforcing her puzzlement.

"I'm about to be ambushed by the women in my family, keen to force me to hold the benighted house party." David sighed wearily.

"Ah. Tell them you will not," she said, eyes on the fishing line bobbing in the water.

"You make it sound easy to deal with determined family members," he said.

"Easy, no. But I certainly have experience doing so." She exhaled.

"Awbury?"

"Of course, but he is easily ignored, at least from my place of peace in Ashmead. Luckily, he has no legal hold on me or my children. My brother is harder to deflect. He's the children's guardian. When you love them, it is more difficult to say no to them, isn't it?" She peered down at him.

David couldn't say why that shocked him. Male family members regularly took the role of guardian. He had simply never considered a mother's point of view. He would have been devastated if another man had power over his children's well-being. "Is he, ah, difficult? Does he bully you about the children?"

"Goodness, no. Not until he wants something. He wants Alf at Eton for reasons of his own, and I have no choice." Her distressed frown troubled David.

"Public school will give Alfred many advantages," he murmured. At least, he always assumed so. *The boy has time with Ashmead's tutor to prepare. That should help.*

"Perhaps. Perhaps I could be persuaded, but as it is, I still have no choice in the matter." She deflected the subject before he could formulate a response to that. "Do you wish to be home secretary? Henrietta Danbury believes you do."

"Yes."

Her expression, wide-eyed, told him that the vehemence behind that one word shocked her as much as it did him.

He looked toward the river and explained, "We spoke of this before. Much is needed. Unrest is seething, especially in the industrial cities. The current office holder does nothing to address it."

"And Danbury believes you're the one to address the issues?" The genuine interest in her eyes wormed its way under his guard.

"He does. And he believes my legislative work and speeches in Lords are not sufficient to advance my interests. I fear he may be right. Politics can be an ugly business." David sighed.

"Perhaps you should listen to him." She turned her eyes back to the river, waiting for his answer.

"Perhaps. Would you attend? Henrietta Danbury says you would be a perfect hostess."

That improper suggestion brought a blush to her cheeks. "Absurd. She'd have us married off in some cloud of gossip and scandal! Your sister should be the one to do it."

"Maddy has the skills; I'm surprised she has the interest. She's much influenced by Henrietta Danbury. She may have withdrawn from London in the years you lived there. Did you know she was a duchess?" He peered up at her.

"But she married a commoner. Yes. She no doubt has the experience you need for a political sortie disguised as a weeklong house party."

He groaned at that. "Who will save me from the hordes of matchmaking mothers?"

Delia turned the full force of her grin on him, taking his breath away. "That I can help with," she said. "So can the ladies of your family."

Their eyes—hers warm, chocolate brown, his, he feared, giving away too much—held for long moments, her pole slack in her lap. A tug on her line broke the moment, and he helped her pull another chub from the water, unhook it, and toss it back.

"Goodness, the sun is high. We are expected for luncheon!" she said.

Soon the boys were herded back to the landau, rudely protesting a luncheon prepared by the girls. Her stern but gentle manner of chastising impressed him. Everything about her that morning had impressed him. She was not at all the wild thing he first took her for, and yet life—vibrant and exuberant—lurked behind her serene façade. His fascination only increased.

Hours later, she walked him to his landau after an interesting but surprisingly edible luncheon. She assured him she would alert him if she heard from the Caulfield and Benson ladies in regard to a house party.

In the flurry of goodbyes and children demanding to know when the next visit would be, he didn't reply.

There will be no such meeting. I don't plan to have a house party. Do I?

CHAPTER SEVENTEEN

DELIA DRAGGED HER feet up the woodland path that was the shortest route to Clarion Hall, the one the children took. An invitation to tea had come from Lady Lucy Benson. That the so-called tea was to occur at the hall rather than Willowbrook, the Bensons' home, meant, she was certain, that she was being asked to be a part of the ambush Clarion feared.

Trudging along, she couldn't shake the thought that Danbury and his marchioness had the right of it. Clarion would be a magnificent home secretary, and the country would be well served. It should be his choice how he pursued the office, however. Everyone deserved a choice.

Harris greeted her formally, took her bonnet and wrap, and showed her to the drawing room. As she suspected, she entered a council of war. Fanny Benson, the steward's wife, and Clarion's half-sister sat next to Lady Benson. Another woman sat with them, one with hair, eyes, and features strikingly similar to Fanny's—and Clarion's.

Madelyn Morgan, no doubt, another Caulfield—sisters and sisters-in-law all. Delia almost turned and fled.

"Lady Fitzwallace, thank you so much for coming," Lady Benson said, rising to greet her. "May I introduce you to Lady Madelyn, David's sister?"

The woman frowned at Lady Benson before turning a benign smile on Delia. "I'm pleased to meet you, Lady Fitzwallace."

Discomfort overcame sense. "Am I meant to call you Your Grace, Lady Madelyn, or Mrs. Morgan?" she blurted out, provoking her friend Fanny to cover her mouth and Lady Benson to laugh out loud.

"Maddy, please," the lady replied, utterly unconcerned. "May I call you Delia? Christian names are so much more comfortable."

Lady Benson rose and rang for tea as if she was the lady of the manor. "Excellent. And call me Lucy, please. I agree with Maddy. We can revert to our most impressive titles when David hosts his ball." Her eyes twinkled conspiratorially. Lady Madelyn—Maddy—rolled her eyes.

"Sit with us please," Maddy said. "We have much to discuss."

"Our first task," Lucy said, "is to convince him to host the thing."

"He fears ambush and truly dreads the thought. Are you convinced it's necessary?" Delia asked.

All three ladies nodded. "Quite," Maddy said. "Lady Danbury had Lucy and me to tea in London, and we discussed it at length. We all read. We all know what is happening in this country, and men underestimate us at their peril."

"My friends in Manchester write often," Fanny put in. "Many are shopkeepers. With wages so low, business is dismal, and the mood of the city is ugly. It is the same, they say, in Liverpool and the mill towns. It can't go on."

"England needs a change, and David is perfect," Lucy added, making no apologies for her bias.

Delia had no argument for that. Clarion had the fortitude and the wisdom for the job, if only he could show more people the man she'd merely glimpsed at the riverside, the caring, personable man she believed lurked inside. "You're convinced he wants the position—and that this house party would further those ambitions?"

Maddy pursed her lips, gathering her thoughts.

Lucy didn't hesitate. "Of course he does. He dedicates his time and formidable intellect to Parliament and seethes over inaction. Even if he didn't, we'd have to push him to it."

"As petty as it seems, he must cultivate the right people. Yes, I believe Danbury is correct about the house party," Maddy added.

"He also fears he'll be besieged by matchmaking mamas and overeager debutantes," Delia said.

"He confided that?" Lucy's brows rose. "It's more than I've gotten out of him."

"He thinks we don't know about Bellwood's granddaughter and the Portland ball," Maddy suggested. "That bit of nonsense subsided weeks ago. The last I heard, the chit was well on her way to betrothal to some baron with a Northumbrian pile."

"I have to admit that he'll be hunted if they think he's ready to look for a wife. Invitations to Clarion Hall would be misinterpreted," Lucy said.

"Task number two, then, is to disabuse the world and his wife of that notion," Maddy said.

Fanny frowned. "How do you propose we do that? You know the *ton*, Maddy. I don't, but even I know we can't send formal invitations with a note tacked on that says, 'To be clear, the earl does not wish to wed.'"

"No, we cannot. We can, however, gently tell everyone we know—the bigger gossips in particular—and let them spread the word," Maddy answered.

"We will be oh so subtle," Lucy said with a laugh. "'Such a pity Clarion has invited political cronies to his estate when he is determined he is not in pursuit of a bride. Such a sad waste.' We sigh sadly when we say it. That won't be hard because we actually do wish he'd—Well, we wish he would consider it."

"It might work, at least with most of the families with eligible daughters. The more determined will try to wriggle their way into the party anyway," Delia said.

"The four of us can handle them if they do," Maddy replied.

Delia grinned at her. "That is what I told him. If we tell him about your whispering campaign to dampen expectations, we might achieve goal one."

"Convincing him? Yes. We should be quite blunt and lead with that," Maddy agreed.

Delia had to admire the women's determination. *Alas, poor Clarion. He doesn't stand a chance.*

"YOU KNOW THERE'S a council of war, don't you?" Eli Benson handed a requested glass of brandy across the desk to David and raised the one he'd poured himself. "Prepare for siege from the petticoat troops, my lord." He pulled up a chair and sat at his ease.

"That became obvious when my sister arrived shortly after breakfast and informed me that she invited Lucy here for tea without so much as an 'if you please,'" David replied morosely. "Have they pulled Fanny into their schemes as well?"

Eli swirled the amber liquid as if studying the light caught through the cut-crystal tumbler. He glanced up slyly. "Of course. I saw Lady Fitzwallace come up the lane a bit ago as well."

Visions of Delia Fitzwallace in the dappled sunlight along the river rose in his mind, her lively expression shifting from teasing to delighted over her fishing prowess, to earnest interest in the concerns of the country. One image would not leave him: the peachy blush that warmed her face as she'd stumbled over her words "married off in a cloud of gossip."

Something about that image of Delia Fitzwallace weakened his determination to have nothing to do with it. "Do we have funds for this house party about which I'm being royally harassed?" David asked.

Benson dropped his eyes to his lap.

"Out with it. What?" David demanded.

Benson drank deeply. "Lady Mad spoke with me. I took the liberty of reviewing her suggestions and developing a budget."

"And?"

"Your investments are doing well. With care, it could be managed." If Benson said so, it was so.

David took a large swallow of his drink. He truly did dread the idea of the cream of London society spilling all over Clarion Hall.

A soft knock warned him of the invasion. When he didn't respond, the door clicked open, and Maddy swept in, followed by reinforcements.

"Good morning, Eli! Come to give aid and comfort to the earl?" Maddy asked.

David's steward beat a hasty retreat, claiming the demands of work. *Coward. Running from a petticoat troop.*

"Do sit down, ladies. Shall I ring for tea? No—wait—you partook of tea in my drawing room," David said.

"We're here on business, my lord earl," his sister said, taking the chair Benson vacated. The others found seats around the room. Delia Fitzwallace, he noticed, gravitated to the window, taking a chair near it but close enough to David to watch his every move. The sunlight sparkled off the highlights in her dark hair.

"Business, is it? Then let's not waste time on trivialities. It's Danbury's blasted house party, I assume. What do you propose?" David caught a faint smile at the corner of Lady Fitzwallace's luscious mouth and took heart.

"You agree?" Lucy chirped from the footman's chair by the door.

"I didn't say that. I said I would listen to the proposal."

"Very well. Let me address the biggest concern before we start." Maddy folded her hands and laid them on the desk. "We are well aware of the irritating, even embarrassing, threats that could be posed to a single man in possession of a title when desperate and ambitious mothers of marriageable daughters get wind that you plan a party."

"You forgot dangerous," David muttered.

"We have a plan for that," Maddy went on.

"You think the four of you can guard me safely the entire time?" he asked with a raised eyebrow. He remembered Lady Fitzwallace's adamant statement that they could.

"Of course. With the help of footmen assigned to watch your bedroom door day and night. Before that, however, we plan a whispering campaign to make certain all of society knows that the Earl of Clarion's interests are entirely political. He is not looking for a wife, nor does he have any intention of doing so." Maddy sat back with a smirk, entirely pleased with herself.

"It won't stop the worst of them," he argued.

"No, but the persistent ones will be easy to identify and track. We'll assign one of us to each of them to watch their every move, leaving you free to focus on influence and power. That is the goal, isn't it?"

It was. His shoulders relaxed. The truth, he admitted to himself, was that he'd teetered close to surrender as soon as he'd heard they were meeting in the drawing room. How could he not allow family to support what was, in the end, his own ambition? He wouldn't let them off easily, though.

"Tell me what you plan. In detail. One word about parlor games in the evening and I'll toss the lot of you out." He folded his arms, raised an eyebrow, and glared at his sister. A quick glance at Delia's grinning face sent a warm shiver through him, and he had to bite his lip to keep from laughing.

Madelyn, of course, ignored his halfhearted attempt to intimidate. Instead, she laid out a perfectly sensible plan for a modest gathering centered on politically connected and interested parties. "We can manage the thing by August, we believe. You, of course, and Danbury will have chief input on the guest list, limiting it to the like-minded and the most needed votes."

His sisters were a formidable force. The minute Delia Fitzwallace had entered his library, however, all hope he could fend off surrender had evaporated. "Very well. If you pledge to keep to your plans, I agree." *God help me.*

CHAPTER EIGHTEEN

S EEING KITTENS APPARENTLY required daily visits to Clarion Hall; house party planning required almost as many. Penny skipped along when Delia responded to an invitation for her third call in ten days. To Delia's relief, the only-with-parents rule had fallen to the side. Delia suspected preparations for the house party would involve many such visits, and she didn't regret it.

The footman who opened the door, Harris being engaged elsewhere, bowed and informed Delia that the ladies were at work in the breakfast room. Invitations had arrived from the printer. The young man, whose name escaped her, let his dignity slip and grinned down at her daughter. "Welcome, Miss Penny. Lady Marjory awaits in the nursery. If you ladies care to follow me, I'll show you the way."

The hall looked brighter somehow and bustled with life. The double doors to the ballroom were open when they walked past, and an army of servants were busy scrubbing wallpaper, polishing, and sweeping. Servants from Willowbrook and the Morgan home augmented the Clarion staff. Joe Holden had reverted to Clarion Hall for now as well. Lucy had mentioned that more—Clarion's skeletal London staff—would be called up, too.

"Where is Mr. Harris today?" Delia asked the footman.

"The chandeliers have been removed to the estate work-rooms. He is overseeing the cleaning. Careful who touches them is Harris."

The stuffy butler had been carried away in delight by the opportunity to open the hall fully. Delia knew this because his eyebrows twitched, and he couldn't prevent the small smile that winked to life—the most expression he'd ever shown—just before he ran off "to alert the staff." He must be in his glory.

"He'll see to the silver next, all those unused pieces that have been in storage," the footman added cheerfully.

They came to the end of the hall, and Penny spied the familiar nursery stairs. Delia pulled her back before she could dart up. "Mind your manners, thank Marj and whoever else assists you, and do not go back home without talking to me first."

"Yes, Mama," the girl chirped, running up the stairs.

The footman opened the door to the breakfast room and announced in his best imitation of Harris, "Lady Vincent Fitzwallace."

Maddy, Lucy, and Fanny, invitations piled around them, grinned up at her. "Thank goodness, reinforcements," Lucy said.

"Am I late?" Delia asked.

"Not at all," Maddy told her. "We were just going over the lists of people to invite. You should take a look as well."

"More than one list?" Delia asked, accepting one that Fanny handed her.

"David began one, Lady Danbury sent one by express, and Lucy and I worked on one over tea on Monday," Maddy told her. "Of course, David has the final say, and he's adamant about not making it too large."

"Our first step is to combine them and finalize the list," Fanny told her. She held a quill and had obviously been in the midst of creating such a final piece.

"Who do you have so far?" Delia asked.

Fanny read it out loud. The Danburys led the list, followed by the entire Tory cabinet. "We just began adding politically prominent peers from both parties—ones David considers moderates."

"Lady Danbury advises including politically influential wives regardless of their husband's leanings or passion for the politics. She also listed some to avoid—cronies of Lord Sidmouth. We have to invite the man himself," Lucy said. Henry Addington, 1st Viscount of Sidmouth, Delia knew, was the current home secretary, the man they hoped to push aside.

"Is that wise? It would be playing your cards rather blatantly," Delia said.

"We're advised to keep him close. Actually, Lady Danbury listed two of his close cronies to invite as well. She rated them both incompetent and more likely to help David's cause than hurt it." Maddy's uneasiness raised the hair on Delia's arms.

"And…," Delia prodded.

"One of them is the Duke of Awbury," Maddy replied.

Delia squeezed her eyes shut briefly. She inhaled deeply. "You are all aware, of course, that he is my father-in-law. Or was."

Maddy nodded. "And we have the impression you would rather avoid the man. Is he horrid?"

"Overbearing. Intrusive. Controlling…"

"So a typical Sidmouth ally. No problem, then," Lucy said, drawing laughter.

"We should leave him off," Fanny declared.

Delia considered it. "Doing that will assuredly harden him against Clarion's cause. And I'll be forced to hear his outrage. I'll just have to play least in sight when he is here and wrap my children in cotton wool." She groaned. "Add him to the list."

They did. "The other is the Earl of Hartwell," Fanny said.

"Is it now?" Maddy mused. "I met Augustus Hobert, the current earl. He struck me as a ninny. The previous earl, his uncle, was a great ally of Sidmouth. Add him. David may need convincing, however. He does not suffer fools gladly."

And so it went. Within an hour, they had a tentative list and began writing invitations to the ones they were certain about. Convivial company made the afternoon fly by, and they had almost finished invitations for all the names Maddy thought certain. Maddy rang for a footman and asked that the carriages be brought around. Delia was startled at the sight of Penny in the doorway with Clarion at her side, dressed and deliciously mussed as if he had just returned from a ride.

"I met this young lady in the stables. She tells me she is to inform her mother that she wishes to go home."

"Marj has schoolwork to complete," Penny added sadly. She gave her mother a pleading glance. Delia assumed she wished not to be reminded of a certain essay she had not completed, at least not in front of Clarion.

"We should go, then," Delia said, rising.

"Productive afternoon, ladies?" Clarion asked, eyeing the pile of finished invitations.

"We finished some we're sure of," his sister said. "We need your final approval of the integrated list. We plan to finish this tomorrow after your input."

"Tomorrow?" Penny said brightly. "May I come again?"

"You may if both you and Marj have your work done by afternoon," the earl said.

Penny looked to Delia.

"Of course. If you finish the essay on cats and their care you promised," Delia said, drawing a chuckle from Clarion.

"May I go up and tell Marj?" the girl asked.

"I see no reason why not," the earl said, catching Delia's eye for permission.

"Come right back. We need to get home," Delia said as Penny darted off.

"The list, David," Lucy said, handing a folded copy to him.

His look of distaste, Delia suspected, had to do with the very idea of the hated house party.

He flipped it open, and his eyes moved smoothly down, his slight frown unchanged until one name caught his eye and his brows rose. He glanced up at Delia, then read on. "Hartwell? The man has more hair than wit. He'll drive me mad in an hour," he said.

Maddy explained Lady Danbury's thoughts on inviting the least effective of Sidmouth's allies. He glanced back at the list and refolded it. "I'll think about it and have it for you in the morning. Have you given thought to those who must be housed here and those we can direct to the Willow? Mr. Benson stands prepared to have every room available."

They agreed to add that to their tasks. "Have you called for your carriages?" the earl asked.

"We have indeed," Maddy said. "Would you like a ride to the dower house, Delia?"

Before she could answer, Clarion interrupted. "If you don't mind a walk on this lovely day, I would be happy to escort you, Lady Fitzwallace."

"I planned on walking, my lord. Escort isn't necessary between your home and mine, is it?" Delia asked.

Penny returned before she could deflect his insistence. She had Marj in tow, begging permission to accompany Penny to the dower house and full of assurances she'd finished her piddly schoolwork and had Miss Walter's permission.

Delia waited while Clarion stooped to speak with his daughter quietly. He appeared to be satisfied, because he agreed that she could go. Both girls had been seized with some brilliant idea about fairy houses that simply would not wait for sluggish adults. They skipped off hand in hand. The ladies beamed at their youthful enthusiasm. Clarion, preoccupied, did not.

"See, David, we have it well in hand. It will be wonderful, just you wait," Lucy said as he helped her into her carriage.

He seemed dubious to Delia, but he didn't argue.

"You will be brilliant, we will be vigilant, and support for your candidacy will envelope you," Maddy told him.

He kissed her cheek and handed her up.

He offered his arm to Delia, who took it automatically.

Maddy leaned out the window and glanced at the two of them, Delia's arm in his. "The one other thing you need is a countess—a political hostess to manage your brilliant dinner parties."

Delia felt his entire body stiffen; his choking sounds alarmed her. His sister's grin disappeared as her carriage drove away before he could make a coherent response.

⟫⟫⟫✶⟪⟪⟪

A GENTLE TOUCH on his arm brought David back to the present. Lady Fitzwallace peered up at him, the concern in her dark eyes warm and penetrating—too penetrating, as if she could see into his very soul.

What a ridiculous notion, Clarion. Remember yourself.

"Shall we?" he asked, gesturing toward the path with a movement of his head.

It took several steps to clear his mind. "Thank you for giving me a moment," he murmured at last "There is something I wish to ask you."

Her puzzled glance touched him.

He hurried on. "I noticed Awbury's name on the list," he said, touching his coat above the pocket where he'd tucked it. "I wondered…"

"If his presence would distress me?" she asked.

He nodded. "I have gathered he made things difficult for you."

"He tried. To address your concerns—it won't make a difference whether or not you choose to invite him. He badgers me from afar and will do so if nearby."

"We don't have to invite him," David said.

"If you don't invite him, he will take offense, particularly because he'll assume my influence and stiffen his resolve to oppose you. Worse, he will probably blame me, and I'll be forced to listen to his complaints. Maddy and Henrietta Danbury believe that his overbearing lordship's heavy-handed bungling on behalf of Sidmouth would work in your favor. Further, that you must invite at least some of Sidmouth's close circle to avoid being too obvious about your ambitions, but should avoid the clever ones. You should invite Awbury."

"What will you do if he accepts?" he asked. It would not do to make her uncomfortable, but he knew she wasn't the sort to shrink from difficult situations.

"He will undoubtedly demand I behave properly (as if I wouldn't!) or even that I stay away from the festivities," she said.

David frowned. He couldn't have a guest intimidating another. He—

"Therefore, I will attend, of course." Her impish grin scattered his thoughts to the winds. It sent his temperature soaring.

What a remarkable woman she is. They reached the woods and its canopy of leaves before he let curiosity get the better of him. She didn't seem the sort to pant after a title. "Why did you marry his son?" He blurted the question out and immediately regretted it. "I'm sorry. That was rude of me."

He paused there, under the cooling embrace of the oaks, setting one hand on hers where it lay on his arm. He regretted the lapse of manners but found he badly wanted to know.

The twist of her lips confirmed his ill manners, but she answered anyway. "I was seventeen and keen to avoid the Season in London my father wished to press on me. I attracted Vincent's interest at a dinner party in Brighton, and Papa seized on it. A duke's son would improve my consequence—and benefit his interests as well."

"You were coerced?"

"Not forced, no. Vincent matched his exquisite good looks— in a highly refined sort of way—with gentleness and basic courtesy. He felt…comfortable."

"Was it? Comfortable?" It seemed such a weak word, *comfortable.* He'd come to expect something entirely different from this woman—joie de vivre at very least.

"With Vincent? Yes. He wanted me for my money, of course, but he was never unkind, much less abusive or cruel, merely negligent. If he was unfaithful, he was remarkably discreet. I saw no sign, and wagging tongues would have loved to tell me about it. The least comfortable part of it, aside from my in-laws, was that I had London society thrust on me after all. I learned to tolerate it." Her smile spoke of long-suffering acceptance. "Besides, I have Alf, Penny, and Percy. Treasures surely."

Ask impertinent questions and you get blunt answers, Clarion. "Did you love him?" he murmured.

"I *liked* him well enough," she replied.

No grand passion. Pity. He'd once wondered if such a thing truly existed. The behavior of his newly wedded siblings seemed to hint that it did, but this woman—passion for life seemed to radiate from her. She deserved no less from a lover. "You've been out of mourning for two years. Do you not wish to remarry?" Rude again, but he needed her answer.

"Good God, no!" she exclaimed, clearly without thinking, and then colored brightly, turning her eyes away and pulling her arm from his, leaving him oddly bereft. She took in a breath and glanced back at him. "Men began pursuing my fortune before it was even proper. I have no desire to put myself, my children, and—what they truly seek—that fortune under a man's control. No, my lord. I do not plan to marry again."

It wasn't what the fashionable world expected, and it wasn't what David had been taught, but he had to respect it. He longed to reassure her that there were honorable men worthy of her. His hand moved of his own accord as if to touch her face. He pulled it back.

"What of you, my lord earl? Why have you never married these several years? I realize you have your heir, but your sister is correct. A man with ambitions requires a wife, one with the breeding to enhance his standing and the training to be a perfect political hostess."

Touché, Lady Fitzwallace.

When he hesitated, she asked, "Did you love your wife?"

Fair enough after my intrusive questions. What sort of man would say he did not love his wife? he wondered. *Most, perhaps.*

"I did. Yes. We were both very young." *Too young to distinguish lust from love, probably.* He had no idea what it might have developed into had she lived. "My parents were horrified. Marjory was a squire's daughter. They believed her beneath them." *Why did you add that, Clarion? What was it about this woman that caused this uncharacteristic need to confide?*

"Did you marry to spite them?" she asked, stunning him.

"Astute observation, Lady Fitzwallace. That may have been a bonus reward. I got Marjory for my wife and showed my father my values were superior to his at the same time," David answered. He could taste his own bitterness. *Was that all my marriage was? My desire to do the right thing by a woman I impregnated and the need to prove I was better than my father?*

She stood a few feet away, studying his face in the dappled light filtering through the trees. "And is that why you never married again—you no longer had added incentive? Or did you love her so very much you can't contemplate another?"

A woman's question, that second part, and he knew it wasn't true. He had loved Marjory—surely, he did—and it left an echo of warm memory. But it didn't haunt him. Why, then? "At first I couldn't bear to bring another woman into the sort of venom my parents unleashed."

"And then?" Her genuine interest touched him.

"The estate needed… It needed everything; I had nothing to give a wife. I got used to being alone." He hadn't considered anything else until this past year, watching siblings marry, one after another.

"But now that has lifted, and you pour your energy into Parliament and the state of the nation. Yet you stiffened when Maddy suggested you needed a partner, someone to help you carry those burdens."

"Why does every love-besotted woman think everyone needs what she has? I'm perfectly fine as I am." A niggling voice deep inside suggested he was more lonely than fine. He silenced it with the reminder there were other solutions to loneliness. Family. Friendship.

"As you say. That seems to make a pair of us. Dedicated to the single state. Shall we be friends, then?" she asked, touching his very thoughts unknowingly.

"Friends," he agreed with a nod, offering his arm again.

"If we're to be friends, you best call me Delia." She sighed, taking his arm and turning her face toward home.

"I would be honored." He hesitated before going on. "I am David. Perhaps we ought to keep that for times when we are private."

"Of course," she said, glancing up with a saucy grin. "We wouldn't like to give people ideas."

Walking home afterward, he berated himself. *What were you thinking, spilling all your maudlin thoughts, Clarion? What must she think of you for probing her hurts?* Worse, he knew with acute awareness that the aching physical attraction he felt for Delia Fitzwallace made something as simple as friendship unlikely.

Another thought came uninvited. *You've been without a woman for too long. A widow with no interest in marriage would make a comfortable mistress.* Except Delia Fitzwallace would never be simply comfortable. He refused to consider it. *And you,* a different, more familiar voice taunted, *are not your father, unable to control your urges.*

He reached the hall and rang for his valet to change out of his riding togs before giving thought to the underlying issue. Perhaps Maddy had been correct. He needed a wife. A proper, well-bred countess. Was it too much to hope he might like her as well?

CHAPTER NINETEEN

S ETTLED IN HER sitting room with her feet up an hour later, Delia slipped a tot of brandy into her tea and reviewed the entire extraordinary conversation in her head. *What happened to our aloof neighbor? His sister must have rattled him badly.*

Sipping her tea, she couldn't help but think his sister was right. A politically astute wife, one with the breeding to enhance his standing and the training to be a perfect political hostess, would not only further his ambitions but ensure his success once he secured the appointment.

You, alas, are not that woman, Delia. Her family background in trade, if not her roots in Jamaica, made her ineligible as a society wife. Hard experience had taught her that. She took a deeper swallow and let the brandy soothe the shard of pain that thought brought on. *Foolish heart. I have no interest in marriage.* Or so she told herself firmly.

If any man might tempt her to foolish impulse, he would, she admitted reluctantly. Clarion's rich baritone, all warm honey, reverberated through her when he spoke as he had that afternoon. His sad green eyes cried out for her to reach up and soothe the lines around them. His lean masculine frame—She cut off that line of thought. *Fruitless, Delia, and a threat to the life you've built here.*

She didn't plan to marry—not even to a man as attractive as David Caulfield. She stiffened her back and let the brandy stiffen her resolve. She had even less desire to wage the battles fought in the ballrooms and parlors of London society as any wife of a cabinet minister would be required to do.

They had agreed to be friends, had they not? What she could do for her friend was support this house party just beyond the trees. She would manage to be proper and above reproach for David's sake until it was over.

She drained her cup and put it down. Enough nonsense. She had another problem. Jeffrey's name had been on the infamous list as well. She knew why. Political ambition required friends with cold, hard cash, and Jeffrey Graham had buckets of it. Clarion hadn't mentioned it, which meant he was open to the idea, but she thought her brother ought to hear from her personally. She wandered down to her secretaire in the drawing room, took a pen, and wrote a letter to her brother with a warning and a question. *Expect an invitation. Do you wish to accept it?*

She hoped he did, if only to annoy Awbury.

SEVERAL DAYS LATER, unexpected company caught Delia at her least respectable. Again. She peered down from her perch on a ladder, Percy held firmly in front of her, to find a duchess in her kitchen yard—at least, a former one in the form of Madelyn Morgan.

Hogswallop! So much for resolving to be above reproach.

Delia had lifted her son up to see the nest full of baby birds that Alf had discovered and Ed had pronounced *brilliant*, and now she had to carry him down again.

"Do you need help with that?" David's honeyed voice called up.

She thought he might be laughing at her and would have been irritated if a worse thought hadn't intruded. *He can see up my skirts.*

Maddy noticed that as well. "She might find it easier to get down if we back away," she suggested, a suspicious wobble in her voice.

"She can do it. Lady Fitz can do anything. It's my turn next," Marj informed her father.

David's voice floated up again. "Shall I take the little one from you?"

Percy, with one of his mother's arms firmly around the waist, wiggled about to see who was speaking, putting both of them in a precarious position. Before she could formulate an answer, she felt David along her back, his heat penetrating her gown; he must be standing a mere step or two lower than she. "Hold on to the ladder with one hand while I…" He reached around to her front, his arm skimming one breast and scattering coherent thought as he took a firm hold on the little boy. Percy went to him eagerly, wrapping his arms around David's neck.

"Hello, my lord," the boy said with a grin. "We're looking at baby birds. Want to see?"

Delia closed her eyes and gripped the ladder with both hands. She leaned her forehead against it and resisted the urge to bang her head. She would have preferred to disappear into the tree.

"Let's back up so your Mama can come down." David's voice faded as he moved away.

There was nothing for it but to climb down with as much grace as she could muster, little though it was. She brushed dirt off her front, pausing before turning.

"Me now," Marj chirped, pushing in front of Delia to take hold of the ladder.

Delia would have gone up behind her for safety, but David broke in. "Not alone," he said sharply.

Delia moved away so he could follow his daughter up the ladder, relieved to have a moment to collect herself. She glanced ruefully at Maddy, trying not to remember that her new friend had once been the Duchess of Glenmoor. "I wasn't expecting callers," she said.

"We ought to have called. Country manners, I fear. David will chastise me on the way back." Maddy dipped her head with a sheepish grin. "We came to ask you something about the invitations. Would you feel better with a moment to freshen up?"

Delia glanced down and patted her coiffure, quickly finding pins that had come loose and anchoring them. *Hogswallop! He's seen worse…*

"You look fine as a sixpence." The deep voice sent her heart galloping. *How did he get so close without me seeing?*

She dropped a shaking hand and peered up into his intense green eyes. "Do I now? I never took you for a liar, my lord."

He tipped his head to hide his smile. "It is all in the point of view, my lady."

"I will invite you to tea, but first we have to secure this ladder so no one takes a notion to climb up unsupervised." Ed's rueful grin was almost as wide as Alf's cheeky one.

Those two do not require a ladder, which is how they found the nest in the first place. Delia gave them a pointed glance. "Do not disturb that nest or molest those birds. Do you hear me?"

"Yes, Lady Fitz," Ed murmured.

"Yes, Mama," Alf said simultaneously.

"Alfred, kindly take Percy up to Joanie. You may play outside with your friends, but—"

"Don't disturb the baby birds," Alf finished. He picked up a protesting Percy and flung him over his shoulder. "Come up with me, Ed. I'll show you my copy of *Ivanhoe*. Barnabas sent it to me from London."

Joe Holden removed the ladder. "I'll lock it up in the shed, my lady," he said, wandering off cheerfully. Marj and Penny skipped after the man, reminding him that he'd promised them bits of wood for their fairy village.

Delia brushed the last bits of dirt from her hands. "Shall we have tea?" She lifted her chin and wrapped herself in the façade of a proper lady.

⤜⤜⤜⬗⤛⤛⤛

DAVID WATCHED DELIA efficiently dispatch both ladder and children, castigating himself for the breach of good manners by appearing without invitation or warning. Outside of proper calling hours. Through her kitchen yard. *And you're flirting with the woman, you blasted fool.*

He definitely shouldn't have called in so ramshackle a manner. Hell, he shouldn't have called on her at all. He'd stayed away for a week after that mortifying conversation in the wood.

Why did you let your sister… He stifled the thought. There had been no coercion and little persuasion. Maddy had merely suggested they update Delia on the guest list and replies—one in particular. He had jumped at the chance to come. The truth was he had missed her.

When Delia gestured around toward the front entrance, he offered his arm to his sister. As he walked behind their hostess, his eyes never left the sway of her derriere. Maddy poked him discreetly with her elbow, suggesting she'd caught him ogling. *That's the reason you should stay away: the woman brings out your basest instincts. She deserves better.*

Delia, on the other hand, behaved like a perfect lady, leading them along a path that wound through the expansive garden, beds of flowers that had once been Madelyn's passion and were now Delia's. She brought them to her drawing room and rang for tea. *At least one of us has decent manners,* he thought morosely.

"You appear unhappy, my lord. Is there a problem with the invitations or other plans?" Delia asked.

"David," he corrected, scowling at his sister, daring her to comment. "We're private here."

Delia colored sweetly. "David, then," she murmured. "Is there a problem?"

"There is no problem with the invitations precisely, but I did have a question," Maddy said, glancing between the two of them, questions David preferred not to answer dancing in her eyes. "Lady Danbury put Jeffrey Graham on the list, suggesting he was a potential donor if we secured his support. I should have made the connection, but I'm afraid I didn't realize he was your brother."

"My time in London didn't coincide with yours. I thought the entire world knew, or I would have drawn it to your attention," Delia said. She stiffened slightly.

David squirmed in his seat. He had seen the name and let it slip by. She'd been so straightforward about Awbury he'd thought she would speak up if she didn't want her brother invited. Hearing Maddy refer so bluntly to him as a potential donor put it in a different light. *Pleased to meet you, Graham. I'm glad to have your money for my political causes, and oh, by the way, I lust after your sister.*

"I apologize for not discussing it with you before we sent the invitation. His formal acceptance came by express courier this morning," Maddy explained.

Delia sighed. "Express courier is typical of Jeffrey—of our family. I confess I warned him it was coming."

The line between her brows boded ill, David thought. *Something bothers the woman.*

She spoke before he could gently probe. "Since we're being open with one another, perhaps I should tell you some things about Jeffery. About the Grahams. We are, as the *ton* frequently sneers, in trade. Business and coin of the realm are Jeffery's primary interests. He views most of life—including, I fear, David's ambitions—in terms of what they can do for Graham Shipping. His generosity is transactional always."

She glanced from one to the other, as if expecting them to leap up in horror. David spoke to reassure but not without thought. "He and your father built their business with that focus. I wouldn't expect otherwise. Neither would I ever make promises in exchange for support. It will be up to him."

Delia smiled then, and David's heart beat more steadily. "He can be direct, but he isn't crude. Nor would he make coarse demands. He thinks more long-term. He will support your cause if he thinks your influence might ultimately benefit Graham Shipping in some way. In fact, he supports many causes you cherish. Better policing, particularly of the docks, for example. He believes the current unrest is bad for business—and conversely that what is bad for business is ultimately bad for the country." She cast him an impish grin. "He can be charming. You might actually like him. He won't embarrass you at the gathering."

"Of course not!" Maddy exclaimed. "Lady Danbury certainly vouched for him."

"But will he make you uneasy, Delia?" David asked, leaning forward.

"I love my brother, overbearing though he can be. It'll be good to see him."

She didn't look as confident as her words, but David believed she meant it. He remembered what she'd told him about the man's rare interference. Perhaps they could speak about Alfred's preparation for Eton. The shared tutoring appeared to be progressing well.

She went on. "He'll stay here, of course, so you needn't factor him into your plans."

David glanced up at the ceiling. "Do you have room here?"

She grinned. "The house is cozy, I'll admit, and I'm prepared for him to harangue me to look for something more impressive, but yes, we have room. The four bedrooms are all currently in use, but Alfred can bunk in with Percy for a week or two. Jeffrey can have his room. We'll put out a pallet in the dressing room or in the attics for his valet."

There seemed nothing else to say. He would be entertaining not only half the *ton* but Delia Fitzwallace's powerful—and no doubt protective—brother. David wondered if he might flee to the Outer Hebrides before then.

"Excellent. I feel much better about that," Maddy said. "Can we discuss flowers and your promise to assist?"

"Of course! The gardens here were your passion, I believe, Maddy. You are welcome to every bloom we can nurse along. The succession houses at the hall should be abundant," Delia suggested.

"They are coming back from long neglect, but they aren't going to be enough. Willowgrove doesn't particularly focus on flowers. Lucy has them in a fever of candle making over there. Thank goodness for her bees. My own gardens are newly planted and no help. I've spoken with a nursery in Nottingham." Maddy raised a cloth folder from her lap. "Notes and ideas. I thought you might help me sort it out."

David stood at the window when the two women went outside to peruse the gardens, studying them as they pointed and gestured before sitting on a convenient bench to take notes. Flowers. Candles. Servants. Silver polishing. Invitations. He needed a woman's help. The thought had nagged him since Madelyn's sly remark and that uncomfortable conversation with Delia. He needed a wife whether he wanted one or not.

He stared long moments at Delia Fitzwallace. *How hard would it be to weaken her determination not to marry again?* The voice in his soul that had held a stranglehold on him much of his life rose again. *Would she even make the sort of countess you need?* He thought of her up a tree and thought she would suit him fine. *In London? At court? As the wife of a cabinet member?* He doubted many would think so. Would it suit *her* ought to be a better question.

Delia laughed at something Maddy said, and David turned away from the window. Henrietta Danbury could be relied on to be discreet. Why not invite a candidate or two to be Countess of Clarion? It wouldn't hurt to look at the field. Then again—*How will Delia behave among the company at the house party?* He quite looked forward to it.

CHAPTER TWENTY

DELIA SPENT THE better part of the next two weeks at Clarion Hall. While her children ran free in Clarion's nurseries, his sisters drew her deeper and deeper into preparations. One day, she joined Maddy on a trip to the nursery in Nottingham. One day, she assisted with the cleaning of the newly opened guest wing. On another, she set up a room assignment chart. On yet another, the sisters planned seating for various meals with Delia's help. Menus took two of them two days to map out. Lucy begged out of that one.

This day, covered in a smock, Delia and Maddy reviewed paintings in the attic.

"Size matters! We want to cover as much wall as possible," Maddy reminded her. The wallpaper in the ballroom had been cleaned but was rather dull. Tall ferns and paintings would liven it up.

Unfortunately, most of the pieces in the attic were small landscapes or portraits of dogs. It quickly became obvious the Caulfields did not indulge in old masters.

Delia eyed two full-length portraits, of the former earl and his countess. Florid and corpulent, the earl seemed to gaze down on her with sneering superiority. The painter's skill had been unable to disguise the ravages of indulgence and debauchery.

"Cover it!" Maddy frowned at her father's image. "David made it clear these are not to be used. I wholeheartedly agree."

"Was there ever a painting of him as a young man?" Delia asked, still studying the painting and saddened by just how miserable her friend's relationship with her parents must have been. "I see nothing of David, much less you, in it."

Maddy narrowed her gaze. "A bit in the eyes if you look closely. Even the hair is faded. It must have been brighter auburn once. Certainly nothing of David in his character. There should be an earlier painting, but I don't know where it is." She turned her back on the portraits.

The countess stood with her nose upturned in her portrait, the same glare of superiority on her face. Blonde and blowsy. Delia thought her manner as avaricious as it was arrogant. Perhaps it was both. She covered them gladly.

An hour of searching revealed no further paintings large enough to be helpful. Flipping through one pile of dogs and horses, Delia discovered the very thing she had asked about, however, a modest-sized portrait of David's father as a younger man. The hair, the eyes, and the build resembled both David and Rob Benson, but the resemblance ended there. An unpleasant scowl and predatory gleam marred the expression. Neither of his sons shared his character, the Almighty be thanked.

She left it in the pile and walked back to Maddy wiping her hands on her smock. "I have a suggestion. That lovely seascape in the gallery leading to the guest wing isn't as large as we hoped, but it might work."

"Yes. But I thought we decided that removing the larger ones would leave obvious evidence on the walls," Maddy reminded her.

"I've been considering that. I suggest we drape some velvet from the ceiling over the empty spot and put one or more of these lovely little landscapes over it. In fact, there are at least three places I can think of where that might work," Delia said. "There's a draper here in Ashmead. If he doesn't have what we need, Graham Shipping's warehouses undoubtedly do. There should be time to order it, but we'll have to act quickly."

"Brilliant! I'm so glad we have your clever mind engaged in this effort!"

The two women selected three midsize landscapes they thought might work and handed them over to a waiting footman. They wandered back down through the bustle of cleaning in the family wing, making their way to the estate offices on the first floor.

Delia's heart sped up when David stood from the table where he'd been studying their various charts. His face lit up, and she dared think the expression was meant for her and her alone.

Calm yourself, Delia. Friends. Remember?

His initial expression turned to a frown. "Word from the Willow is that it has already begun. A young lady twisted her ankle in the stable yard. Her dear parents, Baron Algernon Something-or-Other and his wife, believe she may need weeks to recover."

"Algernon Wadsworth? His wife is a harpy. We won't budge them. Pity they'll take up rooms at the Willow," Maddy said. "I'll encourage Mr. Benson to confine them to one room. He should have no problem when higher titles arrive."

"Shall I begin the list?" Fanny asked, waggling her quill from her place at the table.

"What list?" David asked.

"The security list—ladies that need watching," Fanny said with a grin.

"Excellent idea. I'll hold all of you to your promises." David handed the packet he was holding to Maddy.

"More replies?" she asked, sorting through them. "Fanny is recording the responses." The frank on one caught her eye. She handed the rest to Fanny and frowned over it. "Did we invite the Marquess of Wilbury? Isn't he a Whig?"

David shrugged. "Yes but not a radical. He was on the Danbury list, I think."

Maddy glanced up. "Well, they're coming and bringing their granddaughter. Best add them to those staying in the guest wing.

And add the granddaughter, Lady Estelle Wilton, to the list of ladies to keep under watch." She took a seat next to Fanny.

Delia was left at the side of the room with David, and his penetrating gaze made her heart rush. She could feel his look as a caress on her face. *An illusion surely, Delia, and you know it won't do.*

"Feeling hunted?" she asked, though she thought the emotions in his eyes regret and something altogether different than fright.

He glanced away and breathed in deeply. "Like an elk in the royal reserves. The rapacious mothers are circling."

"It's happening quickly," Delia murmured.

"Sooner over, sooner behind me. Any luck with paintings?" he asked.

I saw your father. It explained much.

She kept that thought to herself. "We found no large enough ones but we have a plan." She explained her ideas, delighted with his swift approval.

"Well done. I'll leave you ladies with my gratitude for your labors," he said, taking her hand and bowing over it. She held her breath, thinking he meant to kiss it. He did not.

His eyes darkened, however, and he reached out a hand as if to touch her face. He pulled it back and rubbed one side of his own nose.

Her hand jerked up to her face, mirroring his actions. She felt her face blush warmly. "Dirt?"

"Just a smudge," he said with his familiar sad smile. "Stay for tea." It wasn't a question.

"It would be my pleasure," she responded. *My increasingly foolish pleasure.* She watched him walk away and tried to recall why she was so determined never to marry.

DAMN. WITH HER *hair coming loose, a smock over her arm, and a smudge on her nose, it was almost all you could do to remember you*

were a gentleman. With an audience. What are you becoming?

David left before he could drag Delia someplace private, determined to think about both Delia Fitzwallace and the subject of marriage rationally. He would see this house party through and focus on his political ambitions—the reason the subject of marriage had arisen in the first place. As for Delia, well, his feelings about her would have to wait until he settled the issue of marriage.

He hadn't told his sisters he'd asked Lady Danbury to suggest a well-bred, well-behaved, perfectly proper young woman with reasonably good looks and a suitable bloodline. He realized too late that he had described precisely the sort of person his mother would have chosen. What he wished for might be an entirely different thing.

Estelle Wilton, Wilbury's granddaughter, he suspected was the recommended lady. Time would tell how suitable the choice.

He joined Eli Benson in the steward's office. An army of guests would stress the estate in a number of ways. Carriages to store. Feed for horses. Housing for ostlers and grooms. His able steward had much of it in hand. David suggested he increase the expected numbers.

"Yes. Da told me some unexpected guests turned up at the Willow already," Benson said.

"Baron Wadsworth and his ambitious daughter," David said morosely.

"Of course, if they aren't invited, we don't need to accommodate their horses," Benson said with a sly grin.

David gave the cheeky remark his best glower. "You know full well we'll have to invite them to the ball at least. They'll insert themselves to come along any time the invited guests travel up from the inn." He leaned forward to add, "But I'll be damned if we foot their bill at the Willow."

Cheered by that shot across the Wadsworths' bow, David rose. "Tea at four. We'll review all parts of this campaign then."

Chapter Twenty-One

T OWARD THE END of July, tea at day's end to review progress had become their custom, and Delia relished the comradery, touched beyond measure to be included in what was essentially a family endeavor. The sisters had become her friends, and planning for this house party—having, as it did, a higher purpose—filled her with satisfaction.

Alone in her room those nights, however, Delia couldn't hide behind the work or her friends. Her thoughts strayed to one thing—one person. David. Her mind—and her eyes—strayed to David every day, awaiting tea, if not a moment alone. When he entered a room, her heart sped up. If he came close, her breathing became erratic. Even caring for her children couldn't keep him from her thoughts.

For her children's sake, she should be more careful, but she felt perfectly safe. David, proper and upright as he was, would never attempt seduction, much less importune her for some sort of long-term liaison she would have to refuse. He needed a wife; even Delia could see that. He didn't need one with Delia's penchant for undignified lapses or her family baggage. She would never do as his countess, even if he decided to ask. Even if she wanted to marry again, which she did not. Or so she told herself, although it became increasingly difficult to believe he had any of the rapacious or autocratic qualities she feared in a husband.

She allowed her secret absorption as a sort of guilty pleasure, a private indulgence. The planning and his presence brightened her days. When it all ended, she would tuck it away as a sweet memory and raise her children in peace. For now, tea at day's end became her great joy, and the days slipped by quickly.

July passed into August, and Rob Benson joined them on the first Monday. It had become his habit. He had taken leave from his security duties for a few weeks and assumed the role of liaison with the Willow, preferring to aid his father rather than get caught up in the frenzy of preparation at the hall, but he would turn up for tea when he came to fetch Lucy. This particular afternoon with less than a week to go before guests descended upon them, he arrived with his son, Kit, on his shoulder. He took the baby to the Willow at old Mr. Benson's request. There were plenty of folk to look after him at the inn.

The ladies vied to snuggle him and exclaim over his blue eyes and strawberry-blond curls. Kit, however, wanted nothing to do with that. He could run and climb as well as walk and was eager to demonstrate. David leaned forward, elbows on his knees, a gentle smile on his face at the boy's antics. When Kit ran up to him, he clapped his hands awkwardly as a man might who had little experience with babies. The sight delighted Delia, but Kit quickly lost interest and ran off.

"How are arrangements coming along?" Rob asked, pulling a teetering vase away from toddler hands. Delia expected David to react in horror; he did not. Her heart turned over when he scooped the boy up to kiss the top of his head. With Kit on his hip, he rang for someone to take the boy upstairs. She had always seen his manner with children as stiff and insecure. *Is he beginning to thaw a bit?*

"Things are going well! We will be ready," Maddy said, picking up the thread of the conversation. She reeled off the day's accomplishments.

"I think the guest list is solid," Lucy added. Kit wiggled from David's arms and ran in circles.

"We're holding two rooms in the guest wing unassigned, for

late changes," Delia added, finally catching Kit's attention by dangling her fringed reticule before him. She corralled him on the settee to play with her reticule, a ploy that had often worked with Percy. She peered over at David, still standing by the bellpull, drawn by some mysterious intuition that his eyes were on her. His smile warmed her down to the soles of her feet. When she smiled back, he came over and picked up Kit so he could sit next to her. Kit leaned against him, chewing happily on her reticule.

Maddy had elected to stay at the hall. Her husband would join them in a few days. The nursery had been augmented by Gwen Morgan and its staff by the Morgans' nursemaid. "Who, besides Brynn and Maddy, are you putting in the family wing?" Rob asked.

"Bachelors!" David, Maddy, and Lucy answered simultaneously, drawing a grin from Rob.

"I have no doubt you will have plenty of unattached young women to make up numbers. One tried to climb into my carriage at the Willow," Rob said, drawing a groan from David.

When a footman appeared, Delia gently extracted her reticule, which now had a well-chewed and sodden corner, and carried Kit to the young man's startled arms, whispering instructions to take him to the nursery, where Maddy's infant and her nurse could be found.

"Let me guess. The Wadsworth chit," David said.

"Yes. She's a determined one. Who is assigned guard duty on that one?" Rob asked.

"I think Lucy can manage her when she is here," Maddy said.

"And I plan to stay away from the Willow completely," David added.

"Having observed her mother's strategies firsthand, I repeat my offer to send for some of my men," Rob said. His "men" were an elite security force at the service of the diplomatic houses in London. "They should be able to handle encroaching females."

"Are you sure of that? Women leave Corporal Goodfellow completely flustered," Lucy teased.

Delia dithered by the door, unsure whether to take the place next to David again. Their so-called friendship left her more confused than it ought. Sitting so close had scrambled her thoughts.

A soft knock presaged Harris. Entering, the butler addressed David. "Forgive me for interrupting, my lord, but a Mr. Jeffrey Graham has arrived asking for Lady Fitzwallace."

Her gasp choked her. *Dear God! He's early.* Her idyll at Clarion Hall was over.

⇶⇴

GRAHAM! DAVID SHOT a quick glance at Delia, who was taken unawares and adorably flustered.

"He must have gone to the dower house and found me gone," she said, twisting her skirt in one hand. "I'll—"

"Show him in, Harris," David said. Delia's eyes flew open; her anxious expression had him doubting he'd done the right thing. He rose to greet the newcomer.

Jeffrey Graham's bulk, tall and muscular, impeccably clad in a well-tailored suit, filled the doorway, where he paused, taking in the people gathered.

"Welcome to Clarion Hall, Mr. Graham. I'm Clarion."

"My lord." Graham's bow, a crisp and precisely correct inclination from the waist, struck David as self-assured. Neither deferential nor defiant. "I don't mean to intrude. I was told I would find my sister here," he said. His eyes—deep brown like Delia's—lit up when she approached.

David might have expected her to throw her arms around a beloved brother, improper though that might be in company. He wondered whether the awkwardness in her posture spoke of her relationship with Graham or the avid observers in the room. She laid a hand on Graham's arm and smiled back at him. "Welcome, Jeffrey. I didn't expect you so soon." Something in the teasing light in her eyes spoke of affection.

David gestured toward a seat. "You've come far, Graham. May we offer tea—or something stronger?"

When the man hesitated, David went on. "You've come upon a family gathering. We've met to review our preparations as has become our habit." Before Graham could respond, David introduced them all in correct order of precedence, beginning with "my sister Lady Madelyn, Mrs. Morgan." *Clumsy, that, but at least I didn't toss in "duchess." She would throttle me.*

"I'm honored, but I truly prefer not to intrude," Graham said.

"Of course. You'll wish to freshen up and rest from your travels. Don't let us impose on you," Maddy responded. "We will have time this week and next to get acquainted."

David looked forward to meeting Graham very much. He had seen his name on the endless lists, and when Delia had made no objection, left him there. As his intense, if confused, interest in Delia grew daily, seeing her brother in a social setting might help him unravel more about her and about his own feelings. His gaze flickered to his shoe tips. *Unravel whether or not the two of you could possibly suit, you mean.*

His attention had wandered. He glanced back up to hear Delia making her excuses and accepting her brother's arm. "Perhaps later, Graham," he said. "We'd be pleased if you would join us for dinner tomorrow."

Graham turned his penetrating gaze on David. "I would be pleased to accept," he said with a bow. He departed, leaving David with the peculiar sensation that he left a vacuum behind, so forceful was his presence.

"Well. That was interesting," Maddy said. "I'm going to quite like getting acquainted."

"THE CHILDREN WILL be down shortly, my lady," Harris said with a proper bow at the door.

"Thank you, Harris," Delia said. "We'll wait outside." A private moment wouldn't go awry.

Jeffrey's coach waited at Clarion Hall's entrance. Delia's brows rose. "I ought to have known you would have ridden. We usually walk," she said with a laugh. Giving him a quick hug, she added, "I'm happy to see you, Jeffrey, even if you did come three days earlier than expected."

Jeffrey shrugged. "My negotiations completed faster than I anticipated."

And in your favor, no doubt, or you wouldn't be here.

"Is Mrs. Morgan the one that was a duchess?" he asked.

"Correct. She is by rights still the Duchess of Glenmoor, since her stepson, the current duke, is as yet unmarried. She prefers 'Mrs. Morgan.' Do you hold that against her?"

Another shrug. "It isn't for me to say. Sir Robert Benson works for Viscount Rockford." That wasn't a question.

Typical Jeffrey, surveying the lay of the land. "I believe that is correct, though what the man does is a mystery to me."

"I'll thank you to acquaint me with the guest list before we go back for dinner."

"I'll do my best. I don't keep the full list," she answered. *Would Fanny think it odd if I borrowed a copy?*

"Uncle Jeffrey!" Penny squealed as the Fitzwallace children spilled out the door and down the steps.

"Greetings, hooligans! Have you made the family proud?"

"Always, Uncle Jeffrey," Alf said.

Her brother handed Delia up and held the door for the children to scramble in before he heaved himself into the coach. His presence gave Delia a familiar sensation—peace, security, safety. Her big brother in both age and size, Jeffrey had always affected her that way.

A twitch of anxiety lessened the feeling. This time, she had the niggling worry that he might upend the peaceful life she had built. *And what will David make of him?* It shouldn't matter, but she very much feared it did.

CHAPTER TWENTY-TWO

S HE DIDN'T COME. Delia had been at the hall every day for weeks. The day after her brother arrived, she didn't come, and David missed her.

He straightened his notes and chided himself. Preparations were well in hand, and there was no reason his neighbor needed to drudge any further on his behalf. That he missed her—missed her laughter, missed her energy, missed the way she studied him when she didn't think he was looking—mattered not one whit. Besides, he would see her at dinner.

Dinner!

He pulled his watch from his pocket. He had an hour before it was time to dress. The Rob and Eli Bensons had refused invitations, for, as Rob had said, "We'll all get our fill of it next week." They'd left after tea. Madelyn, of course, being in residence, would join them at dinner. He hoped the menu was up to Graham's expectations.

David shook his foolish head. *Which one of us is the earl?*

He went back to his notes. His role in preparations had become primarily political. At Danbury's urging, he reviewed attendees, noted each one's political leanings, listing interests. Next to each, he jotted down conversations he wished to have.

He came to Graham's name and laid his pen down. He wasn't entirely sure what he wanted from the man politically. His interest tended toward the entirely personal. He wanted to learn everything he could about the woman who had begun to haunt his nights.

When he returned to his notes, a different name caught his eye. *Wilbury. Damn.* A note had arrived from Lady Danbury that afternoon, confirming David's suspicion. "Give Estelle Wilton a chance, Clarion. She would make a fine wife and an excellent political hostess." He already regretted giving Lady Danbury her head. Now he would be obliged to at least spend time with the girl, and Henrietta Danbury was not likely to give up. He put that problem away as a one for another day and recorded what he knew of her grandfather's politics. Would the support of a prominent member of the opposition help or hinder his cause? He had no idea. The entire enterprise was fraught with traps.

In the end, his work absorbed him, and Harris had to remind him to dress for dinner. By the time Harvey deemed his cravat perfect and suggested, for the third time, that he stop fidgeting with the buttons on his waistcoat, the light through his window told him the sun hung low in the sky.

Entering the drawing room, he found Maddy deep in conversation with Graham. Delia stood at the window, cradling a glass of sherry. She had dressed in a gown he'd never seen, a stunning creation in lavender with alternating panels of deeper purple, bound just below her bosom with pink ribbons that streamed down her back. His mouth went dry.

"Ah, here's David," Maddy said.

David turned and met Graham's knowing gaze. The man had caught him admiring his sister.

"Sorry I'm late," David said. "I got absorbed in my work."

"No apologies needed. I frequently forget meals altogether when work calls me," Graham said, a flicker of amusement in his gaze.

"Not when you expect company, I'll warrant," Maddy said. "I would pour you a brandy, David, but I fear—Ah, there is Harris now," she said at a soft knock on the door.

"Enter," David said.

"Dinner is served, my lord," the butler announced.

"Graham, kindly escort Lady Madelyn and lead us in," David said. He offered his arm to Delia. She accepted with a sweet smile. "You look ravishing this evening," he said, pitching his voice low.

"Ravishing?" she repeated with an impish grin. "That makes me sound like a rampaging Viking."

The joke tickled him, taking the edge off his concern that the massive mahogany table was too large for four people. It had been reduced to a reasonable size, but when he escorted her to a place on one side, it was clear that seating a mere four people around it left distances far from intimate. He took his place at the head, peered down at his sister at the foot, and nodded for Harris to serve the first course.

Harris did so with a verve that brought a twinkle to David's eyes. The retainer gloried in entertaining at last, after a string of dreary years. It was, David thought, just the prelude of what was to come in the next several days.

Picking up the host's responsibility to conduct the conversation, David began with words as formal as the patterns of a country dance, turning first to Delia with a comment on the weather, while Maddy turned to Graham with, "Your niece and nephews seemed delighted to have you visit."

Graham's smile appeared genuine, if somewhat wistful. "They've grown a lot in six months. I rather miss having them around."

Delia's mouth fell open at that statement. She pulled up her serviette to cover it. "The country air has been good for them," she murmured.

David suspected she had other pointed words for her brother. Did he disapprove of her choice to live in Ashmead? Of the house she'd picked?

"Are you comfortable at the dower house, Mr. Graham?" he asked, drawing a frown from Delia.

"My sister has made me comfortable. It is a bit cramped,"

Graham replied.

Dancing on the edge of rude, that. Is he dangling for an invitation to stay at the hall?

"The children love having you, though," Delia put in quickly, "Especially Alf, who truly doesn't mind giving up his room."

"Alfred is a fine lad," David said.

Graham nodded with satisfaction. "Yes, he is. Our father would have been proud of him."

Alf's maternal grandfather was the late Peter Graham, shipping magnate. Was Awbury, his paternal grandfather, proud of him? David doubted it. *The lad deserves better.*

"He and my son have become fast friends," David said.

"He told me he and your boy are sharing a tutor. I thank you for that. He needed to tend to his Greek, and my sister would have difficulty hiring a tutor in this isolated place, even if she had room to house him." There was the sting of criticism in his words; David suspected the modest house was an old issue. Graham went on, "He tells me he is looking forward to starting at Eton in the fall, now that he has a friend to go with him." Graham peered pointedly at Delia, who sighed and put her hands in her lap.

"Did he? That's the first I've heard," she said. "But I'm not surprised. He and Ashmead have grown close." Her sad resignation tore at David, even as he understood Graham's determination to see him in the best schools.

David gazed at Graham directly, but his words were for the boy's mother. "Their tutor tells me he is catching up quickly. I'm grateful for his influence on Ashmead. A friend makes all the difference at that age." *That the friend is an earl's heir won't hurt him in that place, either.*

"Again, my lord, we are grateful for your assistance," Graham said.

"The house will be empty without him," Delia said.

"You are always welcome back. Seascape is—"

"A great barn of a house. I realize you have plenty of room,

Jeffrey. But Bristol remains noisy, crowded, dirty, and utterly lacking in Ashmead's charm," Delia retorted.

David watched the byplay between sister and brother. Did she really hate the city? Bristol had rough aspects, particularly around the docks. So did London, which was arguably dirtier and more crowded. Was she really so set against cities?

"Is it all cities you dislike, Lady Fitzwallace, or is it just Bristol? You grew up there, did you not?" David asked.

"Yes, I did."

"Only from the time you were eleven, Delia." Graham turned to David. "We lived in Jamaica in our early childhood. Our father began his business out of Kingston."

"Yes, I recall now that you told me as much," David said. She had not, he noticed, answered his question about cities. He debated asking again, but she spoke before he could.

"Our house there was surrounded by trees and flowers. It was the flowers I missed most in Bristol. Flowers are what drew me to the dower house," Delia said.

Graham chuckled. "Flowers from the sellers' stalls never satisfied."

"Do you feel the same way about the city, Mr. Graham?" Maddy asked.

The man blinked, as if he'd never considered it. "Not for the same reason. Delia is drawn to the country. My love is the sea. Seascape, my home, overlooks the water. It has what I need to be happy."

"Not near the docks, then," David said.

"Goodness, no! That is no place for a family home," Graham replied.

David nodded. "I've been following reports of crime in the Bristol papers. Liverpool and Manchester as well. My impression—and my research over time appears to back it up—is that it is increasing."

Graham nodded. "Our losses have certainly increased the past five years. The entire country seethes since the wars ended. Too many unemployed."

"How would you prevent crime in that particular situation?" David asked.

"Graham Shipping is large enough to employ its own guards. Smaller operations can't afford it. Consistent prosecution would help," Graham said.

"The bigger firms and associations in London banded together to create a force to police the docks," David said.

"The Thames River Police? Yes. But so far, we have had little luck with such a cooperative venture," Graham said. His next statement surprised David. "Jobs and food for hungry families would make the biggest difference."

David leaned forward. "There are those that say coddling the poor undermines moral fiber."

Graham peered at him steadily. "Is that your platform?"

"On the contrary. My views are closer to yours. I'd like to see consistent policing before it comes to prosecution, however," David replied. "And we can't afford civil unrest."

"The *Manchester Observer* has been beating the drum for reform up north," Graham said. "They claim to eschew unrest and violence, but they keep up the pressure for parliamentary reform."

"I know the paper well." David grinned. "I'm one of their regular subscribers.

"Their demand for more representation in Parliament for the industrial cities, Manchester specifically, is just and reasonable, I believe," Graham said.

David's eyebrows rose. "That idea is not well supported by the business classes, generally."

Graham shrugged. "Not by those who are heavily invested in the status quo. Opening the closed doors to power would benefit them more than they know. The paper's rhetoric is inflammatory, but most of their actual positions are supported in the *Manchester Guardian* as well."

David agreed. "Two more seats for Manchester hardly constitutes universal suffrage, but any change is viewed by some as radical. The *Observer* invited Henry Hunt to speak on the sixteenth, I noticed."

"I heard him once. He's quite the convincing orator but not likely to incite insurrection." Graham surprised David with that.

The conversation flourished, and David found himself outlining legislative proposals and receiving back practical, well-conceived replies as dinner progressed and over their port. His respect for Jeffrey Graham grew. It appeared to be mutual. By the evening's end, he felt certain he had Graham's support.

Watching them depart, however, he realized with a pang that he'd learned little more about Delia than he already knew.

IN THE DARKNESS of Jeffrey's carriage, contentment enveloped Delia. It had been a lovely evening. The men may have ignored the ladies more than manners dictated, but she and Maddy had had no difficulty entertaining each other, and seeing her brother and David reach accord pleased her. To be frank, it relieved her as well. Perhaps she could let herself relax and enjoy the house party.

Jeffrey's disembodied voice, coming out of the darkness, roiled the placid surface of that contentment. "What is between you and the earl?"

"What do you mean? I've become friends with his sisters. I enjoy the comradeship of helping them plan a party," Delia said, grateful for the darkness. She could feel her cheeks heating.

"I can see how he looks at you," Jeffrey replied.

"Nonsense. All men ogle women when they think we don't notice."

"Perhaps. You could do worse," he said. "He could make you—"

"Stop right there, Jeffrey. I told you I have no intention of marrying again. I let you and Father push me at Vincent, delighted that I caught the eye of a duke's son. I won't let you push me at Clarion," she told him.

"I won't attempt to push you, but intentions change. Don't close your mind to it. I think you could have him with a little effort."

What about my heart? something inside Delia cried. "I refuse to become one of the hounds hunting him this week. There's already one parked at the Willow ready to pounce. I won't."

"Then don't," Jeffrey said. "But he's already interested. Don't push him away."

Delia sighed deeply. "He does not wish to marry, but supporters are pressuring him to find a wife, one with distinguished bloodlines and connections. A skilled political hostess. Some English rose with blonde hair and rosy cheeks. I'm not the wife he needs—and, I repeat, I do not wish to marry again." She sank into silence.

They both knew arrangements other than marriage hovered over the discussion, but neither voiced it.

They were halfway up the lane to the dower house when he spoke again. "Was marriage to Vincent so terrible?"

His distress at the thought touched her deeply. She reached over to put her hand on his arm. "Do not fret. It wasn't terrible at all." *It just wasn't the stuff of a young girl's dreams.*

When they came around the bend, she spied another coach in front of the house, the one she assumed carried Jeffrey's baggage and valet. The man alighting from it, however, was someone else.

"Barnabas has come!" Among the many things he was to her, Barnabas McKinney was an old childhood friend, and she loved him.

She opened the door, eager to greet him, but a hand reached up to help her down before she could leap out.

"Barnabas! Jeffrey didn't tell me you were coming." She stepped down, delighted at his familiar dark features illuminated in the light from the window. His joy at seeing her infectious, she couldn't resist giving him a hug.

"Ever impulsive!" Barnabas said with a shake of his head. His deep, rumbling voice went straight to her heart.

"Consorting with earls and duchesses has taught her no manners at all," Jeffrey sighed, alighting. "How was your trip?"

"Fine. It would have been better if that valet of yours weren't such a starched-up whiner. I left him at The Willow and the Rose, demanding rum for his tea," Barnabas said.

Delia opened her mouth to question the sleeping arrangements, but Barnabas interrupted. "Francois can come up days to manage the clothes and whatnot. Jeffrey and I will manage. I wanted to be close to the littles—and I don't mind a pallet on the floor."

Jeffrey, she noticed, seemed to be in full agreement with the odd arrangement. "I'm delighted to have you here, and the children will be, too. Mr. Benson will take care of this Francois," Delia said, not giving the missing valet another thought.

Jeffrey ordered the coaches to the back of the house, and the three of them walked up to the dower house's entrance in familiar accord. Delia reached for the handle to open the door and froze when her brother spoke.

"Just one request, Delia. Whatever you decide about the earl, don't bring down scandal on the family."

✦━◆━✦

CHAPTER TWENTY-THREE

THE REST OF the first week in August passed quickly—too quickly for David's peace of mind. He saw nothing of Graham or of Delia Fitzwallace, although Alf arrived every morning for tutoring and Marj ran off to the dower house twice, bringing home tales of Barnabas McKinney, a favorite of the children.

Brynn Morgan arrived late Friday night and immediately invaded the nursery with Maddy, intent on seeing his "Gwenny," after which he and Maddy disappeared into their suite for a private reunion. Their heated looks and gentle touches reminded David why he'd departed the christening early, and set his confused feelings about marriage and Delia Fitzwallace into a swirling vortex.

Guests were expected to engulf Clarion Hall on Tuesday, August 10. The Danburys arrived first, having agreed to come a day early to review preparations and strategy. Their massive carriage lumbered up the drive, a second less opulent one bringing servants and baggage. Maddy greeted the marchioness with open arms, ordered up bathwater, and pronounced she was eager to show her "the miracles that can be wrought in a month if you set your mind to it."

An hour later, David poured the marquess a brandy in his library, grateful for a quiet talk with the person whose views matched his own the most closely and whose loyalty he could count on. They sat side by side in front of David's desk, with his notes close at hand.

"What have you heard from Liverpool?" Danbury asked.

"The Prime Minister politely declined the invitation. I thought you might like a look at his reply, however." David handed it over.

Danbury read it, frowned, and read it again. "He knows what we're up to. *I hope your endeavors receive the support you wish.* Is that support or flimflam?"

David pursed his lips. "I could take it as support, but that doesn't equate to an appointment or a vote in cabinet. He seems to want to be above the fray until he sees which way the wind blows. At the very least, he doesn't plan to put a spanner in our works."

"Yet," Danbury growled.

"Yes. It is early days," David agreed.

"And Sidmouth?" the marquess asked.

"He's coming."

Danbury snorted. "Always wise to stay close to the opposition."

They went through David's notes. "Leave Cranwick to me," Danbury murmured at one point. "Be careful with Eaton," he said at another. "He can be had, but he doesn't like to be pushed. He needs to think your candidacy is his idea."

Danbury peered up sharply. "Awbury?"

"His acceptance came two days ago. Pushing the boundaries of good manners," David said.

"He probably waited to be sure what Sidmouth would do. We can assume his opposition, but with a little luck, his behavior will undermine his respect from others and limit his influence," Danbury said. "He may even make his man Sidmouth look bad."

"I understand the logic of inviting him. I just hope you are correct. Maddy expressed relief that his duchess will not accompany him. A small blessing, she called it." David went to the cupboard to retrieve a bottle and refilled their glasses.

"Leave it to the ladies. They can get away with more than you can," the marquess advised. He lifted his glass. "And, Clarion, as fine as this is, you'll want your wits about you at all times."

"I'm well versed in the fine art of ostentatious sipping and abstemious imbibing while urging drink on fools like Awbury."

Danbury chuckled without looking up from the notes. "Wilbury accepted. Of course he did."

David glared into his drink without commenting.

Danbury glanced up. "You asked Henrietta's help, Clarion. Regretting that?"

"Yes. Or perhaps no. I understand your point about a wife enhancing my chances. I just—A wife is more complicated than a political ally. I don't know that I have the patience for some miss barely out of the schoolroom." David drained his glass.

"I've met the lady my wife is sponsoring. Poised and proper but not forward. Intelligent but not clever in her manner. She's past first blush. She has a few Seasons behind her," Danbury said.

"Failed to take?" David groaned.

"Perhaps. Perhaps unwilling to be rushed and careful in her choices. She's no flibbertigibbet." Danbury set his glass down and leaned forward. "Wilbury is a Whig and has no say in Tory appointments; however, his support could be an enormous help once you secure the position. You do not want to make an enemy of him."

"And expectations have been raised," David said.

"I fear so. Meet the lady. Give her a chance. Perhaps she will suit very well."

"I promised I would," David said. He felt the jaws of a trap slam shut and his resulting resentment rise. It was going to be a difficult week.

DELIA TURNED THIS way and that in front of the mirror in her suite. Her gown, silk in peacock blue, complemented her coloring perfectly. Shot through with rows of oak leaves dropping vertically from the high waist and diagonally across the bodice, it flattered her form as well. She thought it fine enough, and it had long sleeves appropriate for a day dress and a wide but modest neckline. She rather liked the rows of tiny buttons at her wrists and the way her pearls shone across the expanse of skin. *The dress is perfectly proper. Am I?*

Joanie almost lost patience with her. "You've no need to fret, my lady. You'll be fine as can be for the welcome reception and every day after. Let me do your hair so your brother doesn't lose patience waiting."

And so it begins. I have to endure "every day after"... She raised her chin and put on her Lady Vincent Fitzwallace mask. She resolved to be the perfect neighbor, the respectable friend, the charming sister. She would support David every way she could.

And then what? She grimaced as Joanie pulled her thick black hair into braids and formed a circlet at her crown, and let go of pointless thought.

Jeffrey waited for her as Joanie had predicted, pacing the hall with her shawl over one arm. Barnabas had Percy on his shoulders. Alf had run up to the hall after breakfast because tutoring, he had announced, would continue mornings.

"Mama, you look beautiful!" Penny exclaimed.

Delia hugged her without regard for her gown. "Mind Joanie, help look after Percy, and don't distract Barnabas from his work!"

Penny and Percy were to remain at home except on days specific activities for children were planned. They expected few children, and there was a surfeit of nursery maids to entertain those that came. The primary goal of this party was politics.

Jeffrey correctly insisted they arrive by coach. Hopping through the woods was hardly the impression she wished to make, but she sighed as they turned down one lane, up the road, and down the drive to the hall. She missed the freedom to ramble as she chose.

"Lady Fitzwallace, Mr. Graham, welcome. May I take your things?" Harris intoned. A flick of his wrist had footmen taking her bonnet and Jeffery's hat before he finished speaking.

"The gentlemen have gathered in the billiard room, Mr. Graham. John will show you the way. I'm to direct Lady Fitzwallace to the estate workroom across from the steward's office. I've been informed you know the way," Harris finished with a note of disapproval.

"Thank you, Harris. I do indeed. You, of course, are needed here at your post. Guests will arrive soon," Delia said.

A familiar door separated the public rooms from the servants' world, including the estate workrooms at the far end. She found Maddy, Lucy, and Fanny already in place, poring over lists.

Henrietta Danbury glanced up and broke into a wide smile. "Delia, what a delight. The five of us together will work miracles. Maddy clearly has the details well in hand." They had mapped out leisurely walks, lawn games, cards, parlor games, informal dancing every other night, formal dinners every night, al fresco lunches and balls both Saturdays. Henrietta went on, "Our roles, of course, will be to entertain the ladies—while keeping a sharp ear out for rumors and undercurrents. We'll need to reconnoiter nightly to pass along information."

"As for the list," Fanny said, clearing her throat dramatically. David's half-sister seemed to delight in their determination to protect him from predatory would-be countesses.

"I will handle the Wadsworth interloper," Henrietta, clearly amused, said. "I'm adept at repelling encroaching females. I raised sons."

"I think your talents are best directed at Lady Cillia Effingham, the Earl of Cranwick's daughter. She will be a handful," Maddy suggested.

Maddy declared she would handle Viscount Eaton's daughter, Gemma Albert. "Delia, do you think you can manage the Wadsworth chit?"

Delia swiftly agreed. Miss Martha Darke, daughter of a banker, was another unexpected lady who had turned up at the Willow. Fanny agreed to befriend her—and keep a sharp eye. That left the Honorable Irma Barrington, a baron's daughter, for Lucy.

"Is that all? Our efforts to depress expectations seem to have worked. The numbers came out rather nicely," Lucy remarked.

"Not quite," Fanny said. "You forgot Lady Estelle Wilton, The Marquess of Wilbury's granddaughter. Another one not on the original list."

"Delia, why don't you take Lady Estelle?" Henrietta proposed. "I can manage the Wadsworth chit as well as Lady Cillia." She chuckled. "I know both. Lady Cillia will manage Hester Wadsworth for us, I suspect."

"Are you sure?" Delia asked, not certain she wanted to take on a marquess's granddaughter.

"Quite," Henrietta said, studying Delia rather closely. "Estelle is actually a pleasant person. You will like her."

A little voice distracted Delia before she could respond. "Lady Fitz?" Marj peeked around the door cautiously, eyeing Lady Danbury with some trepidation. "I want to go to the dower house to see Penny. Papa said I had to ask your permission."

"What did Miss Walters say?" Delia asked her.

"She says my work is all caught up."

"Then I don't see why not. Remind Penny you are not to keep Barnabas from his work, or she will try to involve him in all your schemes." She leaned down and whispered in the little one's ear. "I suggest you go out the kitchen and around. Avoid arriving carriages."

Marj grinned, agreed, and bounded off.

"Arrivals will begin anytime, if they haven't already. I suggest we adjourn to the formal drawing room," Maddy said.

The ladies moved off. Delia would endure this day and the two weeks that followed with dignity and propriety under the raised noses of the entire collection of peers and society dragons, Awbury not least among them. She stiffened her spine, determined to do her part for David.

CHAPTER TWENTY-FOUR

A S HE STOOD in the entrance, flanked by Maddy and a phalanx of footmen while guests arrived in waves, David's face hurt from smiling. He wanted nothing so much as to retreat to his library for a brandy in solitude.

What you really want is a walk through the trees with Delia. Or a ride with the boys.

The sun, he noted, had sunk in the west, hovering now over the hills. Many of the guests had settled into rooms and begun to filter back downstairs. Delia and the sisters held court in the drawing room, where the tea trolley was refreshed periodically. Danbury had escorted Effingham to the billiard room over an hour ago. He suspected others had found their way there.

Three more carriages rolled up the lane, following the curve to the entrance. David's shoulders stiffened when the door opened and the home secretary himself stepped out. A physician's son, Henry Addington, 1st Viscount of Sidmouth, thirty years David's senior, had survived thirty-five years of parliamentary intrigue, including two uninspired stints as prime minister.

So it begins. His service deserves respect, not his vision. It's past time for a change. David breathed deeply, and his shoulders relaxed. The jaw he had clamped tight loosened. His back, however, remained rigidly straight.

David greeted the man with an inclination of his head. "Sidmouth. Welcome."

The home secretary peered intently at David as if to verify what he undoubtedly knew—David meant to have his job. "Clarion. Thank you for the invitation." His slight bow somehow failed to acknowledge the higher, older title held by the younger man.

Maddy stepped forward with a curtsey. "Greetings, Lord Sidmouth. We trust your journey wasn't unpleasant?"

"Pleasant enough. On my way to the lake country for a rest," he said.

David narrowly avoided a snort. Sidmouth, London born and bred, rarely left the city.

"We've placed you in the family wing, my lord," Maddy said, gesturing to Harris and a waiting footman. "There are refreshments in the drawing room when you are ready."

Family wing. The home secretary had been widowed a few years before, so Maddy had housed him with the single men. David watched his progress to the stairs and observed a young woman on her way down in the company of her mother. Cranwick's girl, he thought. The mother stepped to the side and bowed, rather obviously prodding the girl to do the same. The daughter tipped her head artfully and smiled at Sidmouth. Perhaps his presence would give the matchmaking mothers another target. David could only hope.

Turning to greet the guests from the carriage that pulled up behind Sidmouth, he clenched his jaw again. *Wilbury. A different sort of worry.* The marquess handed his wife down and reached up again. An exquisitely beautiful young woman stepped into sunlight that gleamed off guinea-gold curls peaking from a fashionable bonnet. She followed her grandparents up the steps.

A warmer exchange of greetings occurred. David genuinely liked Wilbury. He acknowledged the marchioness, whom he'd met socially once or twice. Lady Wilbury turned to her granddaughter. "Lord Clarion, may I make known to you my granddaughter, Lady Estelle Wilton?"

The young woman met his gaze directly as she dropped into

a perfect curtsey. He rather liked that. No artful expressions or batting of eyelashes.

"I'm honored, Lady Estelle. Welcome to Clarion Hall."

She returned his close study with one of her own, neither forward nor shrinking. She obviously knew why she had come. David groped for something to say, wondering if he might actually like this young person.

Maddy's voice interrupted his abstraction. "Delia, well met. You are just in time to greet the Marquess and Marchioness of Wilbury."

Delia. His heart sped up, though he had no idea why Maddy called her over. He had seen her only briefly in passing and wasn't prepared for the vision of her in a glorious blue gown that outshone any he had seen all day. The woman in it glided gracefully across the parquet floor, radiating a life force that must surely be felt by everyone near it.

"Lady Wilbury, may I present Lady Vincent Fitzwallace?" Maddy said, obviously oblivious to whatever David felt. "Lady Fitzwallace, the Marquess and Marchioness of Wilbury, and Lady Estelle Wilton, their granddaughter."

Delia's perfect curtsey, perfect greeting, perfect smile warmed his heart. "We were introduced at one of Lady Danbury's soirees a few years ago," she said.

Lady Wilbury acknowledged the acquaintance graciously. Small talk was exchanged, but David heard none of it. Delia turned to the granddaughter. "Lady Estelle, I've heard much about you from the Marchioness of Danbury. I look forward to coming to know you over the course of the week."

"I would like that very much, Lady Fitzwallace. I'm rather overwhelmed by the exalted company, I fear."

Did she cast a glance at me when she said "exalted"? The chit's father is an earl himself.

"I think you'll like your suite. It is in the guest wing and faces the rose garden," Maddy was saying, but David's attention was on the two younger women who seemed in close conversation to the side.

Maddy handed the family to Harris and a footman waiting to lead them up. Lady Estelle followed her grandmother. David looked up to see a speculative expression on Wilbury's face.

David swallowed hard. "I look forward to a vigorous exchange of views this week," David said.

Wilbury's expression reformed into a grin. "I would expect nothing less of you, Clarion," he said.

David was left feeling like a schoolboy who'd just avoided a failing grade.

"It looks like the guests from the Willow have begun to arrive," Delia murmured, coming up on his side. "I'll go see to refreshments."

"Delia has been assigned to watch Lady Estelle," Maddy murmured under her breath, drawing his baffled frown. She looked toward the new arrivals with a forced smile. "Protection detail, remember? We each have a single woman to watch. Or two."

David's heart sank.

How in God's name can I get acquainted with Lady Estelle with Delia watching every move? The entire enterprise teetered on failure, and they were just getting started.

THE CLARION DRAWING room, refitted for a light supper masquerading as a welcome reception, came alive that evening. A fine and fashionable façade covered what was an assemblage of the most powerful men in England, playing at what Delia began to see as the opening act of a drama seething with plots political, dynastic, and romantic. *And you, my dear, have the role of observer.* She sighed.

She floated among conversational clusters, her ear tuned to any mention of the earl's ambitions. Lord Danbury had assured them he had dropped the need for change in the position of home secretary in the ears of many. Most of what reached her sounded like gossip. She greeted various acquaintances and accepted introductions to others.

Maddy floated up to her. "Can you rescue David? The rum punch is falling low. I need to find Harris."

Delia glanced around the room, finding David in conversation with a man she didn't know. An eager young woman clung to the man, whom Delia guessed to be her father. The father appeared mildly annoyed, and David desperate. They had him pinned into a corner.

"That is Viscount Eaton and his daughter, Gemma Albert, my assignment. I promise I'll return quickly." Maddy scurried off.

As Delia wound her way over, she heard Eaton's belligerent tone. "Nonsense, Clarion. Give Manchester two seats and they'll demand a cabinet post." David gazed at her over the girl's head, and Delia could almost hear him begging for rescue. She shouldered her way around the girl's left.

"Pardon me for interrupting, gentlemen, but Lady Madelyn needs to speak with Lord Clarion." Delia beamed at the girl as a cover for sizing her up. The girl brazenly did the same, clearly judging Delia a threat. *Cold, calculating—and cross with me.*

"I can help locate her. Lady Madelyn has been ever so welcoming to me," the forward little miss said, her eyes determinedly defying Delia to stop her. She'd underestimated her opponent.

"How kind of you, Lady…"

"Gemma," the girl snapped.

"Lady Vincent Fitzwallace, may I present Miss Gemma Albert?" David said.

Delia inclined her head. The girl dipped a perfunctory curtsey.

"As I was saying, Lady Madelyn sent me to re—request Lord Clarion's attention in a family matter. You will excuse us, of course."

Eaton stepped aside to let David pass, drawing a blatant glare from his daughter.

That one is doomed to failure on the marriage mart, Delia speculated, taking David's offered arm.

"I thought she was going to trip you," Delia whispered, smiling at a couple they passed. She felt like the entire room was straining to see what woman had the Earl of Clarion's arm.

"Is there a family matter?" David asked just as quietly, also smiling at those they passed.

"Only that her brother required rescue." She dipped her head to acknowledge the home secretary, expecting to walk on by. Belatedly she noticed his companion, the Duke of Awbury.

David stopped. "I trust you are having a pleasant evening," he said.

"The rum punch is superb," Sidmouth said. "And the company comfortable," he added, nodding at Awbury.

Awbury glared at Delia's hand on David's arm. "As I expected. You've managed to get an invitation for yourself and, unless I'm mistaken, for your brother as well." She thought him close to one of his tirades, but David spoke next.

"All my neighbors have supported this effort," he said. "Lady Fitzwallace provided immeasurable assistance to my sisters in planning it. Your family is lucky to have such a gracious lady as a connection by marriage."

For a fraught moment, Delia feared Awbury would swallow his tongue. She leaned toward David. "Your sister is waiting, my lord," she said.

"We'll have words later, Delia," Awbury growled.

"We're bound to encounter each other this week, Your Grace. Lord Sidmouth, I'm honored to make your acquaintance," she said.

With that, they were past.

"He said 'have words,' not 'chat' or 'catch up,'" David noted.

"He means he has words and I'm to listen," Delia replied.

They had reached the door. Before she could protest, he led her right through it. "Your guests—" she sputtered.

"Will keep for a few minutes while I try to breathe. Where did you say Maddy went?"

"To the butler's pantry, I think. Everyone in that room just saw me leave on your arm. There will be talk," Delia said, skipping to keep up.

Two footmen passed them, carrying punch bowls. David opened the door to the darkened ballroom. "Let them talk in that case. They already are." He led her to the French doors and out onto the terrace.

"Are you trying to cause a scandal?" she hissed.

"I'm trying to remember why I agreed to this entire enterprise," he said, moving his arm to grasp her hand and weave his fingers through hers. "I'd rather be with my friends."

"You agreed because England deserves a home secretary who has more ideas than keeping people down by threat of violence," she said, pulling her hand away.

He leaned closer, breathing deeply. She longed to let him hold her—for comfort, she thought. She longed for more than that. Vincent was gone these three years; she missed the marriage bed. *Clarion is—*

She took a step away. "I really must go back. Awbury's hawk eyes followed us out."

"He can't hurt you."

"Perhaps not, but he can hurt your chances."

"Unlikely according to Danbury," he replied.

"He can and will be ugly and unpleasant. I'll go back and tell them you're looking for Maddy. Take a few moments to breathe as you said. Don't follow me too closely. I don't want Gemma Albert trying to take off my head."

She was to the doors before she heard his whispered, "Thank you."

CHAPTER TWENTY-FIVE

DELIA MANAGED TO avoid her horrid father-in-law for three days. During that time, she and David's sisters among them prevented the banker's daughter from rearranging dinner seating, foiled Gemma Albert's attempt to pull David to the piano bench during a musical evening by reminding him of his "sore throat," and rerouted the Wadsworth chit when she "got lost" and wandered into the family wing.

On the third day, a lovely afternoon, the company divided between those enjoying cards and a light luncheon on the terrace and the more adventurous members who planned to trek through the woodland for a picnic by the waterfall that was one of Delia's favorite spots on Clarion land.

Soon after they started out, Lucy, hovering nearby, was forced to insert herself between Irma Barrington and David when the girl floated to the ground, moaning about a twisted ankle, while David continued on without noticing. Lucy efficiently called for a footman to carry the girl to her maid while holding her hand—firmly—and Delia went for Paul Farley, who had joined them for the day and was several couples ahead, to see to it. The long-suffering physician rolled his eyes as he passed Lucy and Delia, who stood arm in arm, grinning. He followed the footman and a very irritated, not-so-honorable Irma back to the hall.

"I believe I have the easiest assignment," Delia said. "Lady

Estelle is kind, well mannered, and never inappropriate."

"Perhaps she's the shrewdest of them," Lucy said, nodding at David, who now had Lady Estelle on his arm.

"Perhaps. She certainly hasn't put him in any uncomfortable spots. He ought to be able to avoid—"

"Vigilance, Delia!" Lucy said. "Perhaps she plans some devious way to compromise him in the woods."

"Absurd. There are too many people around," Delia said.

"I think he's partnered her the most. He danced with her twice the night before last. They played at the same whist table. They were paired for charades—after we discovered Lady Cillia Effingham attempting to cheat with the drawing. The only one he's partnered more is you."

"I'm safe," Delia said. "I'm practically one of you sisters." She didn't feel safe. She felt…intrigued. Attracted. Confused. She shook her head. *David needs a hostess. Lady Estelle has the breeding, the manners, and the intelligence to fill that role.* She was everything Delia was not, and Delia had begun to realize the girl had honor and character as well. She might just do.

"I FEAR MISS Irma Barrington has fallen, my lord," Lady Estelle said, concern in her voice.

David, who had been attempting to ignore the contretemps, paused. The girl had thrown herself in his direction. He caught her ploy and Lucy's swift intervention out of the corner of his eye. He knew it for transparent manipulation but could hardly say that to the young woman on his arm.

He'd also seen Delia rush past, unsure what that was about. "It appears Lady Benson has it well in hand," he said.

Just then Delia returned, a bit breathless, accompanied by Dr. Farley. "Is all well, Lady Fitzwallace?" he asked with a raise of one eyebrow.

"Quite well, my lord. We've called on this good doctor as a precaution," Delia said.

Paul Farley's skeptical expression spoke volumes. That alone may have been what provoked Lady Estelle to say, "Lady Benson is your sister-in-law, I believe. They are all very protective of you, your sisters. Lady Fitzwallace as well."

He gazed into her face, studying her expression. "And I believe you are a very perceptive young woman."

It earned him a grin.

"It appears they have it well in hand. Shall we go on?" he asked.

"Gladly, my lord."

After a few moments, she tipped her head toward him, holding it back to see out from under her bonnet. "The gossip in London about this party was that it was to be strictly political. I know a number of wives and daughters that stayed away for that reason. And yet—"

"And yet we have had a few unexpected guests, all of them young women?" he said.

She dipped her head, and he couldn't see her face, but he was certain he had put her to the blush.

"I meant no criticism of you, Lady Estelle." *Should I tell her I asked Henrietta to suggest a bride? No. It is too soon to raise expectations quite that high. It is already hanging in the air.*

When she didn't reply, he spoke. She deserved more respect. "An unmarried earl in possession of a full head of hair and all his teeth is an irresistible temptation for matchmaking mothers and their eager daughters. I don't consider you one of their ilk."

"Thank you," she murmured. "I'm not. My grandfather, however, and Lady Danbury, my godmother, have told me we might suit. They asked me to come and spend a bit of time with you. I'm sorry."

"Don't apologize. I have had such encouragement from similar sources. An earl with political ambition, I'm told, ought to consider taking a wife. I would prefer to make my own choice of a wife, however."

She nodded and looked away again. "We should all have a choice in our future," she said, her voice wistful.

Women, he thought not for the first time, *have few choices.*

"I'm glad we're in accord. Perhaps we will suit very well—at least for the duration of this party. We do so far. Shall we see what becomes of our acquaintance, Lady Estelle?"

"I would like that very much, my lord."

Later by the waterfall, she removed her bonnet and sat with perfect grace on one of the blankets set aside for the picnic. David, who had moved off to greet various guests, spied her sitting there, cool and serene. Henrietta Danbury saw the direction of his gaze.

"She is lovely," Lady Danbury said.

"She's exquisitely beautiful," he said, "and I am beginning to think she has a character to match."

Henrietta raised one brow. "No flaws?"

None. Except— He gazed beyond Lady Estelle. In a shaft of sunlight, Delia stood with her head tipped back, laughing in sheer joy while she caught spray on her face from the cataract tumbling down over the rocks. She took his breath away.

"Clarion?" Henrietta's voice came as if from far away.

"I'm sorry, Henrietta, I was woolgathering."

"I asked if you found any flaws in Lady Estelle," the marchioness said.

"None. None whatsoever." *More's the pity.*

CHAPTER TWENTY-SIX

MOST OF THE gentlemen developed the habit of taking coffee in David's library while most of the ladies took chocolate in their rooms and fussed over their appearances in preparation for the day. Footmen came and went replenishing coffee urns, and additional chairs had been scattered about the room, part of David's effort to create an environment that might encourage political dialogue.

Newspapers, normally stacked on David's desk, had been arrayed in overlapping rows in title order along a table. The Willow kept a steady stream of mail coming, and the selection replenished daily to the astonishment of many of the guests. In addition to over forty "national" papers, David received numerous regional and local weeklies.

The Earl of Cranwick surveyed the choices, hands behind his back, as John the footman brought the neatly ironed issues that had arrived the previous day. He smiled at David's approach to check the delivery. "No *Teatime Tattler*, I see," he said with a chuckle. He wasn't the first to complain about a lack of gossip rags.

David knew it for a joke but suspected there were many in this room that would prefer lighter fare. "No room on the table, I fear."

Cranwick nodded at the footman. "Five more, Clarion. Your buffet of information is as substantial as your dinners. And as varied. Should I say spicy?" The earl chuckled at his own wit.

"I try to absorb every viewpoint, Cranwick, so that we don't miss anything," David replied.

"I'm glad someone is doing it," Cranwick said. "I haven't the energy for it. But well done, well done. It explains your thoughtful speeches." He leaned closer and spoke softly. "No one comes close on domestic matters. No one." He took the latest issue of the *Times* and found a seat on the sofa next to an array of bookshelves.

David took the *Manchester Observer* from the footman while the boy filed the others. It was coming daily now, each edition more disturbing than the last. "Rally! Saint Peter's Field," the banner headline shouted once again. Below it, in smaller print, it read, "Manchester, Make Your Voice Heard," urging the entire city to turn out. The coming rally had been in the paper daily. Lurid stories of death and degradation, clearly intended to stir up emotions, filled every issue. David stood in place, riveted there by the story of a child found dead in his bed of starvation. *While I spend a fortune feeding the wealthy…*

Frederick Darke, the banker, pulled out the *London Statesman* with a grunt. The man tended to keep opinions to himself.

"No imagination, that one." Jeffrey Graham surprised David, who hadn't heard him approach.

David smiled. "Not needed in his business." He folded the *Observer* to read later, ignoring the sick feeling it engendered. "You've come up early."

Graham grinned. "I enjoy your library."

Did Delia come with you? David bit back the words. He'd promised Lady Estelle a ride around the estate; thoughts of Delia were best kept locked away. "It is a fine place," he said instead. "I'm happy to share it."

Graham nodded at the newspaper in David's hands. "Anything new?"

"Unfortunately not. More tragedy. More anger."

"Tragedy? Where?" a gruff voice barked.

"Good morning, Awbury. I didn't see you at breakfast," David said.

"Graham. Do you read that trash, too?" Awbury demanded, glowering at the *Manchester Observer* in David's hands.

"On occasion. Always good to keep an open mind," Graham said, picking up the *Bristol Mercury*. "Good selection, Clarion. Thank you." With a polite nod, he left him.

"Did Vincent's gel force that cit on you?" Awbury growled.

David ignored the duke's poor manners. "I believe Danbury invited him, Your Grace."

"Watch Danbury, Clarion. I warn you. Radical tendencies. Be sure others don't see you subscribe to radical papers as well. If I were you, I'd keep that one in your hand a secret. Read it if you must, but a man's reputation can be shredded over something like that. People will talk after this."

"Thank you for the warning, Your Grace. Do take a look at the selection. You should find something to your taste." David made little effort to keep his sarcasm in check but suspected Awbury wouldn't notice it no matter how obvious he made it.

Several men, all absorbed in their beverages and coffee, were scattered around the room. Young Effingham, Cranwick's second son, leaned on the window ledge, absorbed in the *Public Ledger* of all things. The decanter of whiskey, left discreetly next to the coffee urns for those who liked a little spirits in their coffee, was already half-empty. He trusted the staff to deal with it, praying Benson had correctly gauged his ability to pay for this gathering.

There being no other seat, David went around his desk to his comfortable chair. A packet had been laid there with a note in Benson's handwriting. Odd, that; Eli usually brought estate matters to the breakfast room, but of course, the presence of guests made that improper.

A paper had been wrapped around a mail packet. The note on top read, "Fanny thought you ought to see this. I agree. Benson."

He unwrapped it to find a personal letter addressed to Fanny, dated so recently it must have arrived in the mail from the

Willow the day before. Fond as he was of his half-sister, they had never gotten past their awkwardness entirely. She rarely approached him with anything personal. She had grown up over a shop in Manchester. That she tolerated an earl at all was a blessing, he suspected.

He hesitated for a moment, unwilling to read her private correspondence. The Bensons thought he should see it, however, and he quickly understood why. Her friend, a Mr. Abbott, wrote eloquently about the state of his grocery business—failing—and the mood of the city—ugly. City officials decried plans for the coming rally, warning people there would be trouble and urging them to stay away. Abbott wrote that he didn't know anyone who did not plan to attend.

The letter went on with news of her friends, all of it bad. One family's son, who had returned from the war, was unable to find work. The father's wages and hours had been cut. The wife took in laundry, but neighbors couldn't afford to pay for it. The son had tried to enlist in the regiments stationed around the city, against the father's wishes. He had been turned away due to injuries received on the continent. Another family had lost a sick child. Another had no work due to illness. "Hard times have come on us, Fanny. I'm grateful you and your Mr. Benson thrive."

The letter could have been just another issue of the *Observer*. It told him nothing new. He folded it and locked it in his desk. Lost in thought, he tapped his finger.

"I say, Sidmouth, what do you make of the news from Manchester?" Baron Wadsworth called from across the room, holding up a copy of the *Manchester Gazette*. David hadn't noticed the home secretary come in.

"Stuff and nonsense. Mewling of radical journalists to provoke uprising," Sidmouth grumbled, turning to examine the selection of papers with a frown.

"They've invited Henry Hunt to speak," Wadsworth said. "The man is a firebrand. Claims he doesn't believe in uprising or violence, but if any man can drive a crowd into a frenzy, he can."

"Let them try. We're prepared to manage the thing," Sidmouth pronounced, posturing with a hand on his chest as if addressing Lords. His mouth widened in a slight smile, one that didn't reach his eyes. "Come now, gentlemen. Let us not spoil Clarion's splendid house party with talk of reform and politics." His pointed gaze raked David before he returned to his perusal.

Words in Fanny's letter haunted David. Abbott knew no one who didn't plan to attend the benighted rally. If the entire city of Manchester came out to hear Hunt, the crowd would be massive, and the results could be horrible. David wished he had eyes and ears in Manchester. He needed to speak with his brother Rob, who didn't plan to come over from Willowbrook until dinner. He could send a note over, or better yet—*Perhaps I should ride over to Willowbrook with Lady Estelle.*

DELIA FOUND MADDY in the drawing room, among a group of ladies enjoying tea. She sat near a disgruntled Miss Gemma Albert.

"The day is a fine as can be," Delia said. "I noticed the staff setting up for games of pall-mall on the lawn as I walked up. Is that still on offer this afternoon?"

"It is indeed," Maddy said.

"*Some* people are going riding," Gemma complained. "No one told me to bring a riding habit."

Silly chit. It's a country party. Of course you needed one. Her parents must have made a last-minute decision to bring her.

Delia ignored the complaints, grateful the girl was Maddy's assignment, not hers. "Has Lucy arrived?"

"Yes. She's reviewing the dining room settings with the housekeeper," Maddy said.

Seeing no sign of Lady Estelle, her charge, Delia decided to go help Lucy. She stepped back into the entrance hall to find

David dressed for riding. He held his gloves in one hand, tapping them against the other. His face lit up when he saw her.

"Good morning, Delia. How are the little ones?"

"They are well. Penny, Percy, and Joanie have invaded your nursery. Games are on offer today in the side gardens. 'Young gentlemen,' Alf has declared, however, have no use for childish games."

David's grin warmed her heart and sent stirrings through her. "That is because they have plans in the stable when their classes are finished. Did he tell you?"

"He said nothing about today, but he informed Jeffrey two nights ago that riding was a vital part of a gentleman's education," Delia replied.

"It is indeed. At least, the boys he encounters at Eton will expect a duke's grandson to be an expert rider. The grooms tell me he is a quick study." The heart-stopping grin reappeared. "Of course, Ashmead's skills give him some incentive to catch up."

"You put us further in your debt," Delia murmured.

"Hardly. The impact on my son has been priceless. Graham spoke to me this morning about purchasing a mount for Alfred. If you decide to proceed, you can house the beast in our stables," he said.

Jeffrey had gone behind Delia's back. She didn't miss David's tact, assuming the decision to be hers. That gesture of respect further eroded her determination never to marry. *Not that it's on offer.*

She glanced up at that moment, drawn by movement on the stairs. Lady Estelle descended, every movement graceful. She was dressed for riding. The reason for Gemma's disgruntlement became clear. David quickly donned his gloves as she approached.

He bowed to the lady and offered his arm. "We're going to ride over to Willowbrook," he told Delia.

Delia glanced from one to the other, briefly panicked. *Alone? I'm supposed to be on guard duty.*

Her concern must have shown on her face. "We're taking a

groom with us," David assured her.

There was nothing she could do about it now. Her own habit was back at the dower house, and she had no excuse to insert herself. Besides, he didn't seem worried. Delia had begun to wonder if he was actually taking an interest in the poised young woman at his side. She watched them depart through the massive entrance. A groom waited at the foot of the steps with three horses.

She had found Estelle to be lovely in every way. *He could do far worse*, she thought. A woman like Estelle would be right for him. Her heart sank to her shoes; she was grateful she didn't have to witness them together this afternoon.

CHAPTER TWENTY-SEVEN

DAVID LED ESTELLE uphill toward Willowbrook's orchard as directed by the groom who took their horses, skirting a busy beeyard.

"Goodness! Is it safe?" she asked.

"It's a citadel of productivity. They're too busy to bother us as long as we don't disturb them. Willowbrook's bees provide honey and candles to Clarion Hall and the Willow and the Rose—I suspect many homes in Ashmead as well." David leaned over confidentially. "I've often been grateful Lucy manages it so we don't require bees at the hall."

When she grinned up at him, he was struck anew by her beauty. It was an abstract sort of thought, rather as if he admired a fine work of art, hardly heart-stirring. *She would make a comfortable wife, Clarion.* Unfortunately, he no longer believed comfortable was enough.

They found Rob working alongside Willowbrook staff, cleaning pathways through the apple orchard. Coatless, with his sleeves rolled to the elbows, he looked nothing like the polished gentleman who haunted elegant gatherings of the diplomatic corps in London, discreetly seeing to their security.

Rob raised a hand in greeting when he saw them, and gathered his clothing, quickly buttoning on his waistcoat and rolling down his sleeves.

"My apologies, Lady Estelle. I didn't expect a visit from a

lady," he said with a cheeky grin while pulling on his coat. "An extra hand was needed today."

"Not at all, Sir Robert. Your care for your land and its people does you credit," she replied.

Another lady might have simpered with disapproval or openly ogled the man. Lady Estelle did neither. David was torn between admiration for the lady and a twinge of envy, a familiar reaction to his brother's freedom.

Rob escorted them to the house, chatting about bees and apple harvests. He'd become quite the countryman since he'd married Lucy. Once, he'd sworn he never would. Love did things to a man, especially one as utterly in love with his wife as Rob Benson. Envy raised its ugly hand again and reached for David, but he smacked it away. He didn't begrudge his brother his joy.

Rob left them in the Benson parlor, a well-appointed room designed to entertain family and friends.

"This is a pleasant little house," Lady Estelle said.

"Very. I was happy here," David replied.

"You lived here?" she asked.

"From the time of my marriage until my father died. My children were born here."

"How—I'm sorry. I don't mean to pry." Her lashes fluttered downward.

"Lucy is my late wife's sister. She became its caretaker, but then my father left it to Rob in his will." The sharp resentment he'd felt the day the infamous will was read had long ago dissipated. Rob and Lucy cared for Willowbrook, and he was glad for them. He realized with a jolt that the lady must not know about his father's will, though she clearly must see what the whole world knew—that Rob was the old earl's bastard. They took no pains to hide their relationship, and their resemblance made it obvious.

"And you have Clarion Hall," she said, her sweet smile pleasing him.

Willowbrook's housekeeper brought tea and some rather

delicious lemon cake then, likely at Rob's orders. Rob himself rejoined them soon after, groomed and confident, his cravat in place, his clothing brushed.

Rob gazed at David curiously. "To what do I owe this unexpected honor?" he asked, raising one eyebrow.

With a houseful of guests and the knowledge I'll see him at the hall this evening, no wonder he thinks it odd. He probably thinks I brought Lady Estelle to share my past with her. In fact, David had intended to show her the boundaries of the Clarion estate. Fanny's letter had changed that.

"If the lady will forgive me, I actually came to speak with you about Manchester," David said.

Rob's brows shot up. "Trouble?" His shoulders relaxed. "Of course there is. There has been trouble for months."

"Indeed. You're aware that a rally is planned?" David asked. He glanced at Lady Estelle. She appeared neither resentful at the unexpected conversation nor upset. On the contrary, he had her interest.

"I don't read as many papers as you do," Rob said, his tone teasing, "but I'm aware of what is happening."

David pulled Fanny's letter from his pocket. "I was hoping you knew more. Is Viscount Rockford investigating?" Rob's employer's shadowy operation had tentacles across Britain.

"We have people in Manchester, yes. Beyond that, I've heard nothing," Rob said. "There is unrest in Liverpool as well. York, Bristol… Rockford has people watching London's underbelly closely. The country is a powder keg—or perhaps a series of them."

"Poverty, unemployment, and starvation will do that," David said. "Long-term, the answer is improving people's conditions. In the meantime, it's this summer that worries me." He glanced apologetically at Lady Estelle, who seem more sympathetic than distressed.

He handed Fanny's letter to Rob, who glanced up from it with narrowed eyes but read it without question. He grimaced at the end. "Abbott says he knows no one who does not plan to attend. I met Abbott last year when we went after Fanny. He's a good man, sensible, and not one to exaggerate. The crowd will be massive."

"Sidmouth made a pronouncement this morning that he has no worries about the rally. The Home Office is fully aware and will handle it. 'Manage the thing,' he said. If they go after Hunt, or try to shut it down, there will be violence. A heavy-handed response may cause the thing we should hope to avoid."

Rob nodded, deep in thought. "And the timing couldn't be worse. He'll use any violence to justify his authoritarian approach and doom you, my moderate-minded brother, or doom your ambitions, at least. I see your concern."

"I'm concerned for the people of Manchester," David spat. "But yes, the timing couldn't be worse."

"You care for the whole damned country—pardon my language, Lady Estelle. That's why we all support you. What do you want from me?"

"I could use eyes and ears of my own in Manchester." David held his brother's gaze.

"You want me to go there?" Rob choked out his words.

"And take two grooms as messengers," David said.

"Lucy—Kit…"

"My nursery has a small army of nursemaids. Kit would be fine at the hall. Lucy already stays in Maddy's dressing room when needed. Do speak with your wife—and Fanny. See if she knows more. Obviously, I can't order you, but Rob, I would be grateful for a witness to whatever happens. I can't think who else to send."

In the end, Rob agreed to talk it over with his wife. David had no doubt he would go, and it felt like a weight off his shoulders. He and Lady Estelle rode back over the ridge and through the forest, a Clarion groom trailing behind.

"I must apologize, Lady Estelle. That visit wasn't what I originally intended when I invited you to ride," David told her.

"There is no need. That letter must have been important. Thank you for giving me a glimpse of your world—and your political concerns. My grandfather shares them."

Wilbury, he recalled, was a liberal-minded Whig. *Does Estelle share his views?*

"We differ on implementation and the speed of reform, but yes, there are many things Wilbury and I agree on," David said. "What about your parents?"

"My mother died when I was ten, my lord. My father has no interest in politics, much to Grandpapa's disgust," she said. "He's more concerned with horse breeding."

"And you? Are you interested in politics?" he asked.

"Would you think me unladylike if I said yes? A lady is allowed charitable interests, at least."

"Not at all. Observe the Marchioness of Danbury."

She grinned at that. "Yes, my godmother is a superb political hostess. She tells me more of the country's business gets done at her soirees than in Lords."

He laughed out loud. "She may be right."

Henrietta Danbury clearly believed this young woman would make a fine political hostess as well. He'd begun to think she was correct. Lady Estelle might be the perfect countess for an earl with ambitions.

However sure his mind was of that, he struggled to convince his heart. A man needed more than a decorative and charming hostess. He wondered fleetingly what it would be like to kiss her and suspected he ought to put that to the test. Would she take offense if he tried? The clomping of the groom's horse behind them made it impossible.

There would be a ball in the evening. Perhaps he could steal a moment then.

PALL-MALL KEPT MUCH of the company entertained through the

afternoon. Delia would have enjoyed it if Awbury hadn't delayed her. He was leaving the library as she departed the dining room where she had been assisting Lucy.

"Off to cause more trouble?" he growled.

"I'm going to play pall-mall with the others," she said, tempted to storm past him but reluctant to cause a scene. Some of the other gentlemen filed out behind him.

"I've told you before. As long as you carry the Fitzwallace name, everything you do reflects on my son's memory and on my honor. I saw your wanton behavior at the waterfall yesterday. Trucked myself up there just to keep an eye on you, and you met my worst predictions. No lady would dance in the spray as you did. Dampening gowns is for strumpets. And don't think you'll catch Clarion that way. He's too wary a bird for that. He'll never marry you." Awbury dragged his eyes down her length crudely. "Perhaps marriage isn't what you're after. Cause scandal and you'll pay for it."

She left him without a word, grateful that most of the company had filed past before he'd begun his tirade. *How dare he. How dare that beast look at me so.*

She rushed down the now empty hallway, past the dining room, past the ballroom, and into the vast entrance, searching for a private place to break down and fearful that Awbury was on her heels. She was halfway across the parquet floor when David came in, smiling down at Lady Estelle.

She couldn't face him now, not enthralled with Lady Estelle as he was, not with Awbury at her back. *Hogswallop!*

The massive entrance doors hung open behind the couple, and she could see the games on the lawn, and the edge of the trees beyond, where the path to the dower house would take her to safety. She took a step to the side to hurry past them.

David stopped in his tracks, gazing at her with concern. He removed his arm from Estelle and took both of Delia's hands in his, keeping her from passing them. "Delia! Is something wrong?" he asked.

Don't call me that, you blind fool. Not in front of Lady Estelle. "No, I—I'm quite well," Delia said, attempting to pull her hands away and choking back tears.

David lifted one hand to her cheek, his eyes boring into hers. "Something has upset you."

Delia could hear footsteps approaching from the hallway. She pulled herself together. "I'm just late. The—the pall-mall has already started." She pulled her hand free and leaned toward the side.

David gazed past her shoulder, frowning. "Awbury, Lady Fitzwallace is distressed."

Delia's heart froze, as she feared an ugly confrontation. She couldn't move.

Lady Estelle took in Awbury's approach, glancing among the duke, David's anger, and Delia's distress. She made no comment on the fraught situation. "You plan to join the pall-mall? I'm so pleased. I was hoping to play. Would you wait for me? I, too, would feel uncomfortable going late. Let's go together."

"I—of course," Delia replied, blinking rapidly.

"Better yet, come up with me. We can chat while I change," Lady Estelle added, reaching out a hand.

Delia followed the young woman, with her ears attuned to the onset of conflict behind them. "Thank you," she whispered. Lady Estelle patted her arm without answering.

Awbury's voice echoed in the vast entrance, reaching them on the stairs. "Hoydenish women are the bane of society."

She couldn't make out David's reply, but Awbury's final words before he stomped out the door were clear enough. "Watch yourself, Clarion. She'll try to get her hooks into you and bring down scandal on both of us."

CHAPTER TWENTY-EIGHT

T HE BALLROOM GLEAMED under newly polished chandeliers resplendent in Willowbrook beeswax candles. David's sisters had worked miracles in a few short weeks. The newly polished parquet floors needed no embellishment, and the wallpaper flaws he had despaired of faded behind massive ferns and artfully placed paintings. Tonight's ball, meant to be slightly less grand than that planned for the final Saturday, still felt grand indeed.

He greeted guests, Maddy as his hostess at his side, while musicians hired from Nottingham tuned their instruments.

"Where is Brynn?" he asked when Baron Wadsworth and his wife and daughter finally moved past them.

"Fortifying himself on your brandy in the library. He promised to be here when the dancing begins," Maddy replied.

The Earl and Countess of Cranwick, followed by Lady Cillia on her brother's arm, entered next, making proper greetings. The son, Lord Effingham, spoke effusively. "I say, Clarion, your ballroom is a jewel—almost as much as your library."

As humor went, the remark came up to passable. More interestingly, David watched Effingham's eyes stray immediately to Wadsworth's daughter. That was no small relief to see. Perhaps the baron and his wife would give up the hunt for an earl if an earl's heir was on offer. He wondered if that was Lady Danbury's doing.

Lady Cillia made a point of showing her dance card, and he

dutifully signed his name to a country dance.

The Barringtons arrived with Lucy accompanying Irma as always. That one required vigilance.

Lucy let the family move on in front of her.

"Where is Rob this evening?" David asked. "Coming later?"

She gave him a scornful glare. "On his way as you asked, of course. You'll have Kit and me underfoot the rest of the week."

Maddy cast him a curious glance but had no time to ask questions, because guests began to pour in rapidly.

He led Maddy out for the first dance, as they had planned, avoiding any particular lady with ambition as his sisters had instructed.

"Now. Speak with the eager ladies," Maddy said as soon as the set ended. The sisters had insisted that he dance with each of the hounds, as they called the ladies on the hunt for his title. "All or none," Maddy had cautioned, and he had already been maneuvered into signing Lady Cillia's dance card. He felt for the small notebook in his pocket. He'd need to keep track.

He scanned the ballroom, searching for Lady Estelle, hoping to secure the supper dance. If he could find a private moment, he might finally put that kiss to the test. He found her laughing with her grandmother and Henrietta Danbury.

Before he could approach her, he peered around the ballroom one more time, finding Jeffrey Graham, who must have come after David had stopped receiving guests, standing alone. Of Delia there was no sign. He approached the man next. "Where is Lady Fitzwallace this evening?" he asked without preamble.

"Good evening to you, too, Clarion," Graham said, amused. "My sister instructs me to say that Percy is under the weather. She is actually, of course, avoiding Awbury. 'I need a day to restore my backbone' were her precise words. Those words are for your ears only."

"I don't know what he said to her, but I've never known her to be so unsettled," David replied.

"The man is vile. Vincent, to his credit, attempted to keep her out of his father's orbit. Awbury was happy to welcome Delia's money into the family—less happy when he realized neither he nor Vincent had control of it. He has no power over her, only a vicious mouth. Most people see through him. I urged her to face him down. Tomorrow, she said, would be soon enough."

David nodded distractedly. "Her absence is our loss," he murmured. "Enjoy your evening."

David endured the requisite dances. Lady Cillia flirted shamelessly, and Irma Barrington almost thrust her bosom from her low neckline in her effort to fix his attention. Miss Darke, by contrast, appeared utterly terrified of him and would not meet his eyes.

Lady Estelle had wisely saved the supper dance for him, and he took the floor with her with no small sense of relief. Her dancing, like everything he'd seen about her, was refined and graceful.

"Thank you for your kindness this afternoon," he said when the patterns of the dance brought them close.

"Of course. Ladies, as I suspect your sisters have told you, need to look after one another. Awbury is a bully. Besides, I quite like Lady Fitzwallace. Her *joie de vivre* is infectious."

"It is indeed," David said. *This woman is lovely inside and out.*

The dance ended, and people milled about, some hovering near the doors that opened into the dining room, where a buffet had been set out, others seeking air on the terrace. He led Lady Estelle toward the doors to the outside, grateful the presence of others would make their direction unremarkable.

They smiled at various guests when they walked past until David led her to the edge of the terrace, saw no eyes upon them, and slipped unseen around some shrubbery, using his familiarity to lead her through the garden to a private spot by moonlight.

He held one hand while their eyes adjusted to the shadows. She didn't ask him why he had brought her out. Perhaps she didn't need to.

"I enjoyed our ride today," David said.

"I did too," she replied. Her eyes in the moonlight appeared more patient than wary.

He lifted her hand and kissed her knuckles. "You are a lovely young woman."

"And you are very kind, my lord," she whispered, swallowing.

"We've been encouraged to become more closely acquainted, have we not?" At her nod, David leaned closer and whispered, "May I kiss you?"

He didn't wait for a reply. He lowered his head slowly and, meeting no resistance, pressed his lips to hers. She made a flicker of movement, a chaste attempt to return the kiss. He angled his head to move his lips across hers. She made no effort to pull away nor did she freeze. Neither did she respond in any way that encouraged him to go on.

No passion. No fireworks. Little enough response, almost as if she made no effort—

"Do you find kissing distasteful, Estelle?" he whispered, his mouth near her ear, the lady held lightly in his arms.

Her head bobbed up. "Kissing? Distasteful, not at all. I—" She stopped abruptly.

He studied her closely. "You've been kissed before, I think, and found it much more to your liking," he said, loosening his hold on her and taking her hands in his.

"Have I offended you, my lord?" she asked.

"No, you've honored me with that kiss."

"I did not dislike your kiss," she said.

"But it didn't thrill you, either. Who is he?"

She blinked up at him.

"The man whose kisses captured you?" He respected her enough to ask and to expect a blunt answer. She didn't disappoint him.

"The second son of a viscount," she said with a shuddering sigh.

"A soldier?"

"A diplomat," she said, pride radiating in the words. "He is soon to be posted to Saint Petersburg."

"Has your father forbidden his suit?" David asked.

"Not outright. Grandfather said I mustn't pass up an opportunity to be a countess, however, and insisted I come and at least get acquainted. To see, as we've said, if we suit." Her voice had become thick.

"And my request to Lady Danbury to help find me an appropriate bride interfered with your hopes and dreams. I'm sorry," David said.

Even in the moonlight, he could see the moisture in her eyes. He reached for his handkerchief and handed it to her. "Alas, Lady Estelle, it appears we do not suit. You may tell your grandfather that with my blessing."

"Thank you." Her joy was apparent even muffled by his handkerchief. "I wish you well in your ambitions, my lord. The country needs you."

The sincerity of her endorsement touched him. "Shall we see if we can get into dinner without causing talk?" he asked.

"I'm sure we cannot," she answered, taking his arm and letting him lead her through the dark garden.

"Then let them talk. You and I are in accord. We will not suit."

"May I ask you something personal?" she murmured.

"Ask me anything," he replied.

"Have you kissed Lady Fitzwallace?" she asked.

He paused midstep, swallowing a gasp. "No, I have not," he replied.

"You want to, I suspect," she said. "You should do it."

"I'M GLAD YOUR boy is better. Pity you weren't here earlier," Lady Cranwick said, her smirk giving Delia pause.

"Thank you, my lady," Delia said, wondering what on earth

the woman was going on about. Delia had arrived toward the end of supper. A quick glance showed her David seated with Lady Estelle at a small, round table designed to discourage company. She found Jeffrey comfortably seated with Viscount Eaton. The viscount's daughter, Gemma, sat with them, glaring over at David and Lady Estelle. Jeffrey seemed to find Gemma Albert amusing. Delia thought someone needed to instruct that girl to shield her emotions. Jeffrey was unlikely to get hurt, however; she suspected his real interest was in recruiting her father as an investor.

Delia stood at a loss next to Lady Cranwick, who seemed to be waiting for more of a reply.

The woman leaned in conspiratorially. "They thought they were being discreet, but at least three people saw them sneak into the bushes," she said with a knowing look in the direction of David. "Hopes of many will be dashed."

Delia steeled herself against an unaccountably sick feeling in her stomach. *Estelle will make a perfect countess for him. She is what he needs.* She took a breath, grateful she hadn't eaten supper. *We can still be friends.* The fleeting thought died as soon as it rose. Of course they couldn't.

"Ah, Lady Madelyn wishes to speak to me. I bid you a pleasant evening, Lady Cranwick." Delia hurried away.

Maddy had indeed motioned to her. "That didn't look like a pleasant conversation," Maddy said.

Delia shrugged. "She's an unpleasant woman. There are worse." *Much worse.* She saw Awbury glaring from across the room.

"Is Percy truly ill? Mr. Graham implied it was minor," Maddy said.

"Not at all, in fact," Delia said, pitching her voice low.

Brynn Morgan's brow furrowed. "David told us about Awbury. Did he harm you?"

"Not physically. Of course not. But his words were more insulting than usual." *Degrading*, she thought, unable to say the word out loud. "I simply needed a bit of time to recover. The dower house soothed my nerves."

"I understand, and I'm delighted you've recovered. You let the side down, however. You've neglected your assignment."

It took Delia a moment to puzzle that through. "Lady Estelle?"

"Exactly. She lured him out onto the terrace and, if gossip is correct, into the shrubbery. Gemma Albert, for one, is in mourning," Maddy said.

"Dear God, it isn't as if they were discovered in his bed," Brynn grumbled.

"No, but expectations have been raised in the entire company," Maddy replied. "I should have been watching, but he seemed..."

"Eager?" Delia asked. "I think he likes her. I like her as well. She's probably perfect for him. Did you know she's Henrietta Danbury's goddaughter?"

"How do you know that?" Maddy asked.

"Her grandmother told me." Delia shrugged. "Reconnaissance. You told me to watch her."

"I think Henrietta put a cuckoo in our nest," Maddy murmured.

"If he's seriously interested in the chit, a kiss in the moonlight is a logical next step," Brynn said.

His wife swatted him with the end of her serviette. "There is nothing logical about kissing."

Brynn left to refill his wife's tea and fetch a cup for Delia.

Maddy tipped her head and studied Delia closely. "You think he should marry Lady Estelle Wilton?"

"I think he's a grown man. He may have needed a nudge to consider the idea, but he won't be pushed into anything rash. She would be a perfect political hostess, but only he knows if she would suit as his wife."

Maddy continued to regard Delia with unasked questions.

"How do you think the political maneuvering progresses?"

Delia asked, turning the topic. "Jeffrey puts his chances as even or less than that."

Maddy drew breath. "Let me see… I've been preoccupied with the ladies, but I did hear Effingham and his father in a heated discussion in which the son lauded David while listing all the reasons reform is needed. Unfortunately, it's the father who has influence with Liverpool. The invitation alone won him the support of that banker, William Darke, who has some influence in Commons. Has anything struck you about the mood?"

"I'm not certain what you mean," Delia said, gratefully accepting a delicate porcelain cup with steaming tea from Brynn Morgan.

"On occasions when the subject turns to the country, the mood is—I don't know how to describe it. Wary? Waiting? The way it feels before a thunderstorm." Maddy glanced at Brynn, who remained standing. "How are conversations among the gentlemen?"

"If the purpose of this event is to test the waters, I would rate those waters tepid. Most of the gentlemen guests are circumspect and cautious in their speech. They may fear offending the home secretary. Perhaps inviting Sidmouth and his cronies wasn't wise after all," Brynn said before leaving in search of cakes and biscuits.

"It's more than that," Maddy mused. "Even the ladies have an air of worry, as if all their gaiety is a brittle crust on top of a well of concern."

"I know what you mean, but I thought that had to do with the marriage stakes, everyone watching to see who comes up a winner," Delia said. "It might be more honest to put their daughters on auction."

Maddy's mouth twitched at the humor, but she sobered quickly. "David sent Rob to Manchester. Lucy says there's some sort of meeting early in the week, and he wanted an eyewitness."

Delia sat up straight, eyes wide. "That sounds serious." She relaxed back down a moment later. "On the other hand, we're discussing a man who reads a half-dozen newspapers every day, trolling for information. David is obsessed."

Maddy grinned at her. "You may be right." She eyed her husband returning with a plate full of goodies. "And I hear musicians tuning. I have yet to dance with my husband." She gazed at him pointedly.

Brynn sighed, stuffed a biscuit in his mouth, and set the plate down. "For you, Lady Fitzwallace," he said around the mouthful, with a dramatic bow ruined by Maddy's hand tugging him away.

Delia watched them laughing together as they went. She envied their banter. She envied their affection. She envied Rob and Lucy as well. *Don't delude yourself; you envy Lady Estelle Wilton.*

A sharp needle of jealousy wormed its way into Delia's belly and made a path to her heart. *You love the man, you widgeon. How did you let that happen when you know you can't have him?*

She grabbed a ginger bar from the plate, ripped it in half, and took a bite while listing all the reasons she didn't want to marry. Then she listed all the qualities David needed in a wife, few of which she possessed. *But you love him. Doesn't that count?* She feared not. In desperation, she began to note the reasons she would not be his mistress, beginning with the names of her children and her self-respect.

Besides, Delia. A mistress must never, ever, fall in love with her protector. That way lies heartbreak.

She glanced down to see the plate Brynn had left was empty, as empty as her heart. She couldn't be his wife. She wouldn't be his mistress. She couldn't be his friend and watch him with Lady Estelle. She couldn't very well stay his neighbor, either.

Hogswallop, Delia. Life has been close to perfect. Why did you have to fall in love and ruin everything?

CHAPTER TWENTY-NINE

D AVID RETURNED ESTELLE to her grandmother after supper. They had agreed to keep their conversation private for a few days. If the rest of the company thought they were courting, perhaps the other title-hungry females would give him space. He had her gratitude for his kindness and had happily agreed. He'd promised he would speak to her grandfather before the end. She'd told him that, when pressed by her grandparents, she would remain vague and let them draw their own conclusions. She really was a lovely young woman. It wasn't her fault she wasn't Delia Fitzwallace.

Lady Wilbury gave him a penetrating look, as if she saw something in his face. He smiled and bowed over the old woman's hand.

You want to… Estelle's words had unleashed a fierce desire— one he now realized he had been holding in check for some time—to find Delia and kiss her senseless, their pretense of friendship be damned.

He knew she had come; he'd had a glimpse of her at supper. The need to find her consumed him, but as he turned away from the Wilburys, he almost bumped into Gemma Albert. The chit hovered expectantly.

Damn.

"Our dance, I believe, my lord," Gemma chirped.

Of course it was. "I don't believe the sets have begun to

form," he said, looking beyond her.

"Perhaps we can stroll around your wonderful ballroom while we wait," she said, peering up at him with the predatory eyes of a cat before a particularly tasty mouse.

David plastered a polite smile on his face and offered his arm. He may as well allow Gemma the opportunity to preen in front of the entire company for a few moments. It was all she was likely to get from him. Besides, a stroll around the room might lead him to Delia.

Gemma latched on to him as if clinging to the treasures of the Mughal Empire while Estelle's words played over and over in his head: "You want to. You should do it."

Kiss Delia? Hell yes, he wanted to. He'd wanted to since she'd risen from the creek with her gown clinging to her and her eyes shining the day he'd met her. Now he could think of nothing else.

He murmured monosyllables to Gemma, who didn't seem to notice, so busy was she babbling about her plans for the coming Season, her wardrobe, and the deficiencies of every other unmarried woman there.

All the while, he scanned the room. He'd been startled when Delia had entered the supper room, and Estelle had teased him about the way his eyes had followed her. *Am I that transparent?* He ought to be more careful, but he was no longer sure he cared.

Where is the woman?

She'd been sitting with his sister and her husband, but Maddy and Brynn were now standing in the middle of the dance floor, gazing at each other with such heat he wasn't sure if he felt embarrassed or envious. *Both.*

Sets formed, and the music began. Gemma proved to be a good dancer, well trained if uninspired. David's eyes continued to dart around the room. When he saw Delia come from the dining room alone, he missed a step.

His stumble—and the direction of his gaze—drew a glare from his partner, quickly smoothed over.

"She isn't received everywhere, you know," the less-than-honorable Gemma Albert said confidentially. "The taint of trade clings," she added as if it was a dread disease. He really ought to guard his feelings better. Not all ladies were as kind as Lady Estelle.

The pattern of the dance led them apart. David watched Delia speaking with her brother. All too soon, the dance led David and Gemma back.

"I heard Awbury tell my father association with Lady Fitzwallace would doom your ambitions," Gemma told him.

That startled David out of his abstraction. "Did you now?" he asked, moving away with the steps of the dance and then closer. "I didn't know you were interested in politics."

Her artful gaze didn't help her cause. "Your countess will have to be," she murmured with contrived innocence.

The dance ended, to his immense relief, and another began to form, one he had apparently promised to Hester Wadsworth, who almost made him dizzy batting her eyes. At least she didn't try to savage the reputation of other women.

He led her back under the avaricious gaze of her mother, relieved to have done his duty by all the aspirants to the title Countess of Clarion and resumed his search for the one woman who did not seem to covet the position.

He spied Delia promenading on the arm of a recently widowed baronet who kept sending heated glances down her decolletage. David's hands fisted, but before he could do something foolish that would cause a scene, she extracted herself and took the floor with Viscount Eaton.

"You are the host. You aren't supposed to glare at the room as if you mean to chase them all away," a voice hissed. Lucy tugged on his arm. "You're meant to dance and be joyful."

"Then perhaps we should. Another set is forming." He led her out and let her impish grin tease him out of his spat of dismals. Politics—marriage and parliamentary—had become too much for a moment, but David was made of sterner stuff. Or so he hoped. He would wait for the last dance, he decided.

He danced with Maddy and Fanny after that, grateful he had enough sisters to get him through the rest of the program. But there was one woman he hadn't yet partnered with. He went up to the musicians and had a word with the conductor about the final dance. Then he went in search of Delia.

He found her tucked between a fern and her brother, nodded to Graham, and smiled down at her.

"Hiding behind the foliage?" he teased.

"Awbury glares at my every step," she grumbled.

"He's a pompous fool. You shouldn't hide from him," David said.

"So I keep telling her. Brazen it out," her brother said.

"I couldn't agree more. Besides, this is my dance, I believe." When David reached for her hand, she didn't resist.

The pain shadowing her eyes when she gazed up at him grieved him, and he longed to soothe it away. Awbury must have cut her deeply.

She paused near the side, looking about as if for another set to form.

"The last dance is a waltz," he said, disappointed at her obvious distress.

"No. I—"

"Awbury might not approve? You aren't some young miss just out, waiting for permission to waltz. Dance with me. I've looked forward to it all evening," he said.

Something in her eyes melted at that, and she didn't pull away, even when he led her to the center of the floor and nodded to the conductor.

A few notes from a violin, and other couples took to the floor. David put his hand at her waist and tugged her a bit closer, struggling to maintain some sense of proper decorum while a vision of Delia's uninhibited dancing with her children struck him. That was the Delia he had come to know, the forest naiad, not cowed by Awbury and the other sticklers. Every fiber of his being longed to throw propriety to the wind.

The music took him then, and her as well. The stains of the violin and the sway of the woman in his arms wrapped him in an enchanted bower where only they two existed. The room, the other dancers, the scheming mothers, the gossips, the squabbling politicians, and even the fate of the nation all faded away.

Moments—or perhaps hours—passed in a sensual dream until he stood, one hand still at her waist, and gazed into the heat of her deep-brown eyes. When he lifted his other hand to touch her cheek, the hand trembled, and he felt as if he stood on a precipice.

"David!" Maddy's laughing voice, very nearby, sent the illusion crashing down. "The music is over."

Delia gasped and looked frantically around for a brief moment before dropping into a deep curtsey. "Thank you for honoring me with a waltz, my lord. You were correct. It is mesmerizing. But you owe me no thanks. I've been happy to assist your sisters." She turned her back on him, cast a strained smile at Maddy, and spoke in a carrying voice, "Of course. I'd be delighted to help oversee the dessert service."

She walked away.

His whole world had upended, and the blasted woman had turned her back and walked away. He needed to go after her. He needed her.

DELIA STIFLED THE urge to run as she made her way to the door. She smiled and nodded at those she passed, without any awareness of who any one of them was.

A waltz! What was David thinking? The last waltz should have been Estelle's. Not his gauche neighbor's. A friend, as she claimed to be, should have curbed his inappropriate impulse. Except David did not act on impulse. Ever. What, then? Only one thing was clear. She could never be simply his friend.

Hints of whispers followed her. One voice rang clear out of

the cloud. Lady Cranwick. "One has to question the man's judgment. If he thinks he can aspire…" The sound faded away as Delia stepped into the hall and attempted to breathe, one hand clutching her breastbone. *Oh, David, what have you done?*

The sound of the ballroom doors opening sent her scurrying. The company would flow out now that the dancing had ended. Most would simply remove to the late buffet once Harris opened the doors separating the ballroom from the dining room. They were bound to notice she had not gone there as she'd said, but she couldn't bear to face them. Worse, others would come this way.

She ducked into the breakfast room, dark and abandoned, leaned against the wall, and let common sense take over. Whatever people had seen or thought they'd seen back in that ballroom, it had only been a dance. David was a man and an earl. He would be forgiven his impulse. Lady Cranwick and her ilk had no real power to hurt his chances. They would savage her, of course, with Awbury's venom poisoning her standing, but that didn't matter. It wasn't even particularly new.

She walked to the window, staring out into the courtyard garden lost in shadows. It might be best if she stayed away for the rest of the party. Jeffrey would, of course, still attend, and people would think it odd. There would be talk either way. *Which would hurt David least?*

"I thought I saw you come in here." David's rich voice vibrated through her. The door clicked closed behind him.

"What are you thinking?" she hissed. "Your guests expect to see you presiding over the gathering with dignity, not chasing after Awbury's hoydenish daughter-in-law." Her voice faltered as he came closer.

"Maddy has led them to a spectacular midnight dessert display, Brynn is entertaining all and sundry with an amusing story, and Lucy has Irma Barrington and Hester plotting sedate Sunday games for tomorrow while slyly implying they will be anything but. The older ladies are torn between outrage and laughter. The gentlemen are fixed on the food and champagne. No one will miss me."

He stood very close now, his face shadowed, and Delia froze to the spot, unable to move. Tender fingers brushed her cheek, driving the rhythm of her heart to a gallop.

"You mustn't, David," she whispered.

His hand brushed over her ear and touched her hair. "Why?" he asked.

She tipped her head to avoid his hand but couldn't walk away. "Be sensible. Lady Estelle will make you a perfect wife. Carrying on with me may not bring you scorn, but…"

"Carrying on, Delia? Is that what we're doing?" He raised her chin with the crook of a finger.

"No! Nor will we. I won't be your mistress. I can't." Her voice broke on the last word.

"I know. It is one of the things I respect about you." He ran his thumb over her lips. "One of the things I love."

He covered her gasp with his mouth, their breaths mingling. He nibbled her lower lip and ran his tongue along the upper, and Delia melted with each touch until, boneless in his arms, she accepted what he offered, opened to his exploration of her mouth, and returned his kisses.

He kissed from the corner of her mouth to her ear, tickling her with his tongue. As Delia became hot and restless, her hands moved of their own volition under his coat, frustrated by his embroidered waistcoat. When his mouth moved down her neck to her shoulder, she began to undo the buttons.

Her gown gapped, and she realized the ties in the back had become loose. *When did my oh-so-proper earl become so skilled at undoing ladies' garments?* Before she could consider it, he pulled her neckline down, exposing her breasts, and all rational thought fled. He saluted one with gentle fingers and an urgent mouth, and then the other, sending her into a maelstrom of sensation before crushing her against him, her aching breasts against the heat of his fine linen shirt, as he devoured her mouth with his.

"No, ladies. I'm sure this is the other door to the dining room," Lady Cranwick chirped, just outside the breakfast room, her voice shattering Delia's world.

"Damn!" David swore, pulling away just as the door handle rattled.

Delia prayed the floor would open up and swallow her, only vaguely aware of her bodice being restored and the ribbons on the back of her gown being pulled tightly together.

She meant to jump away, but he held her hand, anchoring her to his side at the window.

Light from the hallway blinded her. She made out only shapes of people gazing into the room.

"Lord Clarion! What are you doing in here in the dark?" Lady Cranwick crooned as if it wasn't obvious.

"I'm showing Lady Fitzwallace the glow of the courtyard by moonlight. It is one of the treasures of Clarion Hall," he said, the wretch.

Did he have to use my name? Not that it would have made any difference. Someone had seen him follow her in here.

"Lady Fitzwallace!" Lady Barrington said with a shuddering breath. "You may thank the angels you aren't an innocent maiden or you would be positively ruined."

"As it is, she is not, is she, ladies?" the Cranwick witch sneered. "Perhaps we can forgive Clarion for dallying with the goods on offer before settling down with a proper wife."

Goods on offer? She wanted to slap Lady Cranwick. That would only make it worse.

One woman moved toward the window. In the faint light, Delia made out Lady Wilbury, Estelle's grandmother, and her heart sank. "Lady Cranwick doesn't know Clarion Hall as well as she thinks. We might have missed this enlightening view," Lady Wilbury said under her breath, gazing out the window.

"Lady Wilbury, might I request an interview with you and your husband tomorrow? There are things I need to explain," David murmured.

The lady cast him a sidelong look. "I don't believe explanations are necessary, but Arthur will hear you out."

The Cranwick lizard meant to embarrass Delia, put David on the spot, and crush his chances with Estelle in one fell swoop. Delia might have given her cunning credit, if she weren't enraged on David's behalf.

"I'll make way for the ladies to enjoy the view," Delia croaked with an inclination of her head to Lady Wilbury. She almost added "Estelle should see it too" but couldn't bring the words to her swollen lips. She pulled her hand loose and sidestepped their avid audience, ducking into the hall and walking away without looking to the right or the left until she reached the main entrance.

She accepted her cloak and bonnet from the footman standing duty, asked him to notify Jeffrey Graham that she had gone home on foot, and disappeared into the night.

CHAPTER THIRTY

THE FITZWALLACE CONTINGENT did not appear at church services the following morning. *Thank God neither did the Wilburys,* David thought, taking his seat in the earl's pew alone. Moments later, Maddy and Brynn surprised him by joining him there.

He had intended to kiss Delia the previous night, merely to kiss her, a simple kiss, a test to see—But with Delia, nothing would ever be simple. He should have known; he should have anticipated the raging lust. He couldn't regret it, but he needed to speak with her. She deserved an apology. Or an explanation. Or if he had his way, an offer of marriage. His path had become clear. He could only hope that the stubborn woman who claimed she would never remarry could be persuaded to have him.

Most of the guests didn't venture out to Saint Morwenna, having enjoyed David's hospitality well into the night. His own head pounded from the copious alcohol he'd imbibed in hopes of calming his raging need for Delia and presenting a confident front to the company. He'd only come in hopes Delia would be here, but she was not.

Lady Cillia Effingham, Cranwick's daughter, however, had been clever enough to follow him, with just her maid for company. Her conniving mother had clearly decided he could be compromised. While Mr. Styles, the vicar, gave one of his jovial, heartwarming sermons, David's mind focused on how to avoid her. He was grateful Maddy sat at his side.

Coming out of church, he spied Baron Wadsworth in conversation with Old Robert Benson. He craned his neck and found Maddy speaking with the vicar's wife. At least Hester Wadsworth had parents with her. He decided there was safety in numbers.

"Is all well at the Willow?" David asked.

"Bustling for certain, my lord. The business you sent our way is a blessing," Old Robert said, glancing at the Wadsworths out of the corner of his eye.

"We keep your ostlers busy repairing our sad carriage and ferrying us to the hall," Wadsworth said jovially while his daughter did her best to appear demure and proper.

Give the girl credit. Perhaps she is demure and proper. She isn't a harpy like some of the others. She'll make Effingham a fine wife.

"Lord Clarion, well met!" Lady Cillia Effingham, neither demure nor proper, had a voice that grated on his pounding head.

Hester lit up when Lady Cillia approached. "Is Lord Effingham with you?" she asked.

"Hardly. Reggie is sleeping off whatever the gentlemen did in the billiard room last night," Lady Cillia said.

Old Robert bowed properly. "I best get back to the Willow. Our Sunday midday meal rivals the hall, I'll warrant," he said with a twinkle in his eye. "Care to stop by this Sunday, Lord Clarion?"

"Not this week, Mr. Benson, but Lady Cillia would be well served to go with you. Luncheon will be much later at the hall," David said.

"No! That is, my mother… I need to go back," the Effingham chit babbled. "I seem to be without a ride," she added hopefully.

David swallowed the temptation to ask her how she'd gotten here. She'd no doubt sent back whatever vehicle she had commandeered from his stable. "Pity. I rode over. Perhaps Mrs. Wadsworth will see you safely home to your mama." David tipped his hat, inclined his head, and mounted his horse, smiling at Old Robert's obvious wink. *Maddy will see her home.*

David rode along the river path, soaking in the beauty of the English summer. He put women from his mind and started to catalog his gentlemen guests. Support for his candidacy, he suspected, fell just above half the invited group, almost enough to overturn Sidmouth. Some of it was soft, however, and a few were openly opposed. Watching the sunlight on the water, he found it hard to care about ambition. His wayward heart kept straying.

Should I call at the dower house? More likely Delia and Graham would be arriving at the hall shortly. In any case, he needed to meet with Wilbury first. He'd promised the wife, and he owed Estelle his support. Still, he was desperate to talk with Delia; they couldn't leave their relationship as it had been, not after what had passed between them.

Harris took David's hat and riding crop at the door. Irma Barrington and the banker's daughter tittered on the bench outside the drawing room, trying to draw his attention. *Lying in wait.*

"Has Lady Fitzwallace come up from the dower house?" David asked.

"No, nor Mr. Graham, either. If I may, sir, the Marquess of Wilbury requested your attendance in the sitting room of their suite as soon as can be."

Dread filled David briefly. *Sooner over, sooner done.* He nodded at Harris, ignored the avid attention of the ladies in the corner, and climbed the steps with leaden feet.

Estelle stood by the window when Wilbury answered David's knock. The marchioness put her needlework aside. He thought her gaze held sympathy, but that may have been wishful thinking.

"I understand you wished to have words with me," Wilbury said. "Should we be private or may the ladies stay?"

David glanced at Estelle, calm and confident, and said, "They should stay. This won't take long."

Wilbury raised one eyebrow. "Say your piece."

"Lady Estelle—lovely and charming as she is—" He floundered briefly. "That is, I know you came here with hopes, if not expectations, but the lady and I, having become acquainted, have decided we will not suit. We are both quite certain."

Estelle smiled reassuringly, and it wasn't lost on Wilbury. "I see," he said. "You've discussed the matter."

"Lord Wilbury, I believe your granddaughter's heart is elsewhere, and you would do well to heed it," David said. Estelle colored charmingly.

Wilbury frowned at the girl.

Lady Wilbury bit her lower lip. David would swear it was to keep from smiling. She cleared her throat. "I believe, Lord Clarion, the same is true of you."

"I suspect Henrietta Danbury knew it all along," Wilbury growled. "We should leave tomorrow morning, Martha."

"No, Grandpapa! We can't. I promised Lord Clarion to maintain the fiction of our courtship the rest of the week. To keep the harpies at bay," Estelle said.

"Even after last night?" Wilbury asked. "His behavior insulted you. Perhaps not personally or intentionally, but in the eyes of the company…" He shook his head and glared at David. "You have sisters guarding the harpies as Estelle calls them. You don't need my granddaughter. Let them think she leaves disappointed. When we announce her betrothal to Walter Houseman, society will—"

Estelle threw herself into her grandfather's arms. "You will? Truly? You've made me the happiest of women. I care nothing for the opinions of society."

"Well done, Lady Estelle. I wish you every happiness," David said, his grin sincere.

"The harpies, as you call them, will be on full attack, Lord Clarion," the marchioness warned, unable to dim the radiance of her joy for her granddaughter. "You had best make up your mind about a wife and quickly."

"That is excellent advice, my lady, but there is naught to decide. Only one woman has my heart, and she professes no interest in marriage."

Wilbury glowered under bushy eyebrows. "What sort of cabinet minister would you make if you can't convince one young woman—one, I might add, that is clearly besotted with you—to marry you."

David descended the stairs, his heart lighter than it had been in weeks. The Barrington girl and the banker's daughter had disappeared, probably to tell all and sundry that he'd been summoned by Wilbury. He avoided the drawing room and thought to have Harris order food to the library, but it would be full of politics and intrigue. At the moment, he wanted nothing so much as to clear the harpies and the political squabbling out of his house so he could have his life back as it was, calm and peaceful, but with Delia in it.

Calm and peaceful? Delia? He grinned. He hoped the breakfast room was empty, for hunger made it hard to think. He'd need his wits when he sought her out.

"FOR GOODNESS' SAKE, Delia, you look as if someone died." Jeffrey glared across the breakfast table at his sister.

Delia pushed her eggs around on her plate. She'd been unable to eat a bite after a sleepless night. She had cried until shortly before dawn, and felt a fool. Delia Graham Fitzwallace never succumbed to weeping. Never.

"Explain it to me again. Clarion offered for you, and you refused?" Barnabas asked. He sat back in his chair, tipping two of its legs up, and sipped his coffee.

"He did not. And he shouldn't."

Jeffrey put down the paper and leaned across the table. "Excuse me? If even half of what Lady Cranwick was pouring into the ears of all and sundry last night is true, an offer is the least he owes you."

"He can't marry me!" Delia frowned at her brother. "How

can you be so obtuse?"

"Again, I fail to understand you. He is unmarried, to the best of my knowledge, as are you," Barnabas said, his teasing grin in place. "And I gather the two of you were discovered in a, ah, private moment last night."

"He knows, we all know, that a political wife would help his career. If he wants to be home secretary, he needs a woman with an unsullied English pedigree—preferably one that dates to the time of the Conqueror. A woman raised to manage a fine house, to entertain the Prince of Wales, and to serve dinner to the prime minister and his cabinet. One who doesn't blot her copybook in public at every turn. A born lady. I am not that woman."

Barnabas's chair thumped down onto all four legs, and he clapped. "Bravo. Fine speech. One almost might think you believe it."

"You are as much a lady as any of them," Jeffrey growled.

"The *ton* respects only birth. Our father's grandparents were shopkeepers," she said. She needn't mention her maternal grandfather, the sugar planter.

"And we are shamelessly wealthy merchants whose ships sail every sea," Jeffrey retorted. "If he doesn't think we're good enough…" Jeffrey glared across the table.

"It isn't that. It doesn't matter what he thinks. He'll be judged by his wife. He is going to offer for Lady Estelle. He told her grandmother he would speak to Lord Wilbury today." Delia pushed her plate away. She couldn't eat.

"If he was kissing you as thoroughly as you looked last night and doing God knows what else and yet plans to offer for Lady Estelle Wilton today, he is pond scum, unworthy to be in the same room with you, much less—Tell me he didn't offer you carte blanche!" Jeffrey shouted.

"I told him I would never be his mistress—not that he asked such a thing. He didn't," Delia said, brushing aside the fact that she expected him to. He told her he respected it. *It is one of the reasons I love you… Love you!* Had he actually said that or had she imagined it?

"What are you going to do?" Barnabas asked.

"Stay away from him. At this point, I'll only mar Lady Estelle's triumph. I'll have to move, of course. I love it here, but…"

"But you love this philandering earl," Barnabas said.

"He's not a philanderer! It was a moment of weakness. My foolish heart is the problem. I'll have to move."

Jeffrey grunted. "You can do better than this poky little cottage, Delia. You were raised to better. All three of us were." He set down his serviette and stood. "You've quite put me off my feed with your dismals. I'm going to see what is on offer at Clarion Hall. The overbred guests must have crawled from their beds by now."

Barnabas rose as well. "I'm going down to the Willow. Their coffee is fine and their Chelsea buns world-class. Mr. Benson has been allowing me to use his office to get some work done."

Jeffrey is correct. Giving in to dismals does nothing. With Alf gone to the stables as he did every morning, the house was too quiet. She had accepted that he would attend Eton in the fall, but she hadn't come to like it. She found Penny sketching in the little schoolroom they had set up in the attic. Joanie and Percy were building castles out of blocks.

"What do you think, Mama?" Penny asked, holding up a sketch of some bunnies nibbling grass.

"What a fine drawing! We should take your sketching outside," Delia said.

"I would like that, Mama. I love being out, and I'm so glad we moved here," Penny said.

"I think we shall always live in the country," Delia replied.

"I mean here. With Marj nearby," Penny said, stepping on her mother's broken heart.

Delia didn't even try to reply. She helped Penny pack up her sketching to take outside, but the sound of raised voices interrupted her.

"Enter," she responded to a quiet knock.

Parsons's distress was apparent. "The Duke of Awbury wishes a word, my lady. He is in a rather fierce mood if I dare say.

Shall I tell him you are out?"

Awbury? Tempting— She considered her choices for a moment. "He'll ignore that, I fear. Sit him in the parlor—if he hasn't already bullied his way in—with tea, and I'll be down shortly. Joanie, I will need you to accompany me. And Parsons, please fetch Joe Holden if you can and ask him to stand ready in the kitchen. I may need him."

She left her daughter to her sketching and tried to freshen up. No amount of cool water soothed her obviously red eyes, however. Her frock, a pleasant enough afternoon dress, would do. She straightened her spine and went to confront her obstreperous father-in-law. "Damn it, Jeffrey and Barnabas. You left too early," she muttered on her way down.

Awbury paced the floor like a rabid animal. The man not sleek enough for her to think him a wolf, his short stature made him more a vicious badger than a bear. Vicious certainly. Delia took a few steps into the room, and Joanie slipped in after her. The attack was immediate.

"You think a maid will protect your reputation," Awbury sneered. "It is far too late for that. What have I said to you? You ignored my explicit orders, and your reprehensible behavior tarnished the Fitzwallace name—again!" he shouted. "That waltz—putting yourself forward in such a disgraceful way— unrefined and uncouth. As to what happened afterward, playing whore to Clarion—"

"You will not speak to me that way, Awbury! I'm not yours to abuse." Delia shook with outrage. Had the bully watched for her brother to leave? She wouldn't put it past him. "I'll thank you to leave."

"I'll do no such thing," he said. "You behaved like the strumpet you are in front of the entire company. Lord Sidmouth asked me how I could possibly have allowed my son to marry such a woman—the home secretary actually questioned my judgment!"

"We both know the answer to that," Delia snapped. "You thought you could get your greedy little hands on Graham money through Vincent. More fool you."

He approached so close it took all her will not to step back. She would not be cowed.

"You will stay far away from Clarion Hall this week, while Sidmouth and the others are there. If Clarion wants to keep his mistress in a cozy little cottage on his estate, let him." He stood so close she felt his spittle as he raged. "Whore if you must, but I demand discretion. Stay away from your betters at the hall and for heaven's sake, away from London."

She pulled away then, going around him so that she had her back to the drawing room and opened his way to the door. "Leave now, or I'll have you bodily removed." She glanced at the doorway, where Harris and Joe stood, anxious and ready.

Awbury spun around at them and turned back to bare his teeth at Delia. "You think they can lay hands on a duke with impunity? I'll have them imprisoned. I'll have them transported. As for you, keep your sluttish behavior to yourself. One more incident and I will force your brother to drag you back to Jamaica where you belong, along with that presuming black clod of a factotum of his."

"Jeffrey would never," Delia said, chin high. Unless Awbury found a way to apply pressure. She didn't believe he could but knew the attempt would be unpleasant.

"I've always had a mind to travel abroad," Joe said quietly from the door. "Shall I throw him out now, my lady?"

Delia thought Awbury might expire of apoplexy on her drawing room floor, so purple was his face. He gasped several breaths before turning on his heels and pushing past her servants to the front entrance. "No more, Delia," he croaked. "You've been warned."

The door vibrated behind him, answering waves rippling through Delia. She trembled, unable to move. After a moment, Harris spoke. "Shall I bring you tea, my lady? Or perhaps something stronger?"

She peered at the three of them: Harris, Joanie, and Joe. "Please, Harris. And I thank God for the three of you."

CHAPTER THIRTY-ONE

D AVID FOUND LUCY seeing to early risers in the breakfast room but saw no sign of Delia. In fact, few of the ladies had arisen. Those who had, greeted him politely, but the sharpened interest in their eyes hinted that he—or rather, the episode in this breakfast room in the dark—had been the topic of discussion. Perhaps it was best Delia had not come. He should go to her as soon as he ate.

A few more abstemious gentlemen broke their fasts and made free with his newspapers. Sidmouth sat in the corner, leaning toward his sycophant Hartwell and Lord Barrington, their chairs pulled back from the table. Sidmouth appeared to do most of the talking. Barrington had the hunted look of a man trapped by a particularly aggressive salesman. Hartwell looked bored. They paused when he walked in, but continued to confer quietly when David didn't approach. He could guess the topic and had no desire to confront them.

"Come to join us, Clarion?" the banker, Darke, called from his place at a table.

"Quiet this morning. No fears of the marriage stakes," another wag called, drawing chuckles from most and frowns from some.

A footman appeared at David's elbow, coffee as he liked it in hand. "Eggs, my lord? Kippers?" the young man asked.

His stomach lurched. "Toast, I think."

Darke looked on knowingly. "Long night, Clarion?" He let the possible meanings of that hang in the air.

"We were all up far too late, I suspect," David replied calmly.

"Have you seen the most recent *Manchester Observer*?" Lord Eaton asked, eyeing Sidmouth in the corner. "It came just yesterday."

"No, I have not. Is there any news?" David asked.

Eaton slid it over. It had been folded to an article about the "rising tide of anger." A quick glance showed him another prediction of a massive turnout on Tuesday. He shook his head. "What do you think, Eaton? How can we prevent trouble?"

Sidmouth, it became apparent, had sharp hearing. Before Eaton could reply, the home secretary boomed from the corner, "Prevent? Fear and intimidation are the only things the rabble understands. We increased troop strength. They're to parade through the city in formal march today. True Englishmen will cheer for them."

David looked at the men around the room. Some nodded. Some frowned at the home secretary—Barrington, David noticed, among them. A larger group tried to study their coffee or plates. "Do you think provocation is the most effective way to address hungry, unemployed sons and fathers?" David demanded.

"The most effective way to deal with rabble is to transport them to Van Diemen's Land," Sidmouth declared in a voice meant for the audience in the room, daring anyone to disagree.

"Empty the streets of the cities, Sidmouth? Where will workers come from? How will you fill your pantry? Who will drive your coaches?" Jeffrey Graham stood in the doorway, arms akimbo. "Most importantly, who will unload my ships and fetch my brandy?" he asked. An uneasy spate of laughter met his words.

The gentlemen took it as an excuse to ignore Sidmouth, who left them soon after, followed by Hartwell. Their numbers thinned.

David's attention remained on the door, but Delia did not

follow her brother in. Graham took his time over the offerings before he sat and thanked the footman for pouring coffee. Either the man had an iron stomach or he hadn't had as much to drink the previous night as David had thought.

Questions ran through David's mind, but he didn't want to discuss Delia with her brother in front of an audience.

"She didn't come," Graham said softly.

David didn't ask who. "Am I that obvious?"

"You have been all week. I doubt if the ambitious mothers have missed it," Graham said.

"I need to speak to her. And to you. Privately."

Graham put his fork down, glanced around the room, and studied David carefully. "Indeed, you do, Clarion. I think you should come to dinner at the dower house," he said quietly.

David's heart leapt. But it fell down quickly. He had guests. He had responsibilities.

Graham resumed eating, his eyes darting to David. He waited patiently.

Lucy, who had been about to leave with Mrs. Darke, the last of the ladies, must have heard. She leaned between them to whisper. "Today is Sunday. Supper will be informal and simple. You will not be missed. Especially when we tell them you are indisposed."

"I promised Danbury and some of the others a ride out," David said.

"Do it; I'll confer with Maddy," Lucy said. "Then claim fatigue and take to your bed. Slip out after." She flashed her impish grin and left to see to their female guests.

"Shall we say seven, my lord?" Graham asked blandly. "One thing. She may not be happy with me. She is determined to avoid you for the duration of the week."

Hope that had flared died just as quickly. "Seven it is," David replied.

An hour later, dressed for his ride, David stopped in the drawing room, looking for Maddy. The ladies clustered there discussing evening entertainments.

The Honorable Irma Barrington argued in favor of a scavenger hunt, hoping, no doubt, for an opportunity to invade the family wing. Gemma Albert alternately preened in the company of a duchess and sulked. She cast David a scathing glance, born, no doubt, of her belief that his meeting with Wilbury had included an offer for Lady Estelle.

"May I have a word with Mrs. Morgan, please, ladies?" David asked.

Gemma appeared almost as distressed to lose the company of a duchess as she was the loss of a chance at an earl. She had no notion why Maddy had left the title behind or that Maddy only paid attention to her because of her determination to keep David from the ambitious chit's machinations.

Maddy stepped into the entranceway. "I've spoken with Lucy. Unlike her, I'm certain your absence will be noticed. Are you sure about this?"

"About dinner at the dower house? Yes. I owe Graham a private word," he said.

"That isn't what I meant, and you know it," she said.

"The rest is up to the lady. I owe her a conversation, at least."

Maddy studied him carefully. Before she could speak, the Danburys descended the stairway.

"Ready, Clarion?" the marquess asked jovially.

His lady pinned David with a knowing look. "Lucy tells me we're to cover for you this evening," she said. "I trust you've come to your senses, Clarion. Don't make a muddle of it."

She floated into the drawing room, a man-of-war at full sail. "Lady Cillia!" she boomed. "We missed you at breakfast." She shut the door behind her.

David stared after her. *Henrietta never intended Lady Estelle for me at all.* He suspected the grand dame intended to prod Wilbury into allowing Estelle her desired match. Besides, she was fond of Delia.

Maddy cleared her throat. She had caught him beaming. "You

heard her, David. Don't make a muddle of it." She followed the marchioness.

Left with Danbury's knowing grin, David opened his mouth but couldn't formulate words.

Danbury clapped him on the back. "You heard the ladies!" He glanced to the stairs. "Ah, Barrington and Eaton are here. Shall we ride this fine estate, gentlemen?"

SHE COULD KILL him. Jeffrey rarely interfered in Delia's life, but when he did, it was on a grand scale. *How dare he invite Clarion for dinner?*

"If you invade the kitchen again, Mrs. Parsons will quit, and then where will you be?" Barnabas asked from his comfortable chair.

"What was Jeffrey thinking? Clarion should be with his guests. The whole purpose of this house party is to further his ambition to be home secretary. England needs him."

Barnabas made a rude noise. "England survived Napoleon. It will survive with or without Clarion."

"But he—" A knock at the door interrupted her, and she felt the blood drain from her face. She clasped her hands together, glanced about for a place to sit, and grabbed for her pathetic scrap of needlework, bringing a chuckle from Barnabas.

"The Earl of Clarion," Harris announced.

He took her breath away. Tall, proud, and perfectly groomed, he stood in the doorway. Candlelight reflected the deep auburn of his windblown hair, the slight imperfection making her upright earl even more attractive. Pleasure swelled in her chest, pooled, and flowed to her nether regions. Pain followed quickly on.

Hogswallop. I'm going to make a fool of myself.

David approached, and it didn't help that the hand she presented to him shook. He bowed over it, his eyes boring into hers as if looking for the answer to an unasked question. "Thank you for having me, my lady," he said with perfectly proper diction.

She began to speak, but no sound came out. She heard Jeffrey's heavy tread on the stairs, grateful for his presence. *He caused this confrontation. The least he can do is manage it.*

"Clarion! I trust you extracted yourself from your duties with care," Jeffrey said.

"How could I not with my sisters and the Marchioness of Danbury all conspiring to send me on my way?" he said with a rueful smile.

What does he mean about Henrietta?

"May we offer you a brandy? My sister keeps a good cellar in expectation of my visits," Jeffrey said. He glanced at Barnabas. "Have you met our…operations manager, Barnabas McKinney?"

Barnabas rose to his feet and extended a hand. David took it without wavering. Delia studied the dark hand in David's pale one and wondered if he'd caught the hesitation in Jeffrey's introduction.

"I believe I met Mr. McKinney several months ago at the Willow," David said.

"Quite right. I was passing through on Graham Shipping business and paused to check in on Delia," Barnabas said. He used her Christian name on purpose. And smiled at her. The wretch.

Jeffrey went to the decanter and poured drinks for David and Barnabas. He raised a brow at Delia in question.

Why not? God knew she needed one. Jeffrey handed her a brandy. "Courage," he whispered.

The gentlemen sat. Delia had remained seated, afraid her legs wouldn't hold her. David's discomfort was palpable, and Delia's social skills deserted her utterly.

Harris rescued them by announcing dinner, and Delia let the familiar rituals of etiquette soothe her fragile nerves.

Predictable, polite platitudes about the weather and the state of business only took them so far. Humorous stories about the house party set Delia's nerves on edge. Jeffrey brought it back to the political debates swirling throughout—safer ground surely.

David seemed pleasantly surprised by Barnabas's probing questions. Though he hadn't attended, he knew the players and the stakes. "Jeffrey tells me Sidmouth threatens ironfisted reaction if Hunt's speech causes unrest in Manchester," he said.

Enough! Dining en famille, Barnabas addressed the family by their Christian names. Of course he did. *What must David think of his familiarity? He ought to know.*

Delia gave in to the urge to speak before she lost her nerve. "You may have noticed Barnabas is closer than an employee, David. He's a stakeholder in Graham Shipping." She looked around the table. "He's also my grandmother's nephew." *There. I said it. Let him draw his own conclusions about Grandmother Molly's origins.*

David smiled at Barnabas. "Family has no substitute," he said. "It explains your loyalty. Graham Shipping must thrive on it."

Jeffrey nodded. "That it does, Clarion." He gazed at David with approval as if David had passed some test Jeffrey had failed to mention.

Delia narrowed her eyes at her brother. *Is that what this dinner is about? Making our family connections clear to David?*

Harris cleared plates. "Shall we bring the pudding, my lady?" he asked, "Or would you prefer to take it with tea in the drawing room?"

"We dine informally, David. I'm not accustomed to leaving gentlemen to their port," Delia said. She nodded at Harris. "The drawing room," she said.

As if by agreement, they all rose, but Jeffrey paused in the entrance. "We never covered your views on the situation in Manchester, Clarion, and I'm as curious as my cousin about it, but I don't think that's why you came. You'll want a private moment with my sister—a moment, mind. May I suggest that we leave you two to talk?"

Barnabas grinned. "It's a pleasant evening. A walk would be welcome."

Jeffrey clapped him on the back. "Excellent suggestion."

Before she could object, Delia found herself alone with David. She strode into the drawing room, wringing her hands. She couldn't bear for him to speak, dreading what he might say. "You saw Wilbury, then. Am I to wish you and Estelle happy?"

His face pinched as if he was in pain. She interrupted him before he could speak. "Please, David. Please don't apologize for what happened between us—and don't let it ruin your life."

⫷ ❧ ⫸

CHAPTER THIRTY-TWO

R UIN MY LIFE? *Save it, more like.*
He approached Delia as closely as he dared. He longed to take her hand, but neither her stiff posture nor her tightly clasped hands allowed such a thing. "Wilbury plans to leave in the morning, taking Estelle with him. You may wish her happy. He has given permission for her to marry the man she loves."

Her eyes flew wide. "But you said—"

"I told Lady Wilbury I would speak to the marquess. I did. I told him Lady Estelle and I agreed that we would not suit and that Estelle's heart was engaged elsewhere. I owed her that much before I came to speak with you."

"What is there to say to me? Please don't tell me you came to apologize. What happened was…"

"What, Delia? What was it?" He touched her clenched hands, and they unfolded into his.

"Wonderful." The word, so soft he barely heard it, penetrated to his core.

"I thought so, too," he whispered, leaning closer, their breaths mingling.

She wouldn't meet his eyes. "Wonderful but hopeless. I won't be your mistress, I told you that, and I do not plan to marry again." She looked at him directly then. "But Henrietta Danbury is right. You need a wife to advance your ambitions. To, to—"

"Ambitions be damned," he growled.

"You say that, but I know you. England matters. The acts of Parliament matter. You don't have to accept the ninnies chasing you at Clarion Hall. There are more like Estelle, the right sort of wife, who can manage dinner parties and soirees to further your causes. One who will be an ornament on the Clarion estate. I can't be that person.

"A wife is not an ornament! Damn it."

She attempted to pull her hands away then. "Awbury came today. He called me a strumpet and worse. He's wrong, but he isn't the only one who thinks that. I forget myself. I fall in creeks. I speak out of turn. I—"

"Awbury is an ass, and most of society knows it. Ignore him!"

She stared at their hands, gently trying to extract hers. "He threatened to force Jeffrey to send me back to Jamaica. I would go if it would help you."

David cursed under his breath. "That toad's attempts to make you feel unworthy must stop. I will see that they do." He spoke through clenched teeth. When she didn't respond but continued to stare at her hands, he let them go and ran a hand through his hair in frustration.

"I repeat. A wife is not an ornament or some damned political hostess. A wife is meant to be flesh of my flesh, bone of my bone, heart of my heart." He cupped her face. "You have my heart, Delia. You must know that."

She gaped at him, and the sight of her luscious mouth sent sense to the winds. He leaned closer. She froze before he could kiss her. *Don't force this, Clarion. Give her room.*

He took a step back, holding her eyes with his. "I came here tonight to ask you a question. Will you marry me?"

She began to shake her head in denial.

He raised a hand to stop her. "I came to ask the question, but you don't have to answer tonight. I won't accept your no in any case. Take the question to your heart and let it rest there, my voice whispering, 'Will you marry me?' I won't take an answer until this unbearable house party is over. Can you promise me you will do that?" he pleaded, determined to beg if he had to. "I can be the husband who cherishes and respects you, the one who doesn't bully or attempt to control you. We could be good together. Friends and partners. And lovers."

She looked away and swallowed. "You can still find someone more suitable. Whether you are home secretary or not, you need someone who won't bring gossip." She didn't sound as confident; he could tell she weakened.

When he put his hand on her cheek again, she didn't pull away. When he slid it around her neck, she gazed up at him, her dark eyes wells of sorrow. "You said wonderful," he whispered, inches from her mouth. "It can be wonderful again."

Her breath against his face quickened; her eyes never left his.

"Will you keep my question in your heart?" he asked.

"How can I not? You put it there. I won't be able to remove it," she breathed.

He meant the kiss to be gentle but found it impossible to prevent the flames that ignited between them. She was no more able to stop it than he was.

This, Delia. This is what I want.

⋙✦⋘

Sounds at the entrance brought Delia to herself, or as much as was possible after the maelstrom of emotion and sensation David had unleashed.

Jeffrey and Barnabas made a great show of speaking loudly, giving David time to tug her bodice up. He could do little about her swollen mouth or the state of her coiffure, undone and hanging over one ear. His no longer pristine cravat had come undone, but he managed to button his waistcoat before Jeffrey came in the room.

Jeffrey's gaze missed nothing. Barnabas's smug grin didn't help. "Are we to offer congratulations, then?" Jeffrey said.

"I have asked your sister for her hand in marriage. She has

promised to think about it," David said, back straight, shoulders firmly set.

"Think?" Jeffrey drawled with a raised eyebrow. "Is that what you call it, Delia?"

"I—"

David interrupted her. "She has promised to consider my question and give me her answer at the end of the week. When the house party is over."

"Are you sure that is wise? It might be better to announce it in front of them all," Jeffrey said. "Face the gossips down."

Delia blanched and let David take her hand in his.

"She needs time to think, Graham, and would probably prefer not to face Awbury again."

"Awbury?" Jeffrey glared at Delia.

"Has that dog been bothering you again?" Barnabas demanded.

"He came while you were gone. It was his usual venom," Delia said. She had no intention of giving them detail.

"He threatened to force you to send her back to Jamaica," David told them.

Jeffrey's bark of laughter echoed off the walls. "As if he could force me to do anything."

"I ought to gut the man," Barnabas muttered, and Delia was grateful she hadn't told anyone what Awbury had called him.

"That, I fear, is my privilege. Or it will be once I persuade her to accept me," David said.

"Persuasion. Is that what was going on here before we walked in?" Jeffrey asked.

David's smug grin infuriated her.

"I'm not such a fragile flower that I succumb to persuasion," she sputtered, yanking her hand away. "I agreed to withhold my answer—my refusal—until the end of the week. That's it. Now if you gentlemen will excuse me, I'm going to freshen up."

She swept out with as much dignity as she could muster. Her swell of triumph ended in moments when she heard David say,

"She's a stubborn woman."

"You don't know the half of it," she heard Jeffrey reply. "We wish you luck."

Barnabas's deep laugh didn't help.

CHAPTER THIRTY-THREE

MONDAY PASSED WITHOUT David encountering Delia. Maddy told him she was on the lawn, managing children's games, that morning, but he didn't see her. Her backbone filled him with pride, grateful she didn't let Awbury keep her away. By the time he managed to free himself from a billiard game over which debate raged about the limits of public dissent, however, she was gone.

The ladies insisted on another leisurely walk to the waterfall that afternoon. He looked for her in the milling crowd when they started off, but Maddy told him Delia had gone into Ashmead with Henrietta Danbury and Lady Barrington. Meanwhile, Lady Estelle's departure raised the hopes of every one of the matchmaking mothers, and David felt besieged. Maddy and Lucy did their best. Fanny felt under the weather again as she had been a few times the previous week. Eli had begun hinting at a coming announcement about a happy event, but so far none was forthcoming.

He spied Delia across the drawing room with Graham when they gathered in the evening, but Harris announced dinner before he could make his way to her through the guests who wanted his ear. He wasn't sure who'd arranged the seating that night, but he peered the entire length of the massive table to find her sitting at the far end. She sparkled up at her brother and Mrs. Grant, while David sat in a conversational purgatory with Lady Cranwick on one side and Lady Wadsworth on the other. Sidmouth's stiffly formal presence on Lady Cranwick's other side didn't help. By the time dinner was over and he had extricated himself from the gentlemen's sonorous discussion, she was gone.

He awoke Tuesday morning from fevered dreams of Delia beside him to sweaty sheets, an aching head, and an ominous feeling he couldn't shake. He counted days—four until the final ball. Five—no, six, since most people would not travel on the Sabbath—until they left and he had peace. He would demand his answer then.

He threw his legs over the side and sat on the edge of the bed, determined to avoid Delia, thinking perhaps it would be better if he didn't have time alone with her until then. All he wanted to do was haul her into an empty room and kiss her senseless. And more. His habitual lifelong reserve, his sense of propriety, and his gentlemanly instincts had deserted him entirely. He couldn't even mourn their loss.

Shooting was on offer for the men that morning, he remembered. He loathed it, and he knew Clarion Hall couldn't provide the best of the sport, but a tramp in the woods would at least keep the men occupied. Then he remembered Awbury had said with great relish that he planned to participate, and David groaned. He really didn't want to be around the man with a gun in his hand.

Sidmouth had claimed that a packet of work had arrived and he would be unavailable all day. He had managed to convey that the matter was cabinet business, hush-hush, and of paramount importance. Danbury had told David to ignore "the old bag of air." David was as glad not to see him.

Well and truly tired of the debates, discussion, and maneuvering, David wondered why he had ever sought higher office to begin with. *I should never have let Danbury talk me into this.*

His only consolation was that it was almost over. He rang for his valet.

➤➤➤❮❮❮

"SHOULDN'T YOU BE standing guard on Irma Barrington?" Delia smiled at Lucy. The two ladies sat at the table in the dower house Tuesday morning with Penny and Marj creating lists for the much-awaited scavenger hunt.

"She discovered the men had gone shooting and didn't come down all day. At least, she hadn't before I left," Lucy replied.

"She'll be wanting a rest for tonight," Delia said.

Lucy rolled her eyes. "I'll be running my feet off. We have Brynn assigned to assist the footman at David's bedroom." She covered her mouth with one hand when Delia indicated the girls with a toss of her head. "What do we have so far?" Lucy asked.

Marj read off the agreed-upon list. "This would be easier if we could go outside. Isn't a dried rose an outside item?"

"It could be, but many a lady has one tucked in her journal or Bible."

"That's silly. Why would they do that?" Penny asked.

"Who has a handkerchief with a *B* embroidered on it?" Marj asked. "The Barringtons could make money on this."

They settled, in the end, on ten items that would be hard enough to catch participants' interest, with nothing that might tempt them to intrude in the family wing. Tokens for choosing teams came next.

"I'm counting on you to guard the bag of tokens until it is time, Delia," Lucy said.

"I'm counting on you to oversee the choosing. The debutantes are a devious lot," Delia retorted.

Lucy packed up the game while Delia kissed the girls goodbye and cautioned them to behave for Joanie. Marj planned to stay the night.

"We will, Lady Fitz," Marj chirped. "Barnabas is going to teach us how to play vingt-et-un."

Delia groaned, envisioning David's reaction.

"Don't worry, Mama. We only bet hairpins," Penny added.

"Your brother is going to be unhappy," Delia said as she and Lucy left the house.

"Or not. You've been good for him, Delia. Maddy and I had almost despaired of him coming out of his rigid shell." Lucy looked as if she wanted to say more.

"You mean like the Saturday night breakfast room disaster?" Delia asked.

They reached the wooded path in silence before Lucy burst out laughing. "I mean exactly that. 'Loosen up' indeed!"

Delia couldn't help joining in the laughter over her choice of words. "Just don't get ideas. It isn't what you think," she cautioned.

Lucy looked skeptical but kept her peace.

When the path opened up at the grand front lawn of the hall, they saw a rider emerge from the wooded portion of the lane to their left.

"He's coming fast," Delia murmured.

They sped up and were halfway across when he pulled his horse up and leapt off. "Oh my goodness, it's Rob!" Lucy grabbed her skirts and broke into a run, and Delia ran after her.

The rider didn't pause. He threw his reins to a footman who hurried out, removed a saddlebag, and took the steps two at a time. Delia could see it was indeed Rob Benson, covered in road dirt, with two days' beard and muddy boots.

Rob was across the entrance before Delia came in the door, the man striding into the long hallway, a flustered Harris on his heels. Ladies crowded the drawing room door. Lady Danbury pushed through them and joined Lucy and Delia, hurrying after Harris.

"Did you say the library?" Rob asked over his shoulder.

"Yes, Sir Robert. Or perhaps—" Harris stopped at the library door.

"Where's Clarion?" Rob demanded.

Puzzled faces glanced at one another. "The shooting party

has returned. Perhaps he is changing," someone said just as Delia came in behind Rob.

"I say, Benson, what's so important that you've invaded the library in undress?" Lord Eaton demanded.

Rob reached into his satchel, pulled out a fistful of broadsides, and slapped them on top of the neatly displayed newspapers. He picked up a few and spun around to face Harris.

The butler sputtered. "I shall alert the earl that—"

Rob cut Harris off. "I'll go up. He'll want to see me." He paused long enough to pull Lucy close before taking the back stairs two at a time. Lucy didn't hesitate. She accompanied him at a run.

Delia stared after him while an uproar exploded behind her.

"Blood flowed? How much and whose?"

"I guarantee it wasn't hussar blood!"

"Did they get Hunt? His seditious speeches have been corrupting the people."

"Women and children? Who printed this tripe?"

A few darted out to follow Rob, among them Sidmouth's crony Lord Hartwell, declaring that the home secretary must be informed.

Delia retrieved a scrap of paper from the floor. "Massacre at Saint Peter's Field. Waterloo on Home Ground," the headline read. "Hundreds Trampled."

A regiment had charged a crowd gathered to hear the speakers. Delia remembered the names, known radical agitators all. But had they caused a riot?

The news would be a knife to David's heart. She needed to go to him.

CHAPTER THIRTY-FOUR

THE MORNING HAD been miserable. Awbury had berated the grooms serving as beaters and insulted David's steward's land management when he'd failed to hit any birds. David wanted to throttle the man for his poor manners alone, but his own innate dignity had held him back.

"Perhaps, Your Grace, it isn't your day. You might find the amenities in my billiard room more to your taste," David had told him.

The mood of every gentleman in the party was grim by the time they reached the hall, and David took to his room with relief. He allowed his valet to fuss over his attire while he sipped brandy, being in no mood to face the party.

A disturbance in the hallway cut up his peace, and his temper rose. He exhausted his meager supply of curse words just as the door to his sitting room slammed open. He half expected his sisters, in pursuit of an enterprising would-be countess. He was wrong.

He hurried through the connecting door to find Rob leaning on the door jamb with one hand, looking like the wrath of God, and breathing heavily.

"Good God, Rob. Sit down. Manchester? Tell me every-thing," David said, removing books from a chair so his brother could sit.

Lucy ducked under her husband's arm and put one of hers

around his waist, leading him to the chair. On a gesture from David, Harvey handed Rob a drink. Harris slammed the door behind them. David could hear other voices, Harris's loudest of all, attempting to hold off further entry.

Rob waved it away. "Water, please," he croaked. He leaned on his knees and breathed in deeply. "Bad, David. As bad as we feared. The hussars charged the field, trampled people. Sabers drawn."

"What did Hunt say? Did he whip the crowd into a frenzy?" David asked.

Rob shook his head. "Unprovoked attack."

"Nonsense!" Lord Sidmouth, whose room was across the hall, shook with outrage in the doorway, Harris being no match for the home secretary. "The entire event was a provocation, one planned and carried out by seditious agitators. We expected trouble. We ordered the 15th Hussars to back up the local yeomanry."

"Who ordered them to charge, Sidmouth?" Rob demanded, rising to his feet.

By now others had followed Sidmouth, crowding into David's sitting room.

"How would I know? I was here. The proper authorities, I assume," Sidmouth replied.

"What were your orders?" Rob asked. "What were they expected to do?"

"Break up the meeting at the first sign of a riot, to *prevent* violence. To arrest Hunt and the others if they attempted to provoke the crowd," Sidmouth said, standing erect, one hand against his waistcoat.

"Hunt never spoke. Not one word. The yeomanry moved in to arrest him and the others on the hustings before they spoke. There was grumbling in the crowd—and an attempt by a few to put themselves in front of the speakers—and the cavalry charged the crowd. They slashed at *women*, Sidmouth. Were those your orders?" Rob snapped.

"See here, Benson, are you impugning the home secretary's honor?" Awbury demanded, shouldering past Eaton and Graham.

"Not I. But he best be prepared to defend it in coming days," Rob retorted.

"Could we calm down please, gentlemen?" David said. "Lord Sidmouth, may I offer you a chair?" It felt ludicrous. There was only one more chair at David's little table, and a settee for three—two if one was as corpulent as Awbury. Awbury sat. The rest, including Rob, remained standing. David wondered if he was about to defend a riot in his sitting room.

"Begin at the beginning, Rob," David said. "How was the crowd?"

"They began assembling midmorning, some coming from mill towns, Oldham and the like. By noon they had filled the square and spilled out into the side streets. The atmosphere was anticipatory, cheerful, almost festive. Many groups carried signs, primarily ones demanding the vote."

"Stupid cows," Awbury sneered. "As if we'd allow the rabble the vote."

"How many?" Sidmouth demanded.

"Wroe from the *Observer* and some of the others estimated a hundred and fifty thousand, but that's much too high. I'd say half as many, if that," Rob said, rubbing his chin and smearing it.

Seventy-five thousand would have terrified the local authorities, David mused. He caught Graham's eye. Delia's brother had the same thought.

"The yeomanry had been brought in close. Someone gave an order to arrest the speakers just then—before it started—and then—" Rob swallowed hard and cleared his throat. "Some in the crowd linked arms, thinking they'd prevent the arrest—"

"Clear defiance of law," Sidmouth said in clipped tones.

David spied Delia behind Graham, and his heart took a leap. He held out a hand, and she—the angels and saints be praised—came to his side without question. The feel of her hand in his steadied him.

Rob went on. "The horses of the yeoman were spooked—or the yeoman were drunk—they rode in erratically and began slashing with sabers, trampling people. Almost immediately the hussars attacked, or tried to. Driving even well-trained horses into a crowd that dense is difficult, but they did it, slashing their way in. It was over in ten minutes. The crowd dispersed. They arrested the speakers and some journalists and cleared out."

"Well done, them," Awbury crowed from the settee. "We will have order. We will have no terror on English soil."

"If your lot fears the French terror here, then you are fools," Jeffrey Graham muttered.

Unless our lot provokes it, David thought with mounting despair.

"What then, Rob?" David asked through a sudden thickness in his throat.

"Bodies," Rob said, unable for a moment to complete the sentence. "Filled the square and beyond. Hundreds. Women, children. I wandered through, helping where I could. Others came quickly to minister to them."

"How many dead?" David asked quietly.

"Wroe says a hundred. I think far fewer dead. More serious injuries. I saw one lad go down. He couldn't be saved." Rob's head bobbed up. "I saw them drag a pregnant woman from the platform. I think they had pulled her up because she was feeling ill. I don't know what happened to her."

"Were the London papers there?" Sidmouth asked.

As if that is the most important thing, David thought with disgust.

"The *Times*'s reporter was arrested on the hustings," Rob told him.

"Good! That will delay reports. I need to get to London immediately," Sidmouth said, rushing out. "Have my carriage brought round," he called to Harris in the hallway.

"He has less time than he may think," Rob muttered after Sidmouth left. "One of the organizers, Robert Carlisle, escaped. I heard he was on the mail coach for London by three. He'll have the reformers' version of events on the streets by tomorrow."

"We'll need to organize aid for Manchester," David said, unwittingly putting his thoughts into words. Delia squeezed his hand.

Awbury rose. "See what comes of mollycoddling the masses, Clarion. Your credibility dies today. Don't think the word of your bastard brother will mean anything to people who matter." He glared at Delia. "Entertaining your strumpet in front of the home secretary speaks poorly of your honor as well."

David started for Awbury, red rage blinding him, but Delia's hand pulled him back—hers and Rob's. Less encumbered, Graham started to follow the worm out, but Delia left David's side to grab her brother and hiss a warning. A commoner could not assault a duke with impunity. Graham glanced at David and back at Delia, nodded. He left without a word.

"Not worth it," Rob muttered. He stared in the direction Awbury had gone.

"Graham will bide his time, but Awbury will pay for that," David told him under his breath before speaking firmly to the others. "Gentlemen, this has all been very disturbing. I would like a private word with my brother, if I may." He reached for Delia's hand again to keep her at his side.

DELIA TURNED HER head into David's shoulder as if to block out the horror Rob's words had engendered; David's arm came up to hold her there, one hand making soothing movements on the back of her neck. She sank into the comfort of his body next to hers. Neither Lucy nor Rob said a word.

At some point, Rob sat, and Lucy took the chair across the table. After a while, David's hand slid down Delia's back, sending shivers through her. He led her to the settee, keeping her close, while his valet, Harvey, quietly poured drinks for them all, even the ladies, without being asked, before going into David's bedroom and clicking the door shut behind him.

"Well," Rob said, saluting David with his glass, "I hope you didn't want to be home secretary too badly."

David heaved a breath. "That is the least of our problems."

Our? When David said it, he encompassed all of Britain, Delia thought.

"What will you do?" Lucy asked. "Fight him?"

David kept a firm hold on Delia's hand, his thumb rubbing circles in her palm, sending jolts of electricity up her arm. His brow furrowed, his gaze at his feet, he spoke slowly, thinking through each word. "Sidmouth? For his position? That door just closed for me. Blockheaded conservatism will take over. Anyone still on the fence will be pushed off in the direction of repression, driven by fear."

"Will you retire to the country? Stay out of the whole mess?" Rob asked.

David gazed at Rob directly. "Hell no! We'll need every voice we can muster for sanity in Parliament, first to try to blunt the sword that is about to come down on the people, and second to see to their needs."

Delia's heart swelled with pride in this man. "We can help. We can muster charities. We can…" The heat in his eyes brought her to a stumbling halt.

"Yes," David said softly, gazing into her eyes. "*We* can."

Rob rose with a groan. "I need to speak to Fanny—or at least to Eli. I saw her friends, the Abbotts. She'll want to know they are well. They were among the people who came back to the field to help the wounded."

Lucy studied him with concern. "You need to clean up. And sleep."

"I need to hold my son—then sleep. I'll be up at dawn and on my way to London. Rockford will want to hear everything I told you."

Lucy tugged his arm. "*We* will be on our way to London. Kit and I are coming," she said tartly. "And your leader will want to know everything that was said here this week. Will you follow us to the capital, David?"

He firmed his grip on Delia's hand. "Of course. With luck, most of my guests will be gone in a day or two, but some may hang on. Maddy will help bring it to a close. We'll cancel the benighted ball for the end. That should clear out the title-hungry mothers and their daughters." He gazed at Delia. "That and a quiet word about my intentions."

Neither Rob nor Lucy asked him what he meant. They didn't need to. They left quietly. David turned and put an arm around Delia's shoulders, bringing her closer. She went gladly, her heart fluttering.

"I'm sorry about the position you wanted," she said, her voice muffled in his coat.

He shook his head. "I woke up too late. I should have pressed the government harder four years ago. I should have spoken out more forcefully." His intense gaze wandered over the plains of her face, her eyes, her ears, her mouth…

She held her breath, waiting for his kiss. It didn't come.

"Thank you for standing with me today. You gave me strength," he murmured, his breath warm against her cheeks.

He leaned and touched her lips, his kiss chaste and tender. "I was only half-alive, Delia. A gray ghost of a man walking through life until…" Another gentle kiss, too swiftly over.

"Until?" she asked, her throat tight.

"You, Delia. Until you. You give me life."

She didn't wait this time; she rose to meet him, her mouth insistent and eager. His gratifying response held all she could have asked. She lost herself in the feel of his mouth against her neck, dipping along the edge of her bodice, and of his graceful fingers exploring her body before settling on first one breast and then the other. When his hands wandered up her skirt from ankle to thigh, gently caressing, flames enveloped her.

She whimpered his name, and his mouth came down on hers again, possessive and demanding. So focused was she that she didn't realize his fingers had reached her place of heat and begun to invade until she exploded in a storm of pleasure that left her spent. Only his arms held her upright.

He pulled his mouth away, and she blinked up at his triumphant smirk. "Does this mean yes? You will marry me."

The second part didn't sound like a question. She was tempted to tease that it wasn't the planned end of the party and she still had time to decide, but of course, the party was a moot point now.

"Yes," she whispered. "Yes, I will marry you." She lifted a hand and brushed hair from his brow where it had fallen forward. She could feel his erection, hard against her hip. "But, David, we haven't finished what we started here yet." She wiggled against him.

He sat up straight with a sigh and pulled her upright. "That we have not, and I eagerly look forward to doing that, but now is not the time or place."

She heard it then, Sidmouth barking orders to his servants, traffic in the hallway. "Will we call banns at Saint Morwenna?" she asked.

He kissed her quickly. "We will be in London."

"London?" Her heart sank.

"I'm sorry. This is happening so fast." His eyes searched hers, anxiety stark in them. "I know you didn't plan—"

She put a hand to his mouth to stop his torrent of words. She knew what she had to do. "I heard what you told Rob. You will be needed in Parliament. It means London. It means political dinners and—"

"I can't do it without you," he told her. "Please come. I promise Ashmead and Clarion Hall will be here when we come home. It will always be here."

"That's what I'm trying to say. I can do what must be done, David. For you."

"We'll do it together, Delia," David said. He kissed her again, and she knew his love would make everything possible. "You and the children can stay with Maddy and Brynn while we decide about a wedding," he said. Another kiss. "Where does Awbury attend church?" He took her hand and helped her rise.

"Saint George's, Hanover Square. Where he can see and be seen," she muttered, buttoning his waistcoat and tucking in his shirt.

"Excellent!" he said, kissing the tops of her breasts as he put her bodice to rights. "We'll be married there. A full-on society affair. We'll let Henrietta host the wedding breakfast at Danbury House. Prinny will come and Liverpool as well. My brother who so offends Awbury's sense of correctness will stand up with me, the Fitzwallaces be damned."

She grinned. "Jeffrey will love it."

"He will stand up with us, too, and Barnabas McKinney as well. And all the children. We'll begin as we mean to go on, with God's blessing and the people we care for around us." He winked. "Maybe we'll even collect for relief in Manchester."

"We'll give Awbury apoplexy."

He kissed her well and thoroughly. "We can only hope."

A scratch at the door heralded Harris, his errand likely urgent.

David tucked an errant lock up and pinned it in place. She shook out her skirts while he stood behind her, tying the laces of her gown. He kissed the nape of her neck and leaned near her ear to whisper, "We will finish what we just started, and we won't wait for the society wedding, either. You're mine, Delia Fitzwallace, and I am yours. Now and for the rest of our lives."

EPILOGUE

Caulfield House, London, November 1819

DELIA GAVE HER dining room one last look. All was in order. She had been the Countess of Clarion just over a month. With little by way of honeymoon, she had been thrown into the role of political hostess by rapidly evolving events. For David's sake, she didn't plan to fail. His support and the right set of friends had eased her way so far. It wasn't her first dinner party as Countess of Clarion, but it was a vital one.

Once Liverpool had given his public support to the Manchester magistrates and condemned both marchers and speakers, Prinny had followed suit. Then Sidmouth had called Parliament back; sessions were to begin in a week. David felt duty-bound to be in London. Where he went, there Delia needed to be. She encouraged his efforts to build support among moderate Tories and some of the less radical Whigs, the very people she invited to their table. Aiding his efforts gave her pride.

"Is all in order, my lady?" Harris asked.

"As always, Harris. Well done." The old man appeared satisfied. He'd unbent since she'd become countess, but she still rather missed Parsons, who had been promoted to butler at the hall. An influx of cash from the marriage settlements meant they could fully staff both the hall and Caulfield House. "Kindly have tea sent to my sitting room. I have a bit of time before it is time to dress."

To her surprise, the butler served her himself. She put her feet up, sipped happily, and basked in contentment. She had redone the sitting room in colors that put her in mind of spring. Caulfield House was coming to life and rapidly returning to the showplace it was meant to be. She hoped they could do the same for Clarion Hall, continuing what they'd started for the house party. That alone had won her Harris's support.

The children were thriving. The girls had objected to being removed from Ashmead at first, but once Miss Walters had shown them the delights of London, they'd come around. Besides, they had each other's company. Alf and Ed had gone off to Eton at Michaelmas, and reports had been excellent. She had found that a relief. The week they'd come down for the wedding, the two of them had led her and David on a merry chase. Brynn had had to be dispatched to get them out of a scrape in Green Park.

She smiled to think David thrived as well. Some of it was newfound political confidence. More was his open delight in their marriage. As content as she was to be his hostess, she much preferred to be his lover. He had enthusiastically "finished what they'd started" soon after that day at Clarion Hall. As she had suspected, he was a gentle and enthusiastic lover who needed a little coaxing now and then to give his passion full rein. He'd proven to be a fast learner. He had already possessed the most important prerequisite—a generous and giving heart. The thought of their intimacies the night before brought a blush. Fast learner indeed. She didn't think they needed that trip to the lakes he had promised her on their wedding day as long as they were together.

The sound of familiar boots on the stairs made her heart race. He entered without knocking just as she stood to greet him. Worry lines marred the corners of his eyes, and his shoulders sagged as if under the weight of the world.

Delia went into his arms and put her face up for his kiss. "You are weary."

"It isn't fatigue; it's disgust. Information about Sidmouth's proposals has begun to surface," he said, kissing her forehead.

"As bad as we feared?" She pulled him over to a chair, one she knew from happy experience well fit them both, and crawled into his lap.

He sank his head into her hair. "Worse. Control of military drills and weapons makes sense. But as for the rest—he intends to strangle the press and any sort of dissent. Civil violence benefits no one. But—"

She lifted his head, her hand on his neck, her thumb under his chin. "But?"

He kissed her instead of answering, kissed her until the questions disappeared and he was carrying her into her bedroom beyond the interior door.

Her beloved did indeed learn quickly. He found ways of his own to surprise her, tending openheartedly to her pleasure and driving her mad with arousal until he brought her to completion with care. Basking in the glorious aftermath of passion, she gazed up at David and saw that the worry lines had disappeared. She touched the corner of one eye gently.

He turned his head and kissed her fingers. "You are my bliss," he murmured.

DAVID WATCHED HIS wife greet guests, amused at her poise. One hour before, she had been a wild thing in his bed; no one would ever guess it to look at her, giving her curtsey to the Marquess of Wilbury.

"You may be newly wed, Clarion, but it isn't the done thing to gaze at your wife like that," Danbury said, shrugging out of his cloak and handing it to a footman. "Where is the liquor? Today's news is enough to make one take to drink," the marquess said with the privilege of friendship. "You invited Whigs."

"I'd invite Richard Carlisle and the radicals if I thought it would help."

"It won't. Not in Parliament."

"No, but unless they keep up pressure in the press—even at the risk of imprisonment, God keep them—we'll never have leverage for even moderate reform," David said.

"You and I may never see it," Danbury said sadly. "Sidmouth is determined to squash dissent of any kind. He'll provoke what he wants to suppress. There may be hell to pay for his tactics before we're through."

The two men accepted drinks from a passing footman and clinked glasses. "To the struggle," Danbury said.

"It may be all we have," David answered.

"Nonsense. We have family; it gives us a reason to keeping trying." Danbury winked and leaned in to whisper, "Even one as complicated as yours."

David watched his wife circulating the drawing room. His variety of half-siblings, cousins by marriage, and in-laws were indeed a complex bunch. Their rowdy crew of children all the more so. She hadn't told him yet, but he suspected there would soon be another and that his marriage would be blessed with a seven-month baby. He wouldn't trade any of it.

Complex? No. I have Delia. I have love. She would always be the light of his life. Love made everything simple.

Author's Note

When my Ashmead stories reached 1819, it seemed important to include the historical events surrounding what came to be known as the Peterloo Massacre. I knew instinctively that my beloved earl, David, would care deeply about suffering people. Writing that aspect of the story came easily. I had to give him a heroine who would care as deeply. I hope I've succeeded.

On August 16, 1819, a group of people assembled in Saint Peter's Field in Manchester, demanding reform. Most historians believe the size was in the neighborhood of sixty-to-seventy thousand, not the 150,000 reported by the *Manchester Observer*. They had many grievances—unemployment, industrialization of former crafts, and inflation, particularly the rising cost of bread, among them. Hunger and poverty drove them. Their major demand was election reform at a time when only two percent of the population could vote, the great industrial cities had no seats in Parliament, and major landowners had a chokehold on the House of Commons.

What followed was much as Rob described it in the story. A troop of hussars charged into the crowd on horseback, sabers drawn, before the speakers could start. It was over in ten minutes. Estimates of the wounded range between two hundred and five hundred. At least fifteen people died of saber wounds or trampling on the spot and a few more afterward. Some historians believe women were particularly targeted. Contemporary political cartoons certainly implied that. One unborn child died when his mother was beaten.

After an initial public outcry and demand for an inquest, Liverpool and his cabinet, led by Lord Sidmouth, lowered the hammer. The proposals that so distressed David are now called the Six Acts. One outlawed military drilling by civilians. The Peterloo marchers had drilled in the weeks before, in order to form an orderly parade. Another wrote into law the government's rights to seize weapons, though the marchers apparently had none. The rest were designed to squelch public meetings, hamstring the free press, and suppress dissent in any form.

Danbury's prediction about "hell to pay" was correct. The government uncovered a plot to assassinate the cabinet the following year and five men were hung as traitors for what is called the Cato Street Conspiracy. There would be riots.

As an American, I was struck that these laws were enacted twenty-eight years after the American Bill of Rights while by and large abridging the most dearly held of those rights. Historians have called it an era of unparalleled suppression of freedom, the most repressive in British history. Some of the acts lasted as few as five years. The one banning military drilling wasn't repealed until 2008.

Election reform took thirteen more contentious years until the Great Reform Act of 1832 when Manchester finally got two seats in Parliament and the vote was extended somewhat. It would take over one hundred years for all adults of both genders to have the vote.

Difficult and contentious times have been with us off and on through history. David and Delia navigate through theirs with humor, friendships, family, and above all, love, the stuff of life. May we do the same.

What comes next? Watch for a new series, an outgrowth of the Ashmead world, called Entitled Gentlemen. If you read *The Defiant Daughter*, you may remember Madelyn Morgan's two stepsons. Gideon Kendrick, a wealthy mine owner, should have been a duke. Phillip Tavernash has the title, but the brothers have unfinished business. Jeffrey Graham will join them in the new series.

About the Author

Award winning author of family centered romance set in the Regency and Victorian eras, Caroline Warfield has been many things (even a nun), but above all she is a romantic. Someone who begins life as an army brat develops a wide view of life, and a love for travel. Now settled in the urban wilds of eastern Pennsylvania, she reckons she is on at least her third act. When she isn't off seeking adventures with her Beloved or her grandson down the block, she works happily in an office surrounded by windows where she lets her characters lead her to even more adventures in England and the far-flung corners of the British Empire. She nudges them to explore the riskiest territory of all, the human heart, because love is worth the risk.

Website: www.carolinewarfield.com
Amazon Author: amazon.com/Caroline-Warfield/e/B00N9PZZZS
Good Reads: bit.ly/1C5blTm
Facebook: facebook.com/groups/WarfieldFellowTravelers
Twitter: twitter.com/CaroWarfield
Email: warfieldcaro@gmail.com
Newsletter: carolinewarfield.com/newsletter
BookBub: bookbub.com/authors/caroline-warfield
You Tube:
youtube.com/channel/UCycyfKdNnZlueqo8MlgWyWQ